GOLIATH GETS UP

Starbuck O'Dwyer is a graduate of Princeton, Oxford and Cornell. His novel, *Red Meat Cures Cancer* (Random House/Vintage), was a featured selection of the 2007 One Book One Vancouver reading program and won two national writing awards for humor. Starbuck's work has appeared in numerous publications and has been described as "comic genius" by *Kirkus Reviews*. Visit his website at www.starbuckodwyer.com.

Also by Starbuck O'Dwyer

Red Meat Cures Cancer
How To Raise A Good Kid

GOLIATH GETS UP
A Novel

STARBUCK O'DWYER

Hillary,
May all your dreams come true,
Starbuck

Copyright © 2007 by Starbuck O'Dwyer

ISBN 13: 978-0615493084
ISBN 10: 0615493084

All rights reserved under International and Pan-American Copyright Conventions. No part of this book may be reproduced or transmitted in any form or by any means, electronic or mechanical, including but not limited to photocopying, electronic mail, recording or by any information storage or retrieval system, without permission in writing from the copyright holder. Names, characters, places and incidents either are the product of the author's imagination or are used fictitiously, and any resemblance to any actual persons, living or dead, events or locales is entirely coincidental. Trademarks and service names have been used throughout this book and are owned by their respective trademark holders. Rather than insert a trademark notation at each occurrence of the name, the publisher states that all such trademarks are used in an editorial manner without any intent to infringe upon the trademark.

*This book is dedicated to the citizens of Rochester, NY,
and to every person with a dream
and the courage to pursue it.
I wish you much luck and success.*

ONE

"I'm only going to say this once, so listen up. Mark Twain was right. 'There is no God. No universe. No human race. No earthly life. No heaven. No hell. It is all a dream, a grotesque and foolish dream. Nothing exists, but you. And you are but a thought — a vagrant thought, a useless thought, a homeless thought, wandering forlorn among the empty eternities.'"

When teaching tennis to 10-year olds, it is customary to start with the forehand grip, but I was fired last night from the Eggroll Ranch, where I worked part-time as the assistant head cabbage cutter, so I'm feeling angry and unfocused.

"Mister, did you say there's no heaven?"

I memorized Twain's bitter pronouncement at the end of his life for a public speaking class in high school and, unlike most things, it had stayed with me.

"That's right. The whole heaven thing is a big fat lie."

With Mr. Wang's words "you MUSS chop FASSER!" still ringing in my ears, I find myself face-to-face with seven over-indulged fifth-graders ready to break my heart like the rest of the world and its grasping, grabbing inhabitants. Ordinarily, I wouldn't think of letting my new students step between the lines without committing the first three chapters of *The Inner Game of Tennis* to memory, but I've lost heart and with one look I can tell that these three-car garage nambies don't have the moxie to play the sport of kings. They're doomed, dandified muffins; miserably weak and soft, and wholly unfit for mental and physical, mano-a-mano warfare.

"But if there's no heaven, where'd my dog go when he died?"

"Who knows? It's really anybody's guess."

So how did I get such an enormous, throbbing mean-on? It wasn't just my demise as assistant head cabbage cutter, though that was a shock given my contributions to the organization, including a revolutionary expansion of the menu beyond eggrolls. No, like most people, I had a hostility tree with many roots, some deeper than others.

After yesterday's firing, on my birthday no less, despair accompanied me all the way to my girlfriend Miranda's apartment, where I sought a pair of understanding lips and perhaps a Carvel cake, but instead found a pair of men's zebra-print bikini briefs on the stairs leading to her bedroom. Having risked life and limb to reach my beloved by speeding 85 miles-per-hour through a school zone, I was mortified to discover her twisted like a balloon animal around her yoga guru and moaning to the rhythm of a Ravi Shankar sitar medley. Her claim that they were merely trying a back-bending, Bhagavan Rajneesh prayer position quickly gave way to attempted assault (I took a swing at Casanova with a candlestick) and the sudden departure of Miranda's snake-charming suitor and his stinking exercise mat.

I was devastated. Inside my pocket was a three-quarter carat diamond ring I'd purchased on layaway. I'd finally decided to pop the question and start my life as one half of a legally-recognized, honor-bound institution with all of its rights, responsibilities and semi-regular booty. Unfortunately,

I hadn't anticipated someone else's booty getting in the way. Worse yet, Miranda was the sixth woman in a row to leave me for someone else.

"How could you do this?" I asked.

"What's the difference, David? Our relationship is over," Miranda said. "It's been over for awhile."

"Well, this is a hell of a way to let me know. I think I would have preferred an e-mail or a text message."

"It's taken me awhile to figure it out, David, but I finally get it. I finally understand. You are *incapable* of moving your own life forward."

"That's not true."

"You can't hold a job."

"I haven't found the right career," I said.

"You haven't found *any* career. You're all talk. You never follow through on anything."

"So you start sleeping with this guru guy? That's fair."

"I want to be with someone who's going places. And Guru Ganges, for your information, is planning on franchising his yoga studios across the country. You, on the other hand, have no ambition."

"I can't believe you're saying that to me. You work part-time as a cleat specialist at Lady Foot Locker. That doesn't make you Donald Trump in case you're confused. Does someone with no ambition buy the Tony Robbins tapes?"

"That was a year ago, and you've never listened to them."

"It takes time to awaken the giant within. You have to trust me. I've got a long-range plan to improve every aspect of my life."

"Oh, really? Six months ago, you dragged me to that Carlton Sheets no-money-down real estate seminar at the Dome Arena and charged $500 worth of DVDs to my credit card. Have you bid on a single property since then?"

"The market's soft."

"So's your brain. You've let it atrophy. Look at the book you left on my nightstand. *Who Moved My Cheese?* You want to know who moved your cheese? Nobody. You don't have any cheese to move."

"Maybe not, but I've got five of the seven habits of highly effective people. Two more and I'm golden. *We're* golden."

"I'm not buying it anymore, David. Face it — you're a loser and you'll always be a loser."

Try as I might to teach these ghastly kids standing in front of me now, I couldn't shake Miranda's parting words. By her estimation, I had numerous deep-seated Freudian and ESPN-related issues. In attacking me, she employed hurtful adjectives including insensitive, lazy, emotionally distant and poorly dressed, and said she'd moved beyond me with the Chakra breath work and brain respiration techniques she learned from her yogi. She even had the nerve to tell me that I was spiritually bankrupt while she stumbled around looking for her Wonderbra.

I couldn't see it then but Miranda isn't anything special. She's kind of plain and pudgy; not particularly bright or charming or accomplished. She isn't a woman of incomparable grace or unending patience and, on a scale of one to ten, I'd rate her compassion for pets and old people a three. She just turned 30, the age at which some women panic about being unmarried and begin hunting for a mate with a single-minded ruthlessness. Yet, here I'd been on the verge of doing something that countless men and women do every year — marry the wrong person. Why does this happen? It's complicated, isn't it? For me, the answer resided in my subconscious. I didn't think a bumbler with ebbing testosterone, non-existent job prospects and thirty-four dollars in his checking account deserved better. My disregard for myself, my fear of being alone and my growing sense of mortality were pushing me toward the precipice like an aging convertible being driven by Thelma and Louise.

 In my weakest moment, I listed Miranda's positives and negatives on a piece of paper; desperately trying to quantify her; hoping to find some equation that would convince me of the things I didn't feel in my heart. If this is your preferred method of deciding yes or no on a potential mate, the answer is always no. To let your marital choice become a gradual acquiescence due to pressure, fatigue and a ticking clock rather than an affirmative act powered by illogical inspiration is a mistake.

For months, Miranda had continually talked about rings, china patterns and girlfriends who were getting married, setting up house, having children and moving on with their lives. All the talk, however, was less about me than it was about the deeds; about the need to check these items off some list that would make her complete in the eyes of others. What changed was she found a better prospect.

In retrospect, I admit that ramming her pre-owned Nissan Altima with my '75 Ford Mustang (pumpkin-colored with an odometer stuck at 368,312 miles) was a bit rash, but after explaining that "Gigi" was a curry-flavored freak who satisfied her sexually in ways I never could, Miranda kicked me out of her house. Understandably, this threw me into the type of vengeance spiral I was warned about previously by Judge Stander, a local mediator and hostage negotiator, following an unfortunate incident involving my favorite shirt and a local dry-cleaner.

One piece of advice: never give the woman you love a gift certificate for 24 sessions at the Indo-Aryan Yoga Shack. Now, besides my twice-weekly tennis gig, all I had in life was a part-time job selling slightly-used Tibetan prayer rugs at

Who's Your Llama?, an upscale boutique catering to mooks who say things like, "I'm bringing my iPad to base camp so I can blog." With neither love nor meaningful work to speak of, I took some small comfort in warning my students about life's predators.

"Don't wait. Start your enemies list today," I said.

"What's an enemies list?"

Danny Cohen, a four foot three inch student with a yarmulke pinned to his head and a massive Prince racket in his right hand, was momentarily intrigued. Nixonian paranoia may be unbecoming but, after last night, I realize I should have started scrawling down the names of the awful people who mean me harm much, much sooner.

"It's a record of every subhuman cretin draining the marrow from your bones. Start with your ex-girlfriend's yoga instructor, then add every boss who's ever fired you, particularly ones with cabbage fetishes from cowboy-themed, eggroll eateries located in strip malls."

"I don't get it."

Danny and the rest of the class looked confused.

"Let me try again. It's a list of every bloodsucker plotting your downfall."

Danny never heard straight talk like that. Not even in temple. He pondered my words for a moment before losing interest. He was, after all, only 10.

"Are you a pirate?" Danny asked.

"No, I'm not a pirate. Do you see a parrot on my shoulder?"

"Why do you wear that eye patch?"

"Mind your own business, okay?"

"Why are your shorts so short? They look gay."

This insensitive question came from Willa Nash, the only 165 lb. fifth grader I knew with a monogrammed water bottle, invariably filled with Pimp Juice, an energy drink for malcontents and their snowboarding instructors. By failing to demand a more respectful tongue from their tomboy daughter, Willa's father, Kit, and her absentee mother, Missy, an area veterinarian/plastic surgeon specializing in extreme makeovers of pets and their owners, had loosed yet one more monster on society.

"There is nothing *gay* about these shorts. They're timeless, both in fit and style," I said.

"Timeless, my butt."

"Stifle it, Willa, or I'll drop you like a bag of mulch!"

If this girl, with her low-hanging Bermudas, "Skate or Die" T-shirt, and maddening 'tude, continued her line of questioning, she would soon find her name added to the list of those I would lay to waste. My shorts, which covered the uppermost portion of my thighs at rest and much less upon flight, admittedly challenged most public decency laws, clinging to my rear end like Saran Wrap stuck to a Mylar balloon. But there was a perfectly good reason why I wouldn't abandon them or my shirts, relics from the Ivan Lendl collection, complete with tattered necks and yellowed underarms: I didn't have the disposable income to buy a Blizzard at Dairy Queen let alone a new tennis ensemble.

On most days, my money woes sufficed as a valid justification for my current mental condition and freed me to ponder more pressing concerns like who to vote for on *American Idol* or which whitening toothpaste I needed. Unfortunately, my prior evening's disappointments (e.g. the Eggroll Ranch and Miranda) coupled with the incessant prattling of Willa, the poster girl for childhood obesity, forced me to confront a second, less practical but more honest reason why I wore my old athletic clothes.

The truth was that these aging tennis outfits reminded me of who I'd been at one time during a period in my life when anything seemed possible and stitched to the sleeve of each of my shirts and every pair of shorts was a symbol of strength adorned by my mother.

"What's that stupid lizard on your shorts?" Willa asked.

"It's not a stupid lizard. It's a dragon," I said.

"Well, it looks gay. Are we gonna play tennis or what?"

"Watch your tone, Calamity Jane. And put down the Pimp Juice."

I never knew that "gay" was such a popular word with ten-year olds, but Willa used it more often than an Oscar Wilde scholar discussing his Keith Haring collection.

"Why do you have a dragon on your shorts?" Danny Cohen asked, suddenly interested again.

"It's a long story so never mind. Everybody shake hands with their racket," I said.

I held out my Wilson T-2000, perpendicular to the ground, and demonstrated the Eastern forehand grip. "Today, we're going to learn how to hit a forehand."

"David, am I doing it right?"

"Let me see, Becky."

I pulled my smallest student, Becky Pardi, clad in a pinafore and wearing pigtails, away from the procession of Violet Beauregardes and Augustus Gloops lining up to take their turns on the ball machine. Becky held out her racket to show me her grip.

"Turn your hand a bit to the right," I said.

"Like this?" Becky asked.

"That's it. You've got it. Now try again."

Trying again. Getting the right grip. Actions easier said than done and increasingly improbable in my mind as I assessed my life less than twelve months from my fortieth birthday. Someone once said that 40 is when your life comes together and your body falls apart, but in my case, both were falling apart. Ten years ago, I'd never experienced the joys of lower back pain, acute shoulder bursitis or overgrown nose hair. Today, they were welcome distractions from my plantar fasciitis and sore Achilles that made standing for hours on a tennis court a curse.

"Huddle up, group. We're almost out of time . . . Listen, I owe you guys an apology."

To these imps and the rest of the world, I am David Horvath, part-time teaching pro, late night cabbage cutter and frequent wearer of unmentionable atrocities. But years ago, when I took lessons for everything from tennis to chess to tae kwon do, and competed in spelling bees, soap box derbies and ski races, I went by the name of Dragon, a nickname my mother gave to me for reasons that remain unclear. It may have been just a clever device she used to change my self-perception after I was diagnosed at age two with a degenerative condition in my cornea that caused intense light sensitivity and required me to keep my right eye covered at all times with a patch. More likely, she knew that the absence of my father, and my growing awareness of its significance, created a void in my life and necessitated assurance that I was not merely okay but, rather, indomitable.

Whatever the case, the name change worked for awhile as my mother bolstered my confidence by extolling the virtues of these scaly beasts and, by association, me. According to her, I was going to be great and the records of history, as well as the scrap books she purchased at Woolworth's for $4.99 a piece, were waiting to be filled with pictures and tales of my future achievements. I imagine she thought I would scale Everest, win an Oscar, advise presidents and inspire a dance craze. I would sing at Carnegie Hall, collect gold at the Olympics, marry a princess and end world hunger. No accomplishment was beyond my reach, and the mark I'd leave on this world would be lasting and large. Mind you none of this jibed with the team of specialists trying to teach me to read at school, but this was my mother talking and who was I to disagree? If I hadn't been petrified of heights, I would've grabbed a red cape and jumped off the roof of our house.

My mother was a strong believer in self-fulfilling prophecies and once she started sewing dragons on every pair of Toughskins and second-hand Lacoste shirts I owned (replacing the crocodile), the idea that I would rise to the level of her expectations became less far-fetched. The yellow, red and green threads embedded in my clothes infused me with energy; the tight stitching holding me and my fragile psyche together. I wore my dragons the way a Marine wears his patches — *Semper Fi*. I was an army of one plus one, my mom, who, in addition to using needle and thread, wielded a paint brush to put a fire-breathing hydra with a pair of flaming nostrils on just about everything I owned from the banana seat on my bike to my skateboard to my bedroom wall, all in an attempt to spur me on to the summit. Her technique would have made for a wonderful article in the kind of hyper-parenting magazines you see today, squeezed somewhere between anxiety-provoking pieces about 529 college plans and Sudden Infant Death Syndrome, if not for one fatal flaw: I stunk at everything.

Now, before you think I'm being too hard on myself, let me clarify. When it came to receiving athletic instruction, I was an above-average, some would say highly proficient, listener, but my lack of depth perception prevented me from converting words into deeds and soon I had one of the largest private collections of light blue honorable mention ribbons and certificates of participation on the East coast. If a major league scout from any sport had been watching me, his critique would have read, 'too slow, too short, too weak, but gives it holy hell.' Indeed, nobody tried harder than me, but effort only takes you so far when you're throwing up on the coach after each set of wind-sprints and sweating through your eye patch.

Baseball proved particularly challenging though no sport came easily. Mr. Saunders, my little league manager, who had one tooth, no conscience and a pronounced limp from "killin' a man" in self-defense according to local lore, instructed me to start a fight every time we got behind by spitting a wad of chewing tobacco into the opposing team's dugout or kicking their coach in the nuts. As I recall, we were the only team whose skipper provided each player with sharpened, steel-tipped cleats and a tin of Skoal before all games. Mostly I remember right field in the hot summer and the staring contests I'd enter with random dandelions. Standing firmly in the ready position during my league-mandated two innings, I kept waiting for my volcano of baseball heroism to erupt at any moment, but it never did. All my dreams of hitting a home run over the centerfield fence at Bob Ford Field remained buried in the soil of some Mudville Nine nightmare scenario of strikeouts and weak, Texas-league singles struggling mightily to make it over the first baseman's head.

My mother, who loved Louis Armstrong, thought cornet might be my calling and bought me a beautiful vintage brass instrument from a yard sale. My music teacher, Miss Lovell, wasn't as enthusiastic informing her soon thereafter that I was tone deaf and rhythmically-challenged unlike any other student she'd been affiliated with while suggesting that I give up the pursuit. I can still hear my mother arguing my case until Miss Lovell, in a fit of frustration, said that Stevie Wonder could read music better than me.

When I moved on to the dramatic arts, things looked

promising initially as I landed the role of munchkin number 27 in the junior high school production of *The Wizard of Oz*. After explaining that it was a non-speaking part, Mr. Denison, the drama coach, told me to hide behind a crudely-constructed wooden bush for the entire play, sapping my enthusiasm for acting and, for that matter, set design. Nevertheless, despite the disappointments, I was continually assured by my mother that my time was coming and that these were minor setbacks on the way to major victories.

Athletic, musical and dramatic mediocrity wouldn't have been so bad, but I wasn't much of a wiz in the classroom either. In the sixth grade city-wide spelling bee, I forgot the first 'e' in 'excellent' causing a collective groan in the audience so loud, it's still remembered vividly by event organizers to this day. No matter how much my mother helped me with homework, quizzed me with flash cards or promised me cash, I always came home with a report card full of C's and D's. Notably missing were any remarks about not working up to potential. I wasn't dumb, but my loose grip on phonics put me at a disadvantage when compared to my classmates.

Through it all, Peggy, as my mother was known to the women she worked with at Betty's Beauty Nook, continually tried to help me in ways both obvious and subtle. Among other things, I give her credit for never bad-mouthing my biological father. Instead of trying to convince me that he was a bastard who'd screwed us over, she insisted that he was a handsome, smart, funny man who left with her blessing and loved me though we'd never met. Year after year, she kept the details of his whereabouts sketchy, insinuating that he was off on a quixotic journey far, far away, fighting the forces of evil. And notwithstanding my hurtful discovery that Han Solo was not my dad after three years of insisting everyone call me Chewbacca, I intuitively understood and appreciated my mother's efforts to mythologize this man in order to protect me.

At night, sitting on the edge of my bed made up with NFL sheets, her head eclipsing the hallway light, my mother led us in the Lord's Prayer, read me a poem from her Norton Anthology, and then told me tales about dragons. According to her, ancient civilizations from the Sumerians to the Babylonians to the Aztecs feared dragons as evil, but the Chinese saw them as emblematic of everything good and called themselves Lung Tik Chuan Ren, descendants of dragons. To them, dragons brought abundance, prosperity and good fortune, and were courageous, wise, strong, heroic, perseverant and noble — all the things I was going to be. My mother *insisted* that I, too, was a descendant of Chinese dragons and a celestial creature who would overcome all obstacles in my path on the way to greatness. And though she never focused precisely on how I would become dragon-great as opposed to the slightly above-average yet content person I'd originally envisioned, she insisted my greatness was inherent, pre-destined and waiting to emerge, a theory as water-tight as an Indonesian ferryboat, but one I bought and gladly climbed aboard.

Growing up, I constantly looked to my mother for assurance about my direction and prospects and then, without warning, everything changed when I was nineteen. She died on a Saturday and, immediately, the robust force at my back disappeared and my forward momentum slowed. Soon, thereafter, I stalled out. More than 20 years later I'm stuck, and lately I'm gripped, unlike ever before, by the type of fear that paralyzes a man for whom greatness is predicted, but not yet achieved: the fear of leaving this world without a legacy. Halfway through life, I'm still waiting for the moment to arrive when the promise of the past will be realized and, for the first time, wondering whether my mother was wrong. To wake up one morning and find yourself to be ordinary and average, entirely unremarkable, is easier for those of whom little is hoped. But for those who have feasted on a diet of expectations, it is a staggering blow followed by a creeping sense of dread and moments of panic. Did dragons exist or was I just a mythical beast conjured up for the sake of my self-esteem? Had my mother simply soothed my childhood wounds with her stories or did she know something about me that would yet be revealed?

The answer would seem obvious. Anthropologists agree that dragons never existed. According to these experts, they have always been a mere figment of imagination — a mental morphing of the most feared animals in the Earth's history. Given this fact, maybe I should relegate the winged dragon to the dim place where Santa Claus and the Easter Bunny reside after children no longer believe. After all, overwhelming odds say the experts are right. Plus, I'm not stupid. I can look in a mirror and see that I bear no resemblance to anything other than what I am: a 39-year old, emotionally arrested man clinging to his youth the way a white-knuckle flyer clings to his armrest during severe turbulence. I'm not green. I have no scales or tail. And, except for a brief bout of madness last summer involving grain alcohol and a Bic lighter, I have no ability to spit fire.

Am I a dragon? Is it possible that I'm the latest incarnation of a beast that came before me, imbued with all the characteristics of such a creature as my mother described them? Am I a living heir, like the Lung Tik Chuan Ren? I don't know. What I do know is that I must embrace the dragon dream that something better, some kind of greatness, exists within me just waiting to ignite like flames from the nose of an ancient green monster. I can no longer rely solely on cosmic forces unknown to sweep me up and deliver me to my rightful place and destiny. Instead, I need to act in concert with these forces, consciously reinventing myself, in order to have any chance at something resembling a life; and I need to do it by the time I turn 40.

two

When I look at the *USA Today* weather page, I get incensed. Evidently Rochester, New York doesn't rate as a notable travel destination anymore despite our annual lilac bush festival. Backwater locales like Houston merit Parisian fanfare, but all we get is a small dot on the paper's multi-hued map, making us akin to the nation's appendix.

There was tremendous hope for Rochester when it was founded in 1803 by a hardy band of patriots (some say loose confederation of criminals) who were kicked out of Syracuse. Building along the banks of the centrally-located Genesee River, the great minds of the time quickly harnessed the tributary's water to power one newly constructed grist mill after another; and by 1838, Rochester was producing 500,000 barrels of flour a year. This was a major achievement, and had the world economy continued to revolve around blueberry muffins and peach cobblers, we would've been in terrific shape. Lamentably, the world moved beyond baked goods and Rochester, known by then as the Flour City, needed a new handle.

By planting as many lilac bushes as area soil would hold, local leaders deftly shifted the city's reputation away from a dead industry and toward a dying one, earning the metropolis the new moniker of the Flower City. Tourism is a tough sell in the snow belt but, to this day, our Mayor, Cornelia "Corny" Candee, spends half of our annual marketing budget tricking 80 busloads of Canadians to come to town in May, stand out in the pouring rain for two weeks and wonder aloud why they never planted their own damn lilac bushes.

Sadly, as the area's economy has floundered, an identity crisis has ensued and the suffering self-confidence of the city and its people can be felt in every corner of Monroe County, nowhere more so than at the Sam Patch Saloon, a.k.a. the Patch, a downtown drinking hole located one block from the Genesee River, where most days of the week you'll find my best friend, Walter "Nubby" Jones, who was recently laid off from his sales job by Odorrific, a supplier of bathroom sprays.

"How's it going, Nubby?"

"How do you think it's going? I'm drunk at 11:00 a.m. on a Tuesday."

"Where's Big Nasty?" I asked, wondering about one of the Patch's other daily inhabitants.

"He's getting dialysis," Nubby said.

"Poor guy."

Nubby gulped hard on his mug of Genesee Cream Ale, the only beer he drank. I waited for him to ask me a question about my life, but he remained silent. Our friendship was like many I suppose — no matter what hell I was enduring, I always found myself trying to cheer him up. Nubby played the part of pessimist in our relationship and had a lifetime's experience taking the fun out of everything we'd ever done together. Where some saw the glass as half full, Nubby saw no glass at all.

I can't say I blamed him. He'd had quite a run of bad fortune starting with the loss of his parents, Ruth and Jesse

Jones, when he was seven. He became a ward of the state, but the way he tells it even New York didn't want him since his parents hadn't died, they'd simply left — without their only son and without explanation. Nubby's mother was profoundly deaf, a condition that kept a true bond from ever forming between them. "She tried but we never really connected. Her hearing was like a wall I couldn't climb over. Every night, I'd ask God to fix it but nothing ever changed." All Nubby knew about his father was that he hated him. "I saw him hit her and that was it. I was only five but, right then, I knew he was an asshole. He was always coming and going, leaving my mother alone late at night, and he barely acknowledged me."

I met Nubby in a remedial spelling class in second grade shortly after he was deserted. He thought there was a "k" in dog, and I was convinced cat should have a second t. Unfortunately, his luck, like his spelling, wouldn't get any better. That same year, on a school field trip to a petting zoo known as Lollypop Farm, Nubby lost his right thumb when he decided to feed a carrot to Cocoa Puff, a deranged goat with a ruthian appetite and very sharp teeth. I'm still haunted by the scream that followed and the guilt I feel for handing Nubby the carrot and telling him that Cocoa Puff was harmless. After Nubby emerged from the hospital, he endured weeks of sedation and extensive psychotherapy in order to help him accept his nine-fingered reality. Meanwhile, I vowed that I would make him whole somehow; a pledge I'm still trying to honor.

"Do you know Rochester was just named the most polite city in America?" I asked.

"No shit. How'd they figure that out?"

"From what I understand, they put a few senile old people out in the middle of traffic and counted the number of minutes it took before a citizen brought them back to safety. Of all the cities, it turns out we had the lowest average time. Makes you feel pretty good about your home town, eh?"

"If you like hell holes with manners," Nubby said.

"Have you ever read *Zen and the Art of Motorcycle Maintenance*?" I asked.

"Knock it off, David. I can't handle any inspiration right now."

"Fair enough. . . . How'd your date with whatshername go? Yvette, right?"

"Ten minutes into dinner, she told me she was possessed by a Vatican priest. Any more questions?"

"Coulda worked out."

From Nubby's knothole, finding the right woman, the key to creating the family he never had, was an elusive, though not impossible, mission. Speaking from experience, he rated it, "harder than stealing money out of a blind street musician's guitar case, but less difficult than avoiding personal income taxes for sixteen years running." Lately, however, his tenuous faith that Ms. Perfect awaited him had been shaken badly by an impetuous, six-week stint of living with Lilly Bee, a professed pet psychic who, the one time we met, bit her knuckles until they bled, pausing only to predict many happy marriages for Kim Kardashian's dog. This relationship followed Nubby's self-destructive pattern of giving himself over completely to the first woman who bagged his groceries and left him staring once again into the black chasm of the area's ever-shrinking dating pool.

Rochester had experienced a significant female brain drain and those who left the area after high school outnumbered those who stayed by an eight to one margin. Even worse, the perception, whether fair or not, was that something had gone terribly wrong for those still around. This perception, of course, was not the sole province of women.

To Nubby and me, neither prime marriage material by all but the most forgiving standards, it felt like all the smart and attractive people left town and we were what remained. One December, when we were ten-years old, we watched *It's a Wonderful Life* at my mother's insistence, including the scene where Sam "Hee Haw" Wainwright announces his plan to open up a factory in Rochester. When George Bailey learns of this plan, he asks Sam, "Rochester? Why Rochester?" — a question we'd been trying to answer ever since.

"You're lucky Miranda dumped you," Nubby said.

"I dumped her," I said.

"Sure you did, and O.J.'s still out looking for the real killers."

"That joke's a hundred years old."

"Yeah, but it's still funny."

"Whatever. For the record, my break-up with Miranda was mutual."

"Bullshit. She had you under a spell. All women are witches. Witches or devils. Sometimes both."

Ordinarily, I'd be the first to disagree with Nub, who tended to get wildly (if only temporarily) misogynistic every time he had a bad date but, given my heartache over Miranda, it was no surprise that our bartender, Dixie, beat me to it.

"Nubby, you make the Taliban look progressive. Should I put on my burka before I get your next beer or just quit school and move into a cave?"

Dixie Lee was a 21-year old, Chinese-American who worked at the Patch 20 hours a week. A self-described product of a Shanghai father and a Mississippi mama, she had shoulder-length jet black hair and a pierced nose and topped her boot-cut jeans with tight midriff-baring T-shirts from thrift shops. When she wasn't serving beer, she was in school at Monroe Community College studying the classics: animal husbandry, criminal justice, and butter sculpture. To us, she was smart, frank and the only reality check we had inside the dimly-lit surroundings of the bar. To her, we were regulars, errant older brothers and cautionary tales, all rolled into one.

Dixie's primary goal in life was to create something beautiful out of butter and win the right to exhibit her work at the annual New York State Fair in Syracuse. Every year, in a gigantic refrigerated glass case, a maize-colored masterpiece greeted thousands who passed by in awe. "That's the butter big-top," Dixie would say while sketching out potential subjects for her dairy dreams. "Last year's Elvis nearly brought me to tears. They got the bloating just right."

Dixie embraced causes, large and small, and spent her spare time railing against globalization and fur coats, and demanding that people stop taking such long showers. None of this sat well with her father, Wenshen "Pete" Lee, a successful local builder and businessman who owned a chain of waterslide parks, among other things, and was estranged from his daughter for a variety of reasons, environmental and otherwise. Dixie believed that her father, who was actively grooming her two younger brothers to take over his business, was a chauvinist and she resented it. He brought a patriarchal mentality from his homeland and had not relinquished it, promoting his sons to the exclusion of his only daughter.

After playing the dutiful child and suffering in silence her whole life, Dixie had tapped a wellspring of anger that continued to spout. "I swear he could've cared less where I went to college but for my brothers it was Ivy League or bust. All he wants me to do is get married and let a man take care of me." Just a year ago, Dixie was ensconced at Brattleberg, an undergraduate enclave and spa for the underachieving and wayward children of the rich, located in New Hampshire. One belly ring, two tattoos and three bomb threats to the corporate headquarters of her father's company, Goliath Industries, later, and Dixie was financially on her own. Although the police dropped all the charges, her father wasn't as forgiving, cutting off her credit cards and tuition.

"Dixie, you're smart. Explain to me why women try to change every man they meet," Nubby asked.

"First of all, how do you know I'm smart?"

"Well . . . I don't know . . ."

"'Cause I'm Asian?"

"No . . . I just, uh . . ."

"You just what? Think that all Asians are smart? That we're good at math and science, right? That we spend our lives learning the Suzuki piano method and following our tiger parents' orders when we're not too busy studying or carrying cameras around and taking pictures? Well, guess what? Not all of us are like that and I'm sick and tired of those stupid stereotypes."

"Sor-reee."

"And for the record I suck at math and piano."

"Jeeee-zus, Dixie. I was just asking a question."

"No, you weren't. You were looking for me, little miss smart Asian, to confirm your assertion that all women try to change men — as if you're worthy of our time. Little tip: don't trot out that tired horse, Nubby. Its back is sagging."

"All right, calm down. Calm the hell down. All I know is that Lilly Bee tried to change me."

A look of skepticism swept Dixie's face.

"Let me guess. You ran out to the Pump and Gulp for a third bag of Cheetos and, while you were gone, she picked up the underwear from the floor of your double wide," Dixie said.

"Not even close."

"Wait, I've got it. She tried to throw away the rotting chicken chow mein from your bedside mini-frige, the one covered top to bottom with NASCAR stickers, and you felt threatened by her smothering ways," Dixie said.

"Do *not* disrespect NASCAR. Those men are warriors. And for your information, it had nothing to do with my Cheetos, my underwear, my mini-frige or my trailer."

"Then *do* tell, Romeo. What exactly did she try to change?" Dixie asked.

"It started with sweaters."

"Sweaters?"

"Yes, every time I turned around she was buying me another sweater; each one uglier than the last. And she kept saying, 'Why don't you wear the sweaters I buy you?'"

"What's wrong with sweaters?"

"They're a symbol," Nubby said.

"Of what? Dressing warmly?" Dixie asked.

"No. They're a symbol of . . . I don't know . . . civilization. How can I explain this? . . . You don't put a wild buck in a sweater, you know what I mean? You don't cut Samson's hair. You don't step on Superman's cape."

"Jim Croce knew," I said.

"Damn right he knew," Nubby said.

"So let me get this straight, Superman; you think she was trying to civilize you by putting you in sweaters?" Dixie asked.

"Exactly," Nubby said.

"Good lord. Is that all?" Dixie asked.

"No. She also wanted to re-do the kitchen. What the hell is it with women and re-doing the kitchen?"

"Maybe she wanted a decent place to make you a meal. Did you ever think of it that way?" Dixie asked. "God, you're an asshole. You basically dumped this poor woman because she wanted to buy you a couple of sweaters and fix up your kitchen. You ought to be ashamed of yourself."

"Now wait a minute. When you put it like that, I sound like a jerk."

"I said asshole not jerk."

"Just so you know, it wasn't only the sweaters and the kitchen, Dixie. It was also her dust ruffle," Nubby said.

"What's a dust ruffle?" I asked.

"It's a skirt every woman puts on your bed to mark her territory; like a dog peeing in the corner of your yard. They call it a dust ruffle, but it's really a frilly skirt," Nubby said.

"Nubby, women are not conspiring against you with their nefarious dust ruffles. You're paranoid," Dixie said while filling up Nubby's mug with more Genesee Cream Ale.

"Am I? They turn your bed into a woman and from that point forward it's two against one in the bedroom. They have you outnumbered."

"I don't think one dust ruffle is going to tip the balance of power in a relationship," I said.

"Of course not, but they don't stop there," Nubby said. "They bring in reinforcements to the ruffle: overstuffed pillows. Big ones. Small ones. Embroidered ones that said awful things like, 'Happiness is Being Married to Your Best Friend' and 'I Heart Dan Fogelberg.' They pile up pillows are far as the eye can see. I mean, how many is enough?"

"I've never heard a more immature outlook on love," Dixie said.

"Who said anything about love? This is about control."

"Did it ever dawn on you that women just like dust ruffles and pillows?" Dixie asked.

Nubby was on a roll now, like John Belushi in *Animal House*, but more antic.

"Next come the picture frames. Wood ones, pewter ones, silver-plated ones, ceramic ones, brass ones. And, of course, in order to collect the maximum amount of dust, they've got to put out a complete photo-collage of everyone they've ever met: their parents, their cousins, their prom date, their three-legged childhood dog Mr. Twister, their best friend from third grade who they haven't spoken to in twelve years, and on it goes."

"Nubby, pictures make a house a home," Dixie said.

"Then . . . just when you're about to snap, here come the candles. Soon there's a scented ring of fire surrounding you, and every time you go to relieve yourself, there's a good chance you'll end up in the burn unit at St. Mary's. Lavender. Vanilla. Spruce. They show *no* mercy."

"That's nonsense."

"Going to bed with Lilly Bee was like being an extra on the set of *The Towering Inferno*."

"If you're in love, you don't mind a few candles," Dixie said.

"Well, perhaps that's my problem. Maybe I wasn't in love. Maybe I've never been in love," Nubby said.

Nubby spent five years wondering why he was abandoned until he decided to investigate matters. At the city's Rundel Library, where I helped him scroll through microfilm of old newspapers, he uncovered evidence of what he'd long suspected. A crime, in this case a botched bank robbery, resulted in the death of a security guard and the disappearance of Nubby's father, the leading suspect according to several eye witnesses, and his mother. Faced with the choice between subjecting her child to years on the run with a wanted man or leaving him behind for a better life, Ruth Jones did what she felt was in her son's best interests. Taking custody, New York's child protection officials moved Nubby to Chestnut Ridge, a dilapidated group home, where he spent most of the ensuing years listening to Deep Purple and sniffing glue. He was supposed to be building models to rehab his hand but, because of his limited dexterity and his burgeoning, hallucinogenic habit, he ended up with a bizarre collection of half-finished, classic, 1970's muscle cars, all of which were missing doors, wheels and hoods.

Nubby was a lot like those models: unfinished, unloved and, in the eyes of most, beyond repair. Every Sunday afternoon, prospective parents would arrive at Chestnut Ridge, temporarily raising Nubby's hopes of a new mother and father and an end to his painful existence. He didn't have much clothes; a pair of threadbare jeans and used khakis that he wore to church and always left on after services in anticipation of the coming afternoon's adoption line-up. Every child stood in formation, hands at their sides, as parents entered the group home's cafeteria. Nubby, however, wasn't a cute kid and his missing finger didn't endear him to any father looking for a future star quarterback. As months and then years wore on, Sunday became the saddest day for Nubby as he was overlooked again and again.

And so it went. Nubby grew up without expectations for his future. Teachers passed him along from grade to grade like a dying plant they were determined not to waste too much water or sunlight on. There was no disapproving parent when he screwed up or role model when he looked for one. Deep Purple led Nubby to Eric Clapton, Robert Johnson and the blues, and the hundreds of songs he heard about men who weren't appreciated, understood or loved became his greatest source of comfort. The blues didn't give him any greater reason to live but it did provide solace that there were others just as miserable as he was. Immersing himself in records running from Snooky Pryor and Honeyboy Edwards to John Lee Hooker, Lead Belly and Blind Lemon Jefferson, his all-time favorite, Nubby saw life as one large, ongoing disappointment. So your woman's just run off with your best friend, your car and all your money? That's nothing. Let me tell you about real heartache. In Nubby's eyes, there was something noble about men who'd lost jobs, love and hope, yet still lived on. Both shoes may have already dropped, but you could still make some noise while pinned beneath them.

After barely finishing high school and dropping out of community college, Nubby gained a hundred pounds and got a bad set of hair plugs, removing himself from the remotely attractive category earlier than most. From that point on, he bounced from one spirit-crushing sales job to another until he landed with Odorrific ten months ago. One downturn in the economy, coupled with a corresponding decrease in demand for post-defecation deodorizing sprays with names like Misty Moonbeam Surprise and Sweet Apple Dawn, and Nub was back at the Patch full-time.

"We're just in a rut," I said, trying to rationalize my own rotten love life and appalling lack of direction.

"It's more like a canyon. I think this city is dragging us down. I really do. The economy, the taxes, the aquarium."

"We don't have an aquarium."

"Exactly. We don't have any of the things that make a city great."

"That's not true. We're the most polite city in America."

"Because we're quick to pull crazy old people out of traffic? So what? That doesn't make us Las Vegas you know. In case you haven't noticed, all the companies and jobs are leaving town."

"What about James Cutler? We've got him," I said.

"Who the hell is James Cutler?" Nubby asked.

"The guy who invented the mail chute. He was from Rochester."

"Oh, great, we've got the mail chute guy. Yippee."

"At least it's something."

"Are you talking about those mail slots you see in the hallways of old buildings?"

"Yes. Cutler invented them here."

"Do you know how many lives that guy wrecked?" Nubby asked.

"What are you talking about?"

"I'm talking about all the mail that's gotten stuck in those stupid chutes over the years — all the unpaid bills and love letters — all the Christmas cards that never arrived."

"All right, fine, maybe Cutler was a bad example, but what about George Eastman?"

George Eastman, the inventor of roll film and the portable camera, founded Kodak, Rochester's largest employer, in 1880 and became the city's philanthropic saint, establishing most of its cultural and educational institutions.

"Eastman's legacy is fading fast. It's just a matter of time before Kodak leaves town for China."

"Kodak's not going to China," I said.

"All I know is we'd be better off someplace else; somewhere with a few decent women," Nubby said.

"There are plenty of decent women here," Dixie said. "You're just not what they're looking for."

"What's wrong with me?"

"For starters, take that T-shirt you have on. You wear it almost every day."

"What's wrong with it?"

"It sends the wrong message."

"Dixie, women like to know where a man stands. They want to know his philosophy on life."

"Nubby, trust me. No woman wants a man whose T-shirt says 'See That My Grave's Kept Clean.' It's depressing."

"No, it's not. It's my mantra. I took it from Blind Lemon Jefferson. Like him, I embrace fatalism."

"Well, in case you didn't know it, fatalism is a sure-fire chick repellant so unless you want to die alone, I'd ditch the mantra, the T-shirt and Blind Lemon Jefferson."

"Not a chance in hell."

"You don't get it. Women want to be inspired," Dixie said.

"What does *that* mean?" Nubby asked.

"It means they'll flock to your flame like a moth if you give them a good reason," Dixie said.

"So it's an insect problem?"

"Not exactly, Nubby. They want a co-equal — a partner. But at the same time, they want to bathe in the reflected glow of your love."

"Aw, Christ. I give up. It sounds way too complicated. I think it's mail-order bride time," Nubby said.

Despite its failure to deliver lasting love to Nubby or me, I always took pride in Rochester. Besides Kodak, it was the home of Xerox and Bausch and Lomb, collectively the Big Three, and was known for its cameras, copiers, contact lenses and cold winter weather. I liked being from a place with a clear identity and role in the world, but as Kodak and our core companies weakened and the winters grew milder, Rochester's identity and role had begun to disappear, fading away like an aging starlet whose looks are beyond the salvaging scalpel of even the most skilled surgeon. Every person, like every place, needs something to feel good about, so as Rochester became known as a place whose best days were behind it, I started thinking of myself in the same way. It was an awful thought and the danger of vanishing altogether felt real and frightening. Like dying before your time, it was an unspeakable fate one dared not tempt.

"Maybe you're right, Nub," I said. "Maybe we need to get out of Rochester."

"You two sound pathetic," Dixie said. "Rochester's not holding you back — *you* are. Haven't you heard of setting goals?"

It's one thing for a man to bemoan his own mistakes and the daily disasters that inevitably befall him in the military-industrial complex of America, but it is quite another when someone else, particularly a younger woman, points them out. Unbeknownst to Dixie, she'd hit upon a painfully sensitive subject; the wound I'd been nursing about dragons and greatness, and the fact that I was pushing middle-age with nothing to show for it but my Mustang, my Subway sandwich card and the promises made by my mother.

Although it was hard to admit, I knew that somewhere along the way I had stopped setting goals because of my fear of failure. Too much beer and television and easier options kept my ambitions at bay, idling me like a bit player in a Jimmy Buffett song, but there was always other background music playing, a guilt-inducing melody reminding me that I should be doing something more. The only question was what. It's one thing to decide to make a change. It's something entirely different to actually do it.

"I think you should both do obits," Dixie said.

"Obits?" I asked. "What do you mean?"

"Your obituaries. You should write them out. It's an exercise I'm doing for my American Studies class. Professor Lipshitz says it's important to confront your own mortality."

"Really? That's what Lipshitz says, huh? I don't know about that," I said.

"It's a very powerful tool, you know, facing death and everything. It forces you to think about what you want out of life. Who you want to be. What you're going to accomplish. Who you'd like to marry. Whether or not you want children. All in 150 words or less. Wouldn't you like to do an obituary, Nubby?"

"I don't think I know 150 words."

My obituary? My death? These thoughts equaled a can-clutching spray of lighter fluid on the flames searing my tender psyche, all courtesy of Professor Lipshitz. Dixie was probably right about the benefits of penning my obituary, but I wasn't ready to admit it to anyone but myself.

"Writing your own obituary is empowering," Dixie said. "You can even pick the disease you're going to die from."

"Oh, that's great. You get to pick the disease? How uplifting. I can't wait to get started," I said. "I think I feel bone cancer coming on."

"I'm just trying to help, David."

"I know."

"Dixie, I think we need your help to find love," Nubby said. "Will you help us with that?"

"Wait a second, Nubby. Speak for yourself. I don't need any assistance in that area," I said.

"What the hell are you talking about? Your girlfriend just left you for her yoga instructor. That doesn't sound like the script of *Love Story* to me."

"All right. No need to rub it in. Maybe I could use a small assist."

Dixie brought the glass she was toweling off to the edge of the bar where we sat and looked at us for a moment through the eyes of an outsider. The world is divided between those who are getting ahead and those who are dodging calls from Visa. The latter group drank at the Sam Patch Saloon.

"Okay. I'll help you, but on one condition," Dixie said.

"Name it."

"You'll both owe me a favor."

"What kind of favor?" Nubby asked. "Sexual?"

"No. Believe me it will have nothing to do with sex," Dixie said.

"Too bad," Nubby said.

"And I can call it in at any time," Dixie said.

"How big a favor?" Nubby asked.

"No more questions. Is it a deal?"

"Okay."

"It's a deal, Dixie," I said.

I can't remember when I started frequenting the Patch, but it was right around the time I began buying Lifesavers and Chapstick on credit. The bar was named for Sam Patch, a largely forgotten man whose mustachioed face, captured in an expressionless, pen and ink rendering, greeted you at the door every time you arrived and left. Patch was a drifter who came to Rochester where, on the night of November 13, 1829 with a crowd of eight thousand people watching and cheering his every move, he jumped into the unforgiving grip of the Genesee River with his pet bear, Blackie, and rode over the High Falls, a 100-foot high cliff of churning water and jagged rocks in the center of downtown Rochester. Four months later, Patch was found frozen in a block of ice, dead at 29 and famous around the world as a populist cult hero.

Like the other patrons entering the Patch, I shuffled past the picture of its namesake every day without giving any thought to his ultimate ruin. After all, he was a ghost frozen in time and his life stood in stark contrast to mine. But, like Sam Patch, I was engaged in a fatalistic form of self-destructive behavior: drinking the hours of my existence away; apathetically ignoring my nobler self.

My life and the lives of the people who sat beside me actually stood in much starker contrast to those depicted in the prints that populated the rest of the bar, mostly black and white photographs of early Rochesterians, the men well-dressed in overcoats and bowler hats, the women in hooped, ankle-length skirts topped with petticoats; their heads under bonnets their hands hidden in mufflers. The look on their faces is one of determination as they go about their daily business. Life is not easy for them, but their eyes are filled with a sturdy confidence that hard work will lead to better things in time. Distractions are few and the goals are clear — something that cannot be said for my fellow drinkers or for me. I had always thought of myself as a spectator at the Patch, a witness to the losing ways of others. It never occurred to me that the bar's regulars saw me as one of their own until now.

Had Rochester done this to me? Years of local layoffs had bred bitterness and eventually I was surrounded, night after night, by unhappy people whose woe was contagious. The most frequently requested song on the jukebox had always been *Feels So Good* by native son, Chuck Mangione, but the uplifting notes of his flugelhorn had been replaced by the low moans and pained howls of Nubby's favorite bluesmen, filling the Patch with a mood of mirthless resignation. "Serves you right to suffer, David. That's what John Lee Hooker says," Nubby told me.

Maybe so, but I was sick of suffering. And as easy as it was to blame the city and its declining economy when I was commiserating at the Patch, it was equally difficult to deny the truth that I was at fault for the disappointments of my own life when I was alone. Dixie's assessment that Rochester wasn't holding me back was right, and the sooner I accepted that fact and moved on, the better off I'd be. I may have been stuck, like a piece of mail in one of James Cutler's chutes, but dragons didn't blame others for their failures and neither could I.

three

My break-up with Miranda meant more time at home: a faded tan, two-story walk-up across from the cemetery on Mt. Hope Avenue, a busy road running just inside the southern edge of Rochester's city limit. I still lived with my grandmother, Beatrice, who owned the house, and her second husband, Biff, a man whose entire wardrobe consisted of one olive green, terrycloth bathrobe. My mother couldn't afford a mortgage on her hairdresser's salary while I was growing up so we stayed with Beatie, as she liked to be called, who was happy to have our company as well as someone to feed her nearly-famous peanut butter and banana sandwiches, which she touted as a sure-fire solution to most problems and relied on as a practical distraction from her inability to cook anything other than TV dinners and Chef Boyardee Spaghetti-O's.

When Beatie wasn't making sandwiches for Biff or me or the kid who cut the lawn, she liked to talk about people I'd never heard of, let alone met, who were sick, about to die or newly dead. She had a genuine passion for illness.

"Did ya hear Ray Olson's got the croup, David?"

Beatie used the word croup to describe everything from a mild cough to Lou Gehrig's disease.

"No. I didn't hear that."

"Got a letter from Ursula. Doesn't look good. She says Ray's in a facility in Schenectady."

"That's terrible. Nice guy that Ray."

Even if I didn't know them well, I liked to give the ailing the benefit of the doubt.

"Who's nice? Ray?" Beatie asked.

I nodded.

"Complete and total jackass," Beatie said.

So much for Ray. Fortunately, Beatie and I had a healthier relationship, one that was well-defined. I needed housing and she needed someone to walk her pot-bellied pig, Woofie, a brain-dead but loyal life form who never turned down one of Beatie's sandwiches and never met a lawn he didn't delight in defiling.

Our neighborhood was ordinary, a fact I took comfort in growing up but began to resent the longer I stayed there. Time passed but Mt. Hope remained an ageless, average street with its well-maintained lawns, modest homes, block parties and local gossip queen; in our case, Mona Fuse, who liked nothing better than spreading the word of neighbors going through a nasty divorce or a child with a substance-abuse or weight problem. "Did you hear the Benson's sent Kent off to fat camp?" was a typical refrain I'd hear when walking Woofie. Other than Mona, the people on our street were polite and reasonably friendly, but those who'd lived there for decades were now retiring or dying and many of the houses were being turned into multi-unit apartment dwellings filled with renters I didn't recognize who kept to themselves.

When I left for college at eighteen, I never imagined I'd live on Mt. Hope again. Though my grades only qualified me for Le Pew Chiropractic College, a lesser-known school near Buffalo founded by French missionaries that was still awaiting its full accreditation in chiropractic therapy as well as all other subjects, I blasted out of the neighborhood in my Mustang, all engines thrusting, ready to ride straightened spines to the successful side of the moon. Four months later, besides an occasional bout of homesickness and a roommate who served as founder and president of the Free Charles Manson Society, I felt college was going well. Little did I know that my mother would soon lose a short battle with ovarian cancer and that my interstellar adventure would end with a phone call from my grandmother. "Come home, David."

Unable to stay focused, I quit school and moved back in with Beatie, telling everyone that I wanted to take care of her, a reason that sounded plausible, even admirable, at the time. Five years later, when Biff married my grandmother and moved in with us, however, the explanation started sounding a bit bogus and now it's as tired as the gold, shag carpeting in my boyhood bedroom and the KISS posters thumb-tacked to its walls. I know that living here keeps me from a fully realized adulthood and every time I walk in on Beatie and Biff playing kissy face, I meet my inadequacy quota and then some. Luckily, most of their time is spent sitting in matching La-Z-Boys in the family room watching cable news and arguing about media bias.

"I did something I'm not very proud of today," I said.

"Not now, David. *The Factor*'s comin' on," Biff said. "O'Reilly's going head-to-head with an Al Franken look-a-like."

"I Googled myself at the library. I never thought I'd do that."

"There's nothing to be ashamed about, David," Beatie said. "I google myself all the time. Just change yer drawers."

Beatie had lost much of her Brooklyn accent, but not all of it, so when it cropped up, "pillow" was "pillar" and "oil burner" was "url boyna" in her strange dialect.

"See this," Beatie said, holding up her forefinger and thumb and pinning them together, "I've got no control down there. None. Three rectar operations will do that to ya."

Beatie was nothing if not direct.

"That's not exactly what I meant. I'm talking about the computer search engine called Google. You've heard of it?"

Beatie looked like Artie Johnson and Swifty Lazar's love child. Her small face had deep furrows and countless age spots, and was largely obscured by the wraparound cataract sunglasses she wore at all times. Numerous hairs, poking out at all angles from her cheeks, ears and nose, greeted you each time she demanded a kiss. Her clothes were self-made, shockingly bright smocks with holes punched in the middle and on both sides for her permed head and gelatinous arms. Like the colors in her clothes, Beatie was warm and vibrant, but she could jar you and was entirely without subtlety.

"Biff, try channel 38 for a minute," Beatie said. "There's a movie on with full frontal nudity."

"Biff, you've heard of Google, right?" I asked.

"Don't think so," he grunted while manning the remote. "This damn shooter always sticks."

Apple still meant fruit to Biff and Beatie.

"There's nothing on 38, Beatie," Biff said.

Beatie's biggest loves in life were movies and celebrities, interests that started when she designed a bathing suit for "It" girl Clara Bow to wear in the 1926 motion picture *Kid Boots* as a young woman in art school.

"Oh. Well, check the *TV Guide* and see if *Kid Boots* is on tonight," Beatie said.

"I'm not watching *Kid Boots* again. That movie is asinine," Biff said.

"Yer asinine!"

When not channel-surfing for *Kid Boots*, Beatie liked

showing people her dentures, mastectomy scar and cataracts, often at the same time. Having endured 23 operations, she was akin to the Bionic Woman, with most of her body parts having been removed or replaced, and she was proud to have survived it all. Four different kinds of cancer came to visit during her lifetime but they were all sent away, whimpering like dogs who'd done wrong and been sternly rebuked. Beatie's nightstand contained enough prescription medication to make Rush Limbaugh blush, but she saw her pills as badges of honor and was never embarrassed about taking them or talking about her numerous maladies. Most remarkable of all, Beatie was 100 percent mobile and enjoyed being alive more than anyone I knew.

Every Saturday, I dropped her off at Marketplace Mall where she spent half her time in discount shoe stores, bartering with teenage salesclerks over $1.99 espadrilles, and the other half sitting in the food court drinking free coffee from Panda Express and watching people, an activity she could engage in all day without complaint. Besides observing others, Beatie maintained an abiding interest in Milton Berle, Lindsay Lohan, Katie Couric's hair and an evolving theory that Regis Philbin was the leader of the Irish mafia. She also loved going to Wegmans supermarket, where she could comparison shop in the diet soda, sugar-free pudding and adult diaper categories to her heart's content. Evening's were spent in front of the TV with Biff needle-pointing or writing letters to Steve Danesi, our local congressman, about the lousy service at Damn Fu's, an Afro-Chinese restaurant down the street.

"Is anybody here listening to me? I Googled myself today and nothing came up. No media quotes. No alumni news. No articles. No references of any kind. Nothing. This is the most comprehensive search engine in the world and it has no record of my existence," I said.

"David, have ya tried Schweppes Diet Raspberry?" Beatie asked.

"No. Don't you see what this means?" I asked.

"It means yer missing out on a great soder."

"Quiet, you two. I can't hear Bill," Biff said. "He's about to challenge Alec Baldwin to an arm-wrestling match."

"It means I'm a nobody. It means my life is a complete failure," I said.

"Just shake it off, David," Biff said. "Shake it off."

"Shake it off? This isn't something you just shake off, Biff."

"Throw some dirt on it."

"I'm not talking about a sprained ankle."

"Are you trying to tell me about pain?" Biff asked.

Biff, a WWII veteran, was the only member of the Greatest Generation shot in the groin below deck by a member of his own unit on a war ship headed for France. Investigators ruled that the gun had gone off accidentally, but had difficulty explaining the second bullet lodged in Biff's back. Nevertheless, the assailant was apologetic and Biff was immediately sent home due to the loss of a testicle.

"No. I'm not trying to tell you about pain. I just . . ."

"Good. Because I know about real pain. You ever have a ball blown off?"

"Of course not, Biff. But I'm talking about something bigger."

"Bigger than my ball?"

"This has nothing to do with your ball. I'm talking about my legacy. Do you ever think about your own legacy?"

"There's an expression in the military, David. All gave some. Some gave all. And a few gave a ball. That's my legacy. I left a nut in Normandy."

This was going nowhere.

"Beatie, what about you? Don't you ever worry about whether you've made a mark?"

"Of coyse. Every time I get up."

"She ruined the front seat of my last Crown Vic. Do you remember that car? Best car I ever owned," Biff said.

The highlight of Biff's life, besides having his ball blown off, was a Ford Crown Victoria that he bought with retirement savings and replaced with a new model every three years. A perfectly fine car, yes, but a big enough, worthy enough, end-all be-all accomplishment to hold out as your life's primary achievement? Why were his dreams so small? My only consolation was that we were not related by blood. I knew it was self-indulgent and narcissistic to talk about one's own legacy, particularly with an aging, one-ball war veteran and a professional sandwich maker, but I had been called to greatness by my mother and I couldn't stop until I had some answers.

"I didn't ruin the front seat of the Crown Vic," Beatie said.

"You did, too! I never should've gotten the beige interior."

"It's yer own fault. I told ya I had no control down there."

Biff, who looked like Rueben Kincaid 30 years and 40 pounds past *The Partridge Family*, started wearing a bathrobe the day his first social security check arrived. As he explained it, this monthly check, along with his military pension, enabled him to give the finger to conventional society, including one of its most burdensome constraints: pants. After reading that Einstein always wore the same outfit to eliminate wasted thought before working, Biff hijacked the idea, and then bastardized it by developing his own philosophy that anything worth attending could be done in the terrycloth tank, as he referred to the green garment. This reasoned doctrine got him out of church, cocktail parties, volunteer work and blood drives, but still allowed for the occasional trip to the Pump and Gulp, where he bought gas, lottery tickets, beef jerky and enough batteries to replenish the bomb shelter he'd built in our basement.

Biff was the only man I knew who could spot six enemy combatants during one trip to Home Depot, and his repeated warnings to fellow shoppers to 'watch out for towel-heads' resulted in frequent shouting matches and expulsion from most in-store seminars. Although he never flew anywhere, he loved telling strangers that he'd already paid for his own funeral arrangements on his Master Card in order to get the miles.

In the plus column, he had kept Beatie company for years and for that I was thankful, but I found it impossible to look to him for anything else, whether I sought guidance, affirmation or inspiration. For those things, my only potential source was Beatie who, unlike Biff, remembered my mother's hopes for me and still heard the faint echo of her insistence that I would be successful.

"David, come in the kitchen. I wanna talk to ya," Beatie said.

Beatie loved her kitchen, an all-mauve enclave where she could smoke and worry without interruption. Usually, she could be found at the pine table where we ate most meals with a Carlton pressed between her fingers, debating aloud whether or not we had enough frozen corn niblets to make it through the week. Passing through the butler door that led from the family room with Woofie at her heels, Beatie proceeded to the kitchen counter and began making a sandwich for me, blazing away with a dull knife, a jar of Jif and a peeled banana.

"David, I need yer help."

Seated at the knotted pine table, I read the *Democrat & Chronicle*'s obituary section, trying to find direction in the lives others had led.

"Sure. Do you want me to run you to the mall?"

"No. Not today."

"Wegmans?"

"No thanks. That's not what I need."

Beatie went to the refrigerator and pulled out a can of Budweiser, popped the top and began pouring it into Woofie's water bowl.

"What are you doing?" I asked.

"What does it look like? I'm givin' Woofie a beer."

"You can't give beer to a pig."

"Sez who?"

"I don't know. The A.S.P.C. whatever they are — I'm sure they're against it."

"Don't be a jackass. Woofie's lonely. He needs a drink," Beatie said, sipping the last bit from the can.

Beatie returned to the counter and finished making my sandwich before haphazardly placing the plate in front of me and taking a seat. She pulled a cigarette from her pack of Carltons and lit up.

"I'm ready to die," Beatie said.

I stopped reading and looked up at her.

"What?"

Beatie put her burning Carlton into the serrated edge of an orange ceramic ashtray.

"The cancer's back," she said.

"Since when?"

"Since I sore Doctor Brotherton last week."

"What did he say? Why didn't you tell me?" I asked.

"I'm tellin' ya now. There's a new tumah on my right lung; a bunch actually."

I'd been through this several times with Beatie and the diagnoses were often the most difficult part.

"Okay. So we'll fight it. Just like before."

"Not this time. I don't wanna fight it."

"Why not?"

"'Cause I just don't. Doctor Brotherton sez I've got a year left but I don't want to wait that long."

"What do you mean?"

"Lean here," Beatie said, motioning me to bring my head closer to her hands. "I want to bobby-pin yer hair. It's getting too long."

Beatie pulled a bobby-pin from the ready supply in her bathrobe pocket.

"You can't bobby-pin my hair anymore. I'm a grown man," I said, recoiling from her grasp.

"I can do anything I want. I used to change yer poopie diaper, y'understand?"

Beatie bobby-pinned my bangs off my face.

"There. That's bettah," she said. "Now I've given this some thought and I think ya should use arsenic."

"For what?"

"Whaddya think for what? To put me out of my misery."

"Wait a minute. You think I'm going to kill you? My own grandmother?"

"Don't be so dramatic."

"This is not open for discussion."

"David, it's what I want."

"I'm just in shock here," I said, shaking my head. "You're not kidding, are you?"

"No."

Silence passed between us as Beatie scratched the flaking psoriasis at the back of her head and stared out the window at a red-breasted robin sitting on one of her many feeders. Ordinarily tough as teamster, my grandmother appeared vulnerable to me.

"How are you feeling?" I asked.

"I'm fine. Just a little tired that's all."

"Are you in pain?"

"No."

I rose from my seat and began to pace.

"What about the moral issues?" I asked.

"Whaddya mean?"

"You do remember that murder and suicide are considered sins by the church?"

"Are ya sure? I heard they changed all the rules."

"Some of the rules have changed, but I'm pretty sure these ones haven't been fiddled with too much."

"Well, I don't care. I'm sure God will understand an old woman's desire to die."

"I think you should discuss this with Biff. You realize how lonely he'll be without you, right?"

"Nah, that ninny won't be lonely. As long as the cable TV's working and there's plenty of Reddi-wip, he'll be happy."

"I don't believe that. And what about me? I won't be happy at all."

Beatie remained silent. She wasn't big on tears, but I hoped she was softening her up behind her black plastic shades.

"Don't be a jackass," she said. "Ya don't need me around. Plus, I've done everything I ever wanted to do," Beatie said.

How many people reach the end of their lives and can honestly say they've done everything they ever wanted to do? Sinatra, Mick Jagger and Gandhi come to mind, but the list must be short and I refused to believe Beatie qualified. Suddenly, I saw an opening.

"Now, wait a minute. You've done everything you've ever wanted to do?"

"Pretty much," she said.

"That's hard to believe. There has to be something that you've always wanted to do and haven't done," I said.

Beatie put her Carlton down and shook her head.

"C'mon. There has to be something."

Beatie shifted in her seat; her body language giving her away.

"Okay. I'll tell ya. There is one thing I nevah got to do."

"What?"

"I nevah attended the Academy Awards."

"All right. That's good. That's a start. I can work with that."

"And I nevah had one of those Frappucinos."

"I can get you one of those. No problem. Now we're getting somewhere."

"They didn't start giving Oscars out until 1928 so I nevah got the chance to see if *Kid Boots* woulda won. I always thought Clara Bow woulda had me to the ceremony."

"I'm sure she would have," I said.

"The suit was a real beyoot."

"I bet. What if I got us tickets?"

"To the Oscars?"

"Yes. We could fly out to Los Angeles, hobnob with the stars and eat caviar. What do you say?"

"That's asinine, David. Ya know I'm afraid to fly."

"We could drive."

"In *yer* car? No way."

"She'd get us there."

"I don't think so. It's only two months away."

"Beatie, give me a chance. I can make this happen. Just let me try."

"Forget it, David. It's not important."

"What do you mean it's not important? Of course it's important. It's something you've always wanted to do. All I'm asking for is a chance to try and get us tickets."

Beatie looked at me and sighed. Perhaps she saw the determination in my eyes or was simply too tired to resist.

"Okay, fine. But when this is over, promise me you'll help me die."

"I can't promise you that."

"If ya don't, I'll do it myself."

"Don't say that."

"Then promise me."

"Okay, I promise."

How could Beatie say this wasn't important? Maybe her way of thinking shouldn't have been such a mystery to me. Beatie had never been anywhere west of Ohio or east of Vermont — not to Europe or Asia or even Florida — but she never complained. My grandfather, Red, always said that once you'd vacationed at Lake George in the summer and seen the leaves fall in the Green Mountains in autumn, you'd seen it all and there was absolutely no reason to ever go anywhere else. If espoused by a husband today, this travel philosophy would no doubt be met with fierce resistance by most wives, but Beatie was part of a generation of women that was able to accept such pronouncements, misguided as they might be, and absorb them; indeed embrace them as a sign of love and respect for their husbands. This was in no way subservience. It was something very different; perhaps the product of growing up with a considerably stronger sense of sacrifice than entitlement. Beatie had no need to try to impress others or fill holes in her self-esteem by running marathons or climbing mountains. She had lived through WWI, the great depression and WWII, and she had a keen appreciation for her own small place and importance in the world. She carried no thoughts that others were getting ahead or that she was falling behind. She didn't want to be rich or famous and felt no need to change the world or fulfill any prophecies. She was satisfied with herself and her life; a mentality I could only envy.

Still, I didn't understand why she wanted to die. And as I ambled about Mt. Hope Cemetery walking Woofie, who was tipsy from the beer Beatie gave him, I tried to make sense of it. She didn't want to get sick and suffer. Who could blame her? Fighting cancer again was a daunting proposition. But her lack of will to live said something distressing to me about the nature of life and relationships, though I'd be damned if I could figure out what. Perhaps I was just surprised by her attitude, one that ran counter to everything I'd been conditioned to believe. Wasn't age something to fight and death something to resist? Weren't relationships something to cherish and savor until the end? Everybody else was focused on finding a way to extend their lives and here Beatie was opting out early. As long as I'd known her, she had a spirit as big as a zeppelin and a rear end to match, yet she wanted to go. Was I wrong to object to her request? At some level, I knew I should've taken comfort in the ease with which she accepted death as a part of life and chose to meet the end of her days with dignity, but all I felt was sadness and confusion.

four

"Father Cary Canasta, 106, died last night in the arms of Shirley Stacked, his voluptuous nephrologist and longtime lover. The first person with a colostomy bag to be named *People Magazine*'s Sexiest Man Alive twelve years in a row, Mr. Canasta or Big Nasty, as he was known to friends, diplomats, Billy Graham and six Presidents, burst onto America's arts and letters scene with his unique brand of soul poetry and became an overnight sensation both here and abroad with his one-man Broadway show, *Hurry Up, Jackhole, I'm Leaking*, a gritty and often searing portrayal of a man without control of his bodily functions or life. Command performances for the Queen, a knighthood, Kennedy Center Honors, a Tony, and a Purple Heart, earned during a weapons mishap on his fourth USO tour, did nothing to change the small town boy who grew up wanting nothing more than to share his gift of words with people of all races and religions, and to experience two hookers in a hot tub just once before he died. Father Canasta will be buried with full military honors in Arlington Cemetery this Friday. In lieu of flowers, please send donations to the Big Nasty Fund, a non-profit organization dedicated to the promotion of blow pong."

"Are you done?" I asked.

"Yeah, I'm done. Whaddya think? It's 209 words. Is that all right?"

"We decided not to do obituaries, Big Nasty," I said. "It's too depressing."

"What? Dammit, David. Why didn't you tell me? I spent two days writing that."

"I'm sorry, but we're going in a different direction," I said.

"What direction's that?"

"That's what we're here to talk about," I said.

Big Nasty occupied the booth closest to the bar at the Patch on a perpetual basis with only brief interludes for dialysis, off-track betting and ham radio operation. Six foot six and skinny with an unkempt gray beard, he was never seen without his aquamarine and orange Miami Dolphins jersey (number 13 in honor of Dan Marino) or the giant crucifix that he wore around his neck. Anywhere else he would have been labeled a real Captain Wackadoo but here, over time, he had acquired a tenuous position as the bar's poet laureate and prophet, scribbling furiously into his dog-eared spiral notebook or reading aloud from it. He had no religious training whatsoever but took on the title of Father sometime in the seventies when he performed an impromptu wedding ceremony in Las Vegas for two of Ike Turner's back-up dancers after an all-night bender.

Following a dishonorable discharge from the Navy and 25 years working at the Florida Department of Motor Vehicles, Big Nasty retired and returned to Rochester to look after his mother whose kidneys were failing. When she died and he was diagnosed with the same condition soon thereafter, he started questioning everything about the monotonous life he'd led proctoring the written portion of Florida's driver's test and processing car registrations. Unmarried and childless, Big Nasty sought the proverbial meaning of it all and began writing poetry at the Patch as a way to try and find an answer or at least make some sense of the world. This method, however, yielded few results and gradually devolved into the ongoing exercise in self-delusion and fantasy that it is today.

"If we're not doin' obits, what are we doin'?" Big Nasty asked.

"Yeah, what's the deal, David?" Nubby asked. "Hey, Dixie, can I get another beer?"

"Don't you think you've had enough?" Dixie asked.

"Is a turkey's ass tofu? Give me another pour," Nubby said.

"God, you're rude."

After giving it some thought, I had determined that a collaborative approach to pursuing greatness was the way to go. Misery allegedly loves company so I figured success must, too.

"Okay. Are you ready?"

"We're waiting, David."

"All right. Now, I've got something that's difficult to say and a tiny bit critical so you have to promise me you won't get defensive. Promise?"

"Of course," Nubby said.

"I don't have a defensive bone in my body," Big Nasty said.

"All right. Good. The reason we're here is simple and, again, I don't want you guys to take this the wrong way, but I don't think we're living up to our potential," I said.

"What?" Nubby asked. "Are you out of your mind?"

"That's total horseshit," Big Nasty said. "Total horseshit."

"I just think we could be doing more with our lives."

"I thought we were friends, David. I really did."

"Will you shut-up, Nubby? We are friends. I'm not excluding myself here. Don't you get it? We've got to rise up from these barstools."

"Right now?" Nubby asked. "I just started this beer."

"It's a metaphor, you moron. Don't you see? We've got to rise up, cast out our personal demons and achieve our inherent greatness."

"How the hell are we going to do that?" Nubby asked.

"Look, my personal demons took control of me a long time ago and I'd put the odds of evicting them at pretty much less than zero," Big Nasty said.

"Nonsense. We're going to reinvent ourselves and reinvent Rochester, and in the process we will achieve true greatness."

"What do you mean 'reinvent ourselves'? That's stupid," Nubby said. "I'm not joining some religious cult."

"Aren't you sick of sitting around this place day after day, just watching your life disappear? Don't you want to tap the potential inside you?"

"I've got my poetry. I'm already tapping my potential," Big Nasty said.

"But I just heard your obit and you haven't accomplished any of those things yet."

"So what? If I've learned anything it's that all human endeavors are futile."

"What?" I asked.

"You heard me. All human endeavors are futile . . . pointless."

"You don't believe that, Big Nasty."

"Yes, I do."

"Then what was all that you wrote in your obituary? You've got aspirations. You want to make a mark."

Big Nasty shrugged his shoulders and rolled his eyes.

"You get hooked up to a dialysis machine three times a week for five years and then come talk to me about making a mark. That shit'll bend your aspirations into a goddamn pretzel."

"What's so important about making a mark anyway?" Nubby asked.

"I can't answer that for you. It's different for everyone. For me, I just feel it inside. It's something I have to do."

"Because your mother said so."

"Sure. That's part of it. I'm not ashamed to say that. But it's not just for her. It's for me, too."

"I smell mid-life crisis," Big Nasty said.

"Major mid-life crisis," Nubby said. "Go buy a used Porsche, David."

"This isn't a mid-life crisis," I said. "At least I don't think it is."

"You're not trying to get Miranda back, are you?" Nubby asked.

"No. This has nothing to do with her. But it does relate to women."

"How?"

"By doing something great, you're going to attract great women. Right, Dixie?"

"That's true," Dixie said, rejoining us after a trip to the cash register. "Remember when I told you about the moth and the flame, Nubby? Doing something meaningful with your life is the flame."

"Well, I don't care about doing something meaningful or making any mark," Nubby said. "When Odorrific starts hiring again, I'm going to be first in line."

"To sell bathroom sprays for the rest of your life?" I asked.

"Yes. Wait'll you see their new product line. They're coming out with an aerosol that smells like an Atlantic City casino. It's called Covering the Spread."

"That's pathetic. What about you, Big Nasty?"

"David, I told you. The only chance I've got of making a mark is with my poems."

"Okay. But how are you going to do that if they stay buried in your notebook? Do you ever send them around to publishers?"

"I sent one to *Penthouse* once. It was called *Hooker Without Legs*. I still remember it. *'I see you in my bed and wonder. What lurks beneath the spread? Way down under. Nothin', baby. Absolutely nothin'.'*"

"That's twisted," Dixie said.

"No, I get it. It's an existential ode to a legless prostitute," I said.

"It's the worst poem I've ever heard," Nubby said.

"There's a certain symmetry to it," I said, feigning encouragement.

"To the poem?" Nubby asked.

"No. To the hooker."

"How can there be symmetry? Half her body is missing."

"Perhaps, but the upper torso and the meter have symmetry. The poem's like a haiku. Is that a haiku, Big Nasty?" I asked.

"What's a haiku?" Nubby asked.

"It's not a haiku," Dixie said. "It's a perversion."

"Maybe so, but I'm not going to apologize for the fact that I'm a sexually compulsive person," Big Nasty said. "If God didn't want me to masturbate, he would have made my arms shorter. Did you ever see the documentary film *I Am A Sex Addict*?"

"No. And I'm not going to," Dixie said.

"Guys, guys, slow down. We're getting sidetracked here. I'm going to assume that *Penthouse* didn't publish the poem, Big Nasty, and that you immediately quit sending out poems after that single rejection," I said. "Am I right?"

Big Nasty held his poetry notebook a few inches from his face, angling the spiral pad slightly forward to catch the limited light available from the Coors Light lamp above his head. Slowly, he nodded.

"That's what I thought. Look, I know it's not going to be

easy, but what do we have to lose by trying to make something of ourselves?"

The question hung in the air for five seconds while we each struggled to come up with a plausible answer.

"All right, David. Let's say for a moment that we were going to try and rise up from these bar stools and do all that other shit you're talking about. What would we do?" Nubby asked.

"I don't know. Isn't there something you've always wanted to do?"

"You guys need to get involved in something bigger than yourselves," Dixie said.

"Like what?" Nubby asked. "Monster trucks?"

"No. That's not what I mean. I'm talking about a cause. You guys need a cause. You want my help finding good women? This is step one. Women like men with purpose."

"Dixie's right. What about charity work?" I asked.

"What about it?" Nubby asked.

"I hear it's rewarding."

"Who told you that?"

"I don't know. People," I said.

"People full of crap. I've done the charity thing and it's thankless."

"What charity work have you ever done, Nubby?" Dixie asked.

"I dug graves one summer for a church-sponsored orphanage and I didn't get one thank you note. Do you have any idea how hard it is to hold a shovel with a missing thumb?"

"You're shameless," I said.

"I like the charity idea, David," Big Nasty said. "We could read to the deaf or something like that."

"I don't see how that gets any of us to greatness," Nubby said.

"What if we become organ donors?" I asked.

"In case you've forgotten, I've already got a kidney on the fritz over here," Big Nasty said.

"Yeah, you pretty much have to die to donate organs," Nubby said.

"Or get in a serious wreck," Big Nasty said.

"Okay. Bad idea."

"How about a relief mission to Africa?" Big Nasty asked.

"You were supposed to bring chips to my Super Bowl party and you forgot. Now you want to run a relief mission to Africa?" Nubby asked.

"It's just an idea," Big Nasty said. "I think I still have an old cassette tape of *We Are the World*."

"It's a good idea," Dixie said. "But maybe you could start a bit closer than Africa."

"How about Mexico? I once wrote a poem about a trip I took to Tijuana called *Donkey Show*. 'One spring break in Mexico, I took my gal to a donkey show. To my surprise she gave it a go, and rode that ass 'til the burro blow'd. The more time passes, the more I know, life sure sucks when you're dating a ho.'"

"I'd appreciate it if you would refrain from using the word 'ho' in my presence."

"Sorry, Dixie. It captured what I was feeling at the time. The whole ride home to California she smelled like a bale of hay dipped in donkey turd."

"We could visit sick people in the hospital," Nubby said.

"You can't just show up at a hospital and visit sick people," I said.

"Why not?"

"If you woke up from a coma, would you want to see us sitting at the foot of your bed?"

"Probably not," Nubby said.

"Of course not. Anyway, you have to know the person who's sick to visit them," Nubby said.

"What about people with no family?" Big Nasty asked.

"Even then, I'm sure they wouldn't want to see us. They get top entertainers and athletes to make those visits. Circus freaks. Ventriloquists. Pete Rose. People like that."

"We could entertain them. I could read my poetry. I've written plenty of deathbed poems. I even wrote a very tender one about the intensive care unit called *ICU*. *'So you got hit by a train, and you're in God-awful pain. You got pushed on the tracks, by a junkie on crack. Now just like that thug, you're screaming for drugs. The nurse is your dealer, your muse, your healer. She gives you your fix, like a whore turning tricks. She won't take no shit, or flash her large. . .'*"

"Big Nasty, hold up. I think we get the flavor," I said. "Look, everybody think bigger. We need to find a way to shock the world."

"Right. What about the *Guinness Book of World Records*?" Big Nasty asked.

"What record are *we* going to set?" Nubby asked.

"I don't know," Big Nasty said. "How about making the world's biggest sandwich?"

"That could bring the Rochester community together," Dixie said.

"What kind of sandwich?" Nubby asked.

"How about ham on rye?" Big Nasty said.

"With cheese?" Nubby asked.

"I don't know."

"You have to think about these things. Do you know how expensive cheese is?" Nubby asked.

"Okay, forget the cheese," Big Nasty said.

"What? You can't have a ham sandwich without cheese," Nubby said. "And where are you going to find a big enough piece of rye bread? It would have to be the size of a swimming pool."

"Fine, no rye. Let's use pumpernickel."

"All right, but that brings on a whole host of other problems."

"Jesus, Nubby. Forget the sandwich idea. Just forget it. What if we made the world's biggest sundae?" Big Nasty asked.

"Are you familiar with the cost of caramel?" Nubby asked.

"No, Nubby. I don't know the goddamn cost of caramel, all right?"

"Guys, do me a favor and shut-up," I said. "Forget the *Guinness Book*. We'll find another way to shock the world."

"I still think the sandwich could do it," Nubby said.

"Shut-up about the sandwich, Nubby," I said.

"Wait a minute. I could skip rope for three weeks," Nubby said.

"You couldn't skip rope for three seconds," Big Nasty said.

"Could to."

"I still say you guys need to think bigger," Dixie said. "What about doing something for the city?"

"That's a great idea," I said. "We need to look to our past for inspiration. Rochester has a long history of greatness. Maybe we could do something related to Chester Carlson."

"Who the hell is Chester Carlson?" Nubby asked. "Is he related to the mail chute guy?"

"No, he isn't. He invented the Xerox machine," I said.

"Big whoop," Nubby said.

"Big whoop? Are you joking? Carlson changed the world. Right here from Rochester. If you can't find inspiration in that then you're hopeless."

"I just don't see what some dead dude named Chester has to do with us," Nubby said.

"He's got everything to do with us. See, Carlson was on a quest. After he invented the Xerox copier, he realized that he had created something that could duplicate the past but never change it. No matter what he put into his machine, the same thing always came out on the other side. He began to wonder about people and what happened when they passed to the other side."

"The guy sounds like a crack-pot," Nubby said.

"He wasn't a crack-pot, you idiot. He was a genius with a curiosity about life and this boundary he couldn't get past in the physical world with his copiers bothered him; so much so that he began to explore reincarnation."

"Oh, no. Not one of those. Did he have crystals hanging from the rear-view mirror of his Jetta?"

"Shut-up, Nubby," Dixie said.

One week before, by happenstance, I had come across an article about Chester Carlson while waiting to see my dentist.

"Yes, please. Shut-up," I said. "Carlson came to believe that a person's soul had the ability to transcend beyond this life and take on a new physical form in the next."

"What a flake," Nubby said.

"He wasn't a flake."

"What's the point, David?"

"The point is that Carlson was a great man who lived and died here, and he believed that every man could improve himself — if not in this lifetime then in a subsequent one. He believed that reincarnation or rebirth, if you will, was a part of life, and *rebirth* is exactly what this city and each of one of us needs right now. That's the point."

"All right, fine. If this Carlson guy was so great, why don't we organize an effort to build a monument in his honor?" Nubby asked. "It could be a tourist thing. God knows we need something."

"That's not a bad idea," I said. "How about a tower?"

"We could build a space needle like they have in Seattle," Big Nasty said.

"I hate Seattle," Nubby said. "We need something different."

"What about an arch like they have in St. Louis?" I asked.

"St. Louis is a pit," Nubby said.

"Maybe, but it's a pit with an arch. We're just a pit," Big Nasty said.

"How tall is the Transamerica Building?" I asked.

"Who cares? It's a pathetic attempt at phallic symbolism," Dixie said.

"That's exactly what we need: a huge phallic symbol to energize the people of Monroe County -- right smack dab in the center of Rochester. It would scream 'rebirth,'" Big Nasty said.

"Do you know how sexist that is?" Dixie asked. "The city will never go for it."

"I like that idea," Nubby said. "Think about it. If we build an enormous tower in the shape of a penis, people will come from miles around to see it."

"Sort of like *Field of Dreams*," Big Nasty said.

"Exactly. It'll stand as a reminder of the city's virility."

"I'm not sure about that," I said. "It's a little too crude, don't you think?"

"Not at all," Nubby said.

"It's preposterous. It'll only stand as a reminder of the city's stupidity," Dixie said. "Do we really want to be known as the home of the world's biggest wienie?"

"What are we called right now?" Nubby asked.

"The Flower City."

"No, we're the World's Image Centre because of Kodak, Xerox and Bausch and Lomb. I saw it at the airport," Big Nasty said.

"So, basically, we don't have a nickname that's worth a crap," Nubby said.

"And Home of the Two Thousand Foot Johnson is going to solve all of our problems?" Dixie asked.

"It'll put us back on the map," Nubby said.

"Which one? The map of outsized genitalia? I'd rather stay off it," Dixie said.

"You know, Dixie, it's just a body part; no different than the shoulder or the spleen or the pinky toe," Nubby said. "I'm sick and tired of being made to feel ashamed about it."

"Do you know how fast the protesters would shut you down?" Dixie asked.

"Who's going to protest a penis?" Nubby asked.

"Lots of people. Plus, who's going to pay for it? Do you think the state is going to fund public pornography?"

"We won't tell them what it is. We'll simply apply for funding and keep the design specifications under wraps. As it goes up, the workers can keep it under a sheet," Nubby said.

"Are you insane?" Dixie asked. "Rochester's one of the birthplaces of the women's rights movement. This idea is all wrong. Tell them, David," Dixie said.

The idea of a tower was dead just like the two dozen other ideas we'd thrown around. Rochester was fading off into oblivion and if we didn't do something soon, it would take us with it. Dixie said we needed a cause and I agreed, but the distraction of the discussion was losing its power over me and my worries about Beatie were resurfacing.

"I'm just not sure what any of this has to do with Chester Carlson. Plus, the truth is I've got a bigger problem now," I said, my voice full of resignation. "Beatie's sick."

"Oh, no, David. What's wrong?" Dixie asked.

"She's got cancer again," I said.

"Oh, no. I'm so sorry."

"Yeah, man. That's tough," Big Nasty said.

"Real sorry, David," Nubby said.

"I told her I'd take her to the Academy Awards to try and lift her spirits — dumbest promise I ever made."

"That *was* dumb," Nubby said.

"Be quiet, Nubby," Dixie said.

"I've tried to think of a way to get tickets but it's hopeless."

"I have an idea. If you can't get tickets to the Oscars, you can take her to the High Falls Film Festival as an alternative," Dixie said.

"No, you don't understand. She's lost her will to live. It's got to be the Academy Awards."

"What the hell's the High Falls Film Festival anyway?" Nubby asked.

"I can't believe you, Nubby. Do you *ever* pull your head out of the sand? It's an annual festival held here in Rochester that features films made by women. It also celebrates the city's role in the history of film and the women's rights movement," Dixie said.

"Oh, boy. Here we go. Everything has to be about women's rights with her," Nubby said.

"Don't be a sexist pig," Dixie said. "If you didn't know it, Rochester is where Susan B. Anthony did her greatest work and led the suffrage movement. In fact, they give out a Susan B. Anthony 'Failure is Impossible' Award at the festival every year to honor her spirit and accomplishments."

"Who's Susan B. Anthony?" Nubby asked.

"Are you serious? If it hadn't been for Susan B. Anthony, women wouldn't have the right to vote."

"Women have the right to vote?"

"You're going to die alone, Nubby. You know that, right?" Dixie asked. "You are such an ass."

"Take it easy, guys," I said.

"All I did was ask a question," Nubby said. "What is it a crime if I don't know who this Susan B. Arthur is?"

"It's Susan B. *Anthony* not Arthur," Dixie said. "And it is a crime is because she was one of the most important proponents of women's rights, racial equality and worker protection in history. If you knew a tenth of what I've learned in my women's studies class, you'd know that many of the things she fought for have benefited you."

"I doubt it. Where was she when I got laid off from Odorrific?"

"I wrote a poem about Susan B. Anthony once," Big Nasty said. *'Sweet Susie B., with your corset pulled tight, and your smooth velvet gams, glistening in the light. They say you're a prude, but I know better. 'Cause me likes what me sees 'neath your tight-fitting sweater.'* . . . That's pretty much as far as I got."

"Tough topic," I said.

"Yeah, the civil rights stuff is always challenging," Big Nasty said. "Such a broad canvas to paint on . . . it can be overwhelming frankly."

"You know it figures that we'd get stuck with some crummy, little film festival for sober chicks who like to vote while Los Angeles gets the Oscars," Nubby said.

"The High Falls Film Festival is not a crummy, little film festival for sober chicks who like to vote, you moron. It's an important festival that's only going to grow. And, FYI, step two toward meeting the girl of your dreams: stop belittling the accomplishments of women and being an all-around jerk," Dixie said.

"Hey, don't go ape-shit on me. All I'm saying is that I wish the Oscars were held here instead of some chick flick festival. What's wrong with that?" Nubby asked.

My mother's favorite poet was Ralph Waldo Emerson, whose work she often read to me at bedtime. In one of her favorite passages, Emerson said, *'A man should learn to detect and watch that gleam of light which flashes across his mind from within, more than the luster of the firmament of bards and sages. Yet he dismisses without notice his thoughts, because they are his. In every work of genius we recognize our own rejected thoughts; they come back to us with a certain alienated majesty.'* Today, sitting in the Patch, I would not make the mistake of dismissal or rejection.

"Nothing's wrong with that. In fact, it's perfect," I said.

"What's perfect?" Dixie asked.

"Our cause. It's perfect. It's big. It's communal. It's aspirational. It's absolutely perfect. I can't believe I didn't think of it before."

"David, what are you talking about?" Dixie asked.

"I'm talking about the Oscars. I'm talking about holding the Academy Awards here in Rochester."

"Did you suffer a head wound recently?" Big Nasty asked.

"No. This is the quest for greatness we've been searching for."

"First of all, that's never going to happen," Nubby said. "Second of all, *we* have not been searching for any quest for greatness. *You* have."

"So, you're not in?" I asked.

"No, I'm not in. There's *nothing* to be in. Where are we? *Fantasy Island*? Oh, wait. I think I see Mr. Rourke and Tattoo."

"I think we can do it," I said.

"You're nuts. Why would anyone ever agree to hold the Academy Awards in Rochester?" Nubby asked.

"Because this is where film started. This is the home of Kodak. This is home of the International Museum of Film and Photography," I said.

"So?"

"So Rochester is the World's Image Centre, remember?"

"I thought we were the Flower City."

"No, we nixed that."

"So what's your point?" Nubby asked.

"My point is that this is our chance to prove we *are* the World's Image Centre. Think about it. Where are the Academy Awards held in Los Angeles every year?" I asked.

"I don't know," Nubby said.

"The Kodak Theatre. If they switched things up for a year and gave Rochester — the home of Kodak and the place where film started — a shot, they would generate incredible publicity. Now, why *wouldn't* they do that?"

"One, because they don't have to and two, because it's 20 below zero here in February and celebrities hate the cold."

"We'll just have to be persuasive."

"We've got no chance," Nubby said.

"What do you think, Dixie?"

"I'm in. I think failure is impossible. Just like Susan B. Anthony did."

"Oh, no. Not her again," Nubby moaned.

"Nubby might have a point. What makes you think the celebrities and the media will be willing to come to Rochester?" Big Nasty asked.

"Maybe they won't, but it can't hurt to try. Don't you see? This is our mission. This is our moment. This is our chance to put Rochester back on the map for a reason that doesn't involve oversized genitalia. We've got to try."

"All right, David. I still say this is pointless and I want to go on the record that I prefer the idea of a big penis monument, but what the hell . . . I'm in," Big Nasty said. "I'll be dead soon anyway."

"That makes you the only hold-out, Nubby" I said. "What's it gonna be? Are you in?"

"I don't know," Nubby said.

"This is the way we can shock the world, Nub," I said. "This is the one."

"Just make up your damn mind. I've got a dialysis appointment in 20 minutes and I've got to get going," Big Nasty said.

As John Lee Hooker sang the *Lonely Boy Boogie* in the

background, Nubby took a look around the Patch and considered his options. The look in his eyes told me he was feeling a lot like me. The days of our lives were passing; piling up like old newspapers — frayed and yellow with headlines already forgotten.

"Do you think I could sit next to Julia Roberts during the show?" Nubby asked.

"I can't promise you that, but maybe."

"Okay, screw it. I'm in."

"Should we do a group hug?" I asked.

"Touch me, David, and I'll slug you. I swear I will," Nubby said.

Five

Mayor Cornelia Candee was the richest woman in Rochester, having leveraged her ownership of a dozen trailer parks into a commercial real estate gold mine of strip malls, strip clubs and a chain of restaurants called Cockeye's. She fit the profile of a textbook psychopath — alternatively charming and insane — but after making one large donation to a local hospital, she rode into elected office on a wave of good feeling and relative anonymity. Unfortunately, the power went to her head like eight shots of espresso on an empty stomach. The product of an overbearing stage father who wanted a son, she'd grown up like a weed through rocky soil while traveling the vaudeville circuit as a ukulele prodigy; an experience that brought little money, much heartbreak and prompted her father to brand her a loser. At 87 years of age, she was still trying to knock that chip of failure off her shoulder.

In the shortest political honeymoon ever, Rochester voters began regretting their choice for Mayor during her inauguration when she put the Chippendales bikini team on the dais in order to add "majesty" to the event. In the ensuing three years, she alienated every key constituency through a series of ego trips and blunders, none greater than her "Too Cold for Terrorists" tourism campaign which took an already moribund Rochester sightseeing industry and piled six feet of snow on it. With an election approaching, Mayor Candee was desperate to sway public opinion in her favor and she believed she could do so by turning Rochester into a legalized gambling and prostitution mecca. This proposition, however, had been roundly rejected by the city council, making it an opportune time for us to bring our Oscar idea to her.

Dixie, who moved in the right circles prior to her estrangement from her father, had attended the Mayor's annual Christmas party for years and was able to get us on her calendar. Arriving at City Hall, we checked in with her appointment secretary and took seats in the waiting area outside her office, where we could hear her twisted wisdom echoing off the walls. Lewd, rude and crude aptly described Mayor Candee's governing style.

"Who appointed those morons to the city council?" Mayor Candee asked.

"You did, ma'am," said an obviously frazzled underling.

"Then I got bad advice. Fire 'em all!"

"I can't do that, Madame Mayor. It violates the city charter."

"Then tear up the charter."

"It also violates the bylaws."

"Tear them up, too."

"I don't think that's advisable, ma'am."

"Then tell me how the hell can I improve tourism if those toe-lickers on the council won't let me legalize gambling and prostitution?"

"Madame Mayor, if I may, I think what the citizens really want is to have their trash picked up on time and better mass transit."

"Mass transit is a myth. People love their cars."

"But the latest polls . . ."

"Shut it right there, Denton. You know I don't run this city on polls. I run it on bribes. They're a lot more reliable."

"But, ma'am . . ."

"Don't *but* me, Denton. I've got tubes of ointment older than you."

Denton Fink, a Brooks Brothers sort in his forties who served as the Deputy Mayor, emerged from his boss's office looking browbeaten.

"The Mayor will see you now," Denton said, signaling us to follow him into Mayor Candee's fiefdom. Trailing behind Dixie and Big Nasty, Nubby and I shuffled forward.

"Well, there she is," the Mayor said. "Little Dixie Lee all grown up."

After hugging Dixie and enduring the obligatory introductions, the Mayor instructed us to be seated on three hot pink couches in front of a dark marbled fireplace. Her office was decorated in a style best described as Barbie Dream House meets early American war bunker. I don't think she'd ever been in the service actually, but she wasn't going to let that small fact get in the way of creating the impression. Mayor Candee wore an all-white pantsuit with a black string tie and looked like the disturbed daughter of Colonel Sanders right down to her white shock of hair and black horned-rim glasses.

"So, Dixie, tell me why you and your little friends are here."

"Madame Mayor, we've got an idea that we think could revive Rochester."

"Revive Rochester? You make it sound like the city's on life support. I'm not sure I like your tone. I'm in here two sometimes three days a week trying to make this a better place to live for everyone. I hope you appreciate that."

"Of course, I do. We all do," Dixie said, sensing the need to be diplomatic — even obsequious. "That's why we're here. Our idea is something that can't happen without your commitment to it."

"Few things can, am I right?"

"One hundred percent," Dixie said.

Satisfied that we were sufficiently respectful, the Mayor relaxed.

"Hey, before we count the legs on this centipede, who wants a toddy?" Mayor Candee asked, standing up and opening what could only be described as a walk-in liquor closet.

"I'll take one," Nubby said. "How about a Jack and Coke?"

"Coming right up."

"Nubby, we're not here to drink," I said.

"Aw, c'mon man. I'm just being social."

"No drinks for us, Madame Mayor," I said.

"I respect your discipline," Mayor Candee said, pouring four fingers of scotch into a tumbler. "Just say no. Keep kids off drugs. Don't drink and drive. I'm for all of that nonsense."

With one concerned look from Dixie, I knew she was already wondering if our visit was a mistake.

"Swisher Sweet?" Mayor Candee asked.

"Ma'am, if I may remind you, there's no smoking allowed in public buildings," Denton said.

"I know that, Denton. I'm the one who signed the stupid law, remember? Now, where was I? Oh, right. Tell me about your idea, Dixie."

"The idea is actually David's," Dixie said, looking my way. "So I'm going to let him tell you about it."

"Okay, Davey, fire away," Mayor Candee said, taking her seat.

"Madame Mayor, we think that Rochester, with its unique connection to the film industry, would make a great host for the Academy Awards next year."

"You mean bring the Oscars here?"

"Yes."

Mayor Candee pondered it for a minute.

"That's not bad. That's not bad at all. Would there be gambling involved?"

"No, I don't think so."

"What about prostitution?"

"That's not really part of our vision for it."

"Of course not. You let me worry about all that. Vegas can set the line and I'll pack the place with ass. You add those ingredients and, hell, this jackrabbit just might make stew."

"Madame Mayor, our plan to convince the Academy of Motion Picture Arts and Sciences to hold the Oscars here has two parts."

"Got it. Two parts. I'm tracking."

"The first part is to emphasize to the Academy the incredible tradition in photography and film we have here in Rochester. We can talk about the origins of Kodak and the International Museum of Film and Photography, and we think the Eastman Theatre would be the perfect venue to hold the event, both logistically and symbolically."

"Couldn't agree more. And let me cut you off right there, because I already know the second part of the plan."

"You do?"

"Sure. Blackjack tables and call girls."

"Again, Madame Mayor, none of that is currently part of our plan."

"Hey, don't rush to judgment."

"I don't think I am, it's just that . . ."

"'Cause if the Spandex fits, you must acquit," Mayor Candee continued, chuckling at her own joke.

Feeling frustrated and fairly certain the Mayor was certifiable, I turned the floor over to Dixie to describe the second part of our plan.

"Mayor Candee, as you know, Rochester hosts a film festival at the High Falls every November celebrating the accomplishments of female filmmakers," Dixie said.

"It does?"

"Yes."

"Oh right, right. I think I drove by it one time."

"Anyway, at the festival, they honor the memory of Susan B. Anthony."

"Why is that name is familiar? Was she one of *Charlie's Angels*?"

"No, Madame Mayor, she was a famous suffragette who lived here in Rochester."

"This may be too personal but may I ask what she was suffering from?"

"I don't think you understand. She was the most famous proponent of women's rights in the 19th Century and she did most of her work here."

"Well, I'll be. Is she still working?"

"No, she's dead."

"So how's she going to host the show?"

"Ma'am, please hear me out. The film industry is always talking about the lack of good roles for women over 40 and the rampant Hollywood sexism, but nobody ever seems to do anything about it. Given this fact, what better place to hold the Oscars than one of the true homes of the women's rights movement? We could present it to them as a way to express the industry's gratitude for all the contributions made by females."

"I think I get it. You guys want to blackmail them. I love it!" Mayor Candee exclaimed.

"No, that's not what we want," Dixie said.

"Sure, it is. You want to use women's rights as a wedge issue against the Academy. This is just like an election campaign. Let's swift boat these suckers."

"Madame Mayor, I don't think I'm following you," Dixie said.

"It's simple. We tell the Academy that we're the home of women's rights and that unless they demonstrate their commitment to women by holding the Oscars here in Rochester, we'll go to the media and make a big, fat stink. And, of course, we'll also mention we're the home of film and Susan B. Anthony, one of *Charlie's Angels*. It's your garden variety blackmail."

"Mayor Candee, I assure you that is *not* what's intended. The description of Rochester's role in the women's rights movement would in no way be exploitative or coercive," Dixie said.

"Of course not, we need to do something much, much worse."

"Madame Mayor, I think you're missing the point," Dixie said.

"Not at all. We need to ride this horse buck naked 'til we break her. You're talking about the most powerful weapon of the new era: political correctness. Your plan is perfect. All this p.c. crap plays real well out West."

Dixie appeared exasperated so I thought I'd try to reason with Mayor Candee.

"Mayor Candee, I think what Dixie means is that Rochester's role in the women's rights movement would be presented as something substantive and heartfelt, but would not be intended to pressure anyone."

"Then what's the point? Not only do you need to pressure them, you also need to raise the stakes."

"What do you mean?"

"Davey, let me tell you something. There's only one way to make this Oscar thing happen. We need to play the race card."

"Say what?"

"The race card. We need to play it from the bottom of the deck. Otherwise you're missing one of the major legs of the p.c. stool."

"Madame Mayor, with all due respect, that is one of the worst ideas I've ever heard," Dixie said. "And he goes by *David* not Davey."

"Ouch — if it has tits or wheels, expect problems eh, Davey?" Mayor Candee asked, fixing her eyes on me.

"Mayor Candee, to Dixie's point, using race does strike me as a potentially volatile strategy," I said.

"That's the whole idea. I've got an election coming up and I don't want to rely on voter suppression and intimidation alone. How do you sad sacks think you get any attention for a city our size? You have to do the unconventional. Remember when I married those three people in clear violation of state law? Pure publicity stunt. CNN covered it for days arguing about the ethical implications of the tri-nuptial trend. It's all theatre."

"Theatre or not, I don't think it's worth using a divisive issue such as race to hamstring the Academy," I said.

"Look, Denton's been prepping me for black history month in February and I've learned a few things. Did you know this city was the long-time home of Frederick Douglass, the first black man to run for President? Did you know he ran a paper here advocating freedom for all blacks and is even buried here? Did you know Rochester also played a major role in the Underground Railroad and has a long history of supporting civil rights?"

"Yes, I knew all of that," Dixie said.

"Well, it was news to me, but you pair that up with the women's rights issues and you have a stick of p.c. dynamite that'll blow up the Academy. Correct me if I'm wrong, but doesn't Hollywood get just as much criticism for its treatment of minorities as it does for women?"

"That's true, Madame Mayor, but our objective is not to *blow up* the Academy; it's to entice them to bring the Oscars to Rochester."

"Of course, of course. We'll entice the bejeezus out of them. That's where the dice and the girls come in. But, first, we'll shove a stick of p.c. dynamite straight up their Hollywood butts. Bringing the Academy Awards to Rochester would be the greatest thing ever to happen to this city. We need to do whatever it takes, including under the table cash payments to the Academy board members if our p.c. ploy doesn't work. I'm telling you, this is just the thing we need in order to get Candee Land off the ground."

"Candee Land?" I asked.

"Oops. Denton, you didn't tell them about the theme park?"

"Uh, no, Madame Mayor."

"Well, I haven't announced it publicly yet and if you tell anyone I'll deny it, but I'm planning to turn the High Falls into a combination waterslide park, casino and adult entertainment center. That's why I need the city council to approve my measure to legalize gambling and prostitution. Hosting the Oscars will be the perfect way to publicize the project and push it over the endline. If I can show the viability of a downtown entertainment district, the city council will be forced to approve my measure and the state will have to cough up some public funding. Once that happens, my reelection is all but assured."

"Did you say waterslide park?" Dixie asked, suddenly mindful that her father might be involved. "Are you working with my father on this?"

"Of course, Dixie. I figured you knew about it. His company, Goliath Industries, is going to be the general contractor. Candee Land will be the first theme park in the country to offer genuine fun for the whole family: slots and shots for dad, spas and shopping for mom, and waterslides for the little monsters."

"But you'll destroy the whole High Falls area if you commercialize it like that," Dixie said.

"Destroy it? To the contrary, I'm going to turn the High Falls into a major tourist destination, like the Grand Canyon."

"Nobody goes to the Grand Canyon for gambling, prostitution or waterslides," I said.

"That's because the National Park Service doesn't offer any of that, but they should. They'd get a lot more visitors."

"You can't do this," Dixie said.

"Of course I can. And your Oscar idea is gonna help make it all happen."

We left the Mayor's office in stunned silence. Dixie, whose ears were emitting steam, immediately called her father, violently punching numbers into her cell phone from the passenger seat of my car.

"Daddy, it's Dixie," she said. "What the hell do you think you're doing?"

"Lambchop," Mr. Lee said. "I knew you'd come around. When's my little Dixie chick coming home to her nest?"

Pete Lee was a bastard to most people he met, but was relative putty in his daughter's hands.

"I am not your little *Dixie* chick and I'm not coming home."

"Are you getting married?"

"No, I'm *not* getting married. I'm calling you about the High Falls. How could you agree to build a waterslide park and casino there?"

"Oh, you heard about that?"

"Yes, I heard about it. It's despicable. That's one of Rochester's most historic sites. You're going to ruin it."

"Dixie, that project is going to be good for downtown. The Mayor needs to find a way to convince families from the suburbs to spend time in the city and this'll do that."

"Families? There's going to be gambling and, if Mayor Candee has her way, prostitution."

"Now, hold on a minute. *Prostitution* is such an ugly word.

Think of it as a way for mommies and daddies to make new friends. You're young, but someday you'll realize that they need to have fun, too."

"You disgust me."

"Watch your tone. You didn't seem so disgusted when I was paying for your new clothes and ski lessons. Where do you think that money comes from?"

"I demand you pull out of the project."

"If I don't build it, Dixie, someone else will. It's my chance to get your brothers involved with a big project. They need to cut their teeth and this is perfect. There's nothing you can do to stop it. I'm sorry."

"If you think you're sorry now, just wait."

Dixie hung up on her father and fumed.

"I'm going to need that favor you guys promised," Dixie said.

"What favor?" I asked.

"Yeah, what favor?" Nubby asked.

"The one you promised me in exchange for my help with your love lives."

"Oh, right. That one. What do you need?" I asked.

"I want you to help me burn down Goliath Industries."

"Your father's company?" I asked.

"Yes — the headquarters and the warehouse out by Honeoye Lake. We've got to stop this High Falls project."

"Dixie, that's a bit extreme, don't you think? There's got to be another way to stop the project without resorting to arson," I said.

"I don't know. It sounds kind of exciting to me," Nubby said.

"I agree. I'm in," Big Nasty said.

"Shut-up, you guys," I said.

"We could blow it up," Dixie said. "Big Nasty, what do you know about C-4 explosives?"

"Dixie, I know I promised you a favor, but I didn't know it would involve a felony. I can't do it," I said.

"David, we're not going to get caught," Dixie said.

"What if we do? Is this really worth going to jail? When you said we'd owe you a favor, I thought you meant something like a ride home from work."

"David, a promise is a promise. I'll help you find love, and you'll help me exact revenge. It's a perfect bargain. I want to see the look on my father's face when his whole empire is reduced to smoldering ashes. Don't you get it? My stupid family is going to trash the High Falls. We're talking about the best part of downtown, our city's last untouched natural resource. You have to help me."

"Dixie, I will, but I don't want to burn anything down or blow anything up. Just give me a little time to think of something else."

I added Dixie's deranged demand to my growing list of concerns and wondered about Mayor Candee's assertion that the Oscars would be the greatest thing ever to happen to Rochester. Would we end up like one of those sad Olympic cities left with nothing but overpriced souvenirs and a monumental tax burden to pay for the cost of hosting the event, or would it change the face of the city forever creating lasting memories, an image makeover and unforeseen economic opportunities for years to come? I wasn't sure. Would it renew the spirit of Rochester and its citizens, including me? On that account, surely the answer was yes, but there was something inherently wrong about Mayor Candee's scheme to blackmail the Academy and her plan to build Candee Land. Somehow, we had to stop the Mayor and find another way to lure Oscar.

SIX

Out on court six, my disciples, the princes and princesses of overindulgence, were beginning to gather. Each of them was dressed head to toe in the latest fashions, whites only of course, with brand new shoes and at least two if not three rackets a piece, except for Willa Nash, who appeared to be holding a three-foot long two by four.

"What's with the wood, Willa?" I asked. "You realize you need a racket to play tennis."

"This is Plank," she said.

"Plank?"

"Yes. I'm going to play with him today instead of a racket."

"Willa, I might be willing to indulge that request if you were Ilie Nastase, but since you're not, I'm only going to say this once: put down the wood and pick up a racket."

"But Plank's my friend."

"I don't care if he's your AA sponsor. Put him down."

"Who's Ilie Nastase?"

"Nevermind. Just get your racket."

These were not the kids I grew up with in the 1970's. The boys knew the difference between a BMW and a Buick, the girls were all on the latest diet and tennis was an unpleasant obligation interfering with their ability to get back online, send text messages or watch the latest age-inappropriate movie for the twelfth time in their parents' personal home theatre room.

"It's hot in here," Willa said, racket in hand, as she untucked her shirt and exposed a blubbery waistline.

"Yeah, can we have a water break?" Danny Cohen, my resident lawyer-in-training, asked.

"What are you wearing on your head, Danny?" I asked.

"It's a bike helmet. My dad says tennis can be dangerous."

"Take that thing off, right now," I said.

"What about our water break?" Danny asked.

To these kids, suffering was a car without a DVD player and personal climate control. Suffice to say, the amply heated indoor bubble, erected every winter at Royal Flush golf and tennis club, was not their favorite place.

"We're not having a water break. We haven't even started yet. Now, everybody line up."

"I need to stay fully hydrated, David, and away from dark colas," said Zandra McNeil, a doctor's daughter. "I could get kidney stones."

"If one of us dies, you're gonna get sued," Danny said. "My dad lives for these kind of cases."

"Will everybody shut-up, please? We're not here to talk about water breaks or lawsuits. Today, I'm going to teach you how to serve," I said.

"Oh wait, David. I just got an IM," Zandra said, running over to her tennis bag to retrieve her beeping pager.

"My mom says it's wrong to say 'shut-up,'" said Becky.

"Zandra, turn that thing off. From now on, there will be no IM'ing during class. In fact, I want all pagers, cell phones, pda's, Gameboys, beepers, buzzers, iPods, iPads and anything else electronic turned off and out of sight," I said.

The entire class returned to their tennis bags to silence their equipment.

"Like I said — today, I'm going to teach you how to serve."

"Sounds boring," said Blaise Wentworth, a dark haired kid with glasses and a budding affectation.

"I agree," echoed Boyle, Blaise's twin brother.

"I assure you there is nothing boring about the serve. I want you to think of the serve as your chance to unleash hell on the world. How many of you know who Roscoe Tanner is?"

"Roscoe who?"

"'Hell' is a bad word, David."

"Yes, it is, Becky, but it's appropriate here because the serve is your statement to the world about who you are. See, you have to ask yourself: 'Is my serve going to be a weak, wimpy piddler or a lightning strike to the heart of my opponent?'"

"Is there anything in between?"

"Good question, but the answer is no. As Helen Keller once said, 'Life is either a daring adventure or nothing at all,' and the same holds true of the serve."

"Who's Helen Keller?"

"That's not important. But if you must know, she was a legendary tennis champion."

After teaching these monsters about the back-scratch position and the toss, I set them loose to try and make contact. Some met with more success than others.

"Everybody focus on the ball. Control your toss and you control your serve. Blaise, bend you knees a bit more."

"I'm trying."

"Remember what Yoda said to Luke Skywalker in *The Empire Strikes Back*. 'There is no try. There is only do.'"

"Yoda sucks," Willa said.

"Yoda does not suck," I said.

"He looks totally fake."

"No, he looks like a big booger," Danny said

"Yeah, he does look like a booger," Zandra said.

Somebody started chanting booger and all the kids eagerly joined in.

"Boog-er, boog-er, boog-er, boog-er."

"Stop that! Whether or not Yoda looks like a booger is not important. He happens to stand for the power of belief, which is one of the biggest lessons in tennis. You must believe in yourself."

"I like Yoda, David," Becky said.

"Then *you* must like boogers."

"Shut-up, Willa."

"Willa looks like Jabba the Hut," Danny said, causing the class to break out in laughter.

"Shut-up, Danny, or I'll pound you," Willa said, waving Plank in her tormenter's general direction.

"Enough, you two," I said. "And for God's sake, put down Plank, Willa."

The class finally stood at attention. It wasn't their fault, but all the chauffeuring and coddling and excusifying done by their parents, teachers and the team of nannies surrounding them had softened them to life's cruel realities and made them more vulnerable to sudden upset when they encountered something difficult that they couldn't master immediately.

"Guys, my goal here is to teach you about more than just tennis. I also want to teach you about life."

"Sounds boring."

"There are no boring lives, Blaise; only boring people. Look into it. Let's pick up the balls."

Hopper-time was a great opportunity to get to know my students better.

"So, Boyle, what do you want to be when you get older?"

"An investment banker."

"Really?"

I nearly choked on his reply.

"Yeah, I plan to work for Goldman Sachs. First, though, I'm gonna go to Yale. Where did you go to college?"

"Uh . . . Le Pew."

"What's that?"

"It's a chiropractic college."

"Is it Ivy League?" Boyle asked.

"No, not technically, but it's a good college."

"My Dad says you travel along a broader success curve if you go to an Ivy League college."

"What does that mean?"

"It has to do with probabilities."

"I see."

Had Boyle's parents considered the probability he might become a spree killer?

"Where did your dad go to college?" I asked.

"Colgate."

"That's not in the Ivies either," Zandra said.

"I know. My dad can't seem to get over it. Even counseling hasn't helped. He says I'm his last hope."

"What about you, Blaise? What would you like to do when you're older?"

"I'm gonna run a hedge fund."

"Got it."

"Can we have our water break now, David?" Becky asked.

"Sure. I could use one myself," I said.

One of the worst parts of my job is talking to the parents who pick their kids up after class. On a good day, only nannies who can't speak English arrive thereby precluding any kind of special request or uncomfortable exchange. Today, however, I didn't get so lucky. Kit Nash, Willa's father, had me in the crosshairs from the moment he valet parked his X5.

"David. Do you have a minute?"

Kit trapped me as I tried to duck into the men's locker room.

"Oh, Kit — hey. I didn't see you coming. You know — my bad vision and all," I said, fingering my eye patch.

"May I speak with you privately for a moment?"

"Sure," I said, as Willa walked up behind her father.

"Willa, I'll just be a minute," Kit said.

"My name is Tony Montana," Willa barked.

"Okay, Tony. You and Plank watch TV, all right?"

"Whatever," Willa said.

The two of us took a couple of quiet seats near the organic juice bar in the club's lobby while Willa sat in an adjacent TV room watching a *Seinfeld* rerun. Kit was in his mid-fifties and fighting to keep his looks. Having sired his only child late in life, he was part of a growing breed; a man of appointments; the type who spoke openly of the dozen or so people he used monthly to keep himself as youthful as possible. He was well-meaning but out of touch, the direct result of having too much money and too little self-worth.

"David, we're having some trouble with Willa at home. Have you noticed anything unusual during your lessons?"

"Well, she seems to have grown awfully close to a piece of wood."

"I know. I told her to leave Plank at home but she refused. It started out as something like a security blanket but I'm afraid it's evolved into an imaginary friend. We're building a new home and I think she feels neglected."

"Have you spoken to her?"

"Of course. I sat her right down and told her that custom-made backsplashes and Brazilian hardwood floors don't select themselves. I made it very clear that Daddy and Mommy had to focus on these important matters but she just doesn't get it. She's very self-absorbed that way. She can't see that between my spa treatments and interior design obligations, not to mention ordering take-out every night and planning vacations, I'm just stretched way too thin."

"Maybe you should try talking to her again."

"Don't be so naïve, David. It won't work. I've tried talking to her and everything else: high-calcium Sunny-D, Xanax, Horny Goat Weed and half a dozen other things, but none of it seems to do any good."

"Kit, I'm no parenting expert, but I don't think having an imaginary friend or a security blanket is too unusual or anything to worry about."

"I agree, but that's not the only problem."

"What else is wrong?"

"For starters, as you just heard, she insists Missy and I call her Tony Montana."

"Sounds like she's been watching too much *Scarface*."

"Is that a television show?"

"Actually, no. It's a movie. The main character is Tony Montana."

"Is he one of the good guys?"

"Not exactly. He's a murderous coke dealer."

"Dear God. My daughter is turning into one of those gangster thugs. I *knew* Direct TV was a bad idea. I *told* Missy to put parental block on the new plasma but of course she never did. Missy's very self-absorbed, too, in case you haven't guessed."

"Seems to be going around these days."

"Tell me about it. . . . David, I need your help."

"You do?"

"Yes. Willa likes you . . . at least she seems to like you."

"Look, I don't know much about kids. The only thing I do know is that they appear to like it when you spend time with them. That's all you really need to do I think."

"But I can't."

"Why not?"

"My doctors won't allow it."

"Doctors?"

"They're recommending I spend less time with Willa. They say I'm toxic to her. Evidently, it's like a food allergy. Something about all the soy milk I drink and the botox in my face. Plus, she hates my guts and her psychiatrist says I'm stunting her emotional development."

"What about her mother?"

"Oh, no. She can't spend any more time with Willa. She's never home. She's too busy with her plastic surgery practice. Everybody wants their poodles nipped and tucked and all the bulldog owners want jowl jobs."

"For themselves or the bulldogs?"

"Both, usually."

"What about friends? Doesn't she have any from school?"

"Not really. Her teachers tell us she's a loner. They say her trench coat intimidates the other children. She has grown close to one of our Lithuanian nannies but she's an illegal and the INS has been poking around. I don't have the heart to tell her but Ona is about to be deported."

"Jesus, Kit, I'm not sure what to say."

"Say you'll be her mentor."

"What?"

"I need you to be Willa's mentor; her big brother. You know the deal; you take her to the mall and tell her about the dangers of drug use, video games and poor study habits — all the basic good advice crap. She'll believe it coming from you."

"That's very flattering. It really is, but this isn't a good time for me to be taking on that kind of role. There are a lot of things going on in my personal life."

"David, I don't think you understand. I'm in agony. Do you get that? Agony? We're talking intense human suffering. My daughter hates me. My contractor ordered the wrong kind of Italian marble for our map room and, to be very blunt, my wife lost interest in the physical part of our relationship about six years ago. So you can see I'm a man in need."

"I'm sorry. I really am, but I just don't think . . ."

"David, this is a critical year for Willa. In June, her school will designate which 45 percent of the class is gifted and if she doesn't make it, her future will be ruined. *Ruined*, do you hear me?"

"That sounds a little extreme."

"No, it's not. Once they start sixth grade, there's academic apartheid. The gifted kids ride in the front of the bus and the dummies get thrown under the wheels."

"Willa's not dumb," I said.

"Maybe not, but she's wild. Just last week her choral director called me and told me she keeps inserting the word 'bitch' into the chorus of *Jingle Bells*. I'm terrified that if Willa keeps acting out, she's going to blow everything."

Kit eyeballed Willa, who was trying to pick her nose with Plank in the TV room.

"She'll end up at Lehigh or some other junior college," Kit said.

"I sympathize, Kit, but I'm not sure I'm the right . . ."

"I'll pay you $85 an hour."

"Eighty-five dollars?"

"Yes. Plus expenses. You know — for food and medications — her Paxil and what not."

Money was at it again; making a whore out of a decent man.

"It ought to be easy for you," Kit continued. "All she ever wants to do is skateboard. She spends hours in our new garage going off these stupid wooden jumps she built. I almost hit one with my car. She nearly killed me."

"Is she any good?"

"I don't know. Our neighbors took her and their kid to a couple of competitions and I hear she did pretty well, but I don't want her to be some skate punk. I've spent thousands on every other kind of lesson imaginable — piano, skiing, tennis, calligraphy — and she's taken no interest. All *she* wants to do is skateboard. Go figure."

"If it makes her happy, then it must be a good thing, right?"

"No, it's not. College admissions directors do not care about kids who skateboard; so it's a complete waste of time. This whole *happy* childhood thing has gotten way, way out of control. I've spent the best years of my life paying someone to wrap Willa's gifts, change her diapers and push the little cretin around in a top-of-the-line stroller and look what I've got: an ingrate who complains about the macrobiotic diet we've put her on, shoplifts *Grand Theft Auto* and blathers on incessantly about something called the X Games. . . . Anyway, will you take the job or not?"

Suddenly, in a refreshing change, I felt sorrier for Willa than for myself.

"All right, I'll do it."

"Oh, thank God."

Kit pulled his wallet out and handed me two $100 bills.

"Here's an initial deposit. . . . You must think I'm awful," Kit said, his candor catching me off-guard.

"No, I . . ."

"I wasn't always like this, you know."

"You're fine. I really . . ."

"I used to be a genuine person. . . . a nice person . . . I really was. I'm not sure what happened. I've been pretending to be someone else for so long, I finally became someone else. I'm just not sure who."

Kit's moment of self-awareness didn't last long.

"You'll start a week from Thursday," he said.

He was used to people doing what he wanted whether they were on his payroll or not.

"Yeah, sure. Thursday will be fine," I said, without giving it any thought.

I blinked once and, without a criminal background check or a single reference, I was a mentor. I'd never thought of myself as a molder of young women but I liked the idea and, besides, I needed the money. Willa may have been a terror, but I refused to be rattled by a fifth grader. Young Ms. Nash was about to meet her match.

seven

"Hey, good news. I've set you guys up for a double date."

"No, Dixie. No blind dates," I said.

"Yeah, that's a bad idea, Dix," Nubby said. "Last time I went on one of those it led to a restraining order."

"Didn't you get maced, too?" I asked.

"Yeah, the whole thing was pretty painful," Nubby said.

In a booth by the window at Hicks and McCarthy's, a busy diner, Dixie sat across from Nubby and me eating an Egg Beaters omelet.

"David, you need to get over Miranda and Nubby you need to get over Lilly Bee. What are you two afraid of?"

"I'm not afraid of anything," I said. "And I *am* over Miranda."

"I haven't thought about Lilly Bee for six hours," Nubby said.

"Look, you asked for my help finding love. If I'm going to do that, I need to see how you respond to today's modern woman," Dixie said.

"Whoa, whoa, whoa," said Nubby. "What do you mean *modern* woman? Are you talking about someone with a job and a car? A checkbook? Those kinds of things? Chicks who wears pants to work?"

"Yes, Nubby. These *women* wear pants to work. They're not strippers. They're two of my professors from Monroe Community College."

"Dixie, may I remind you that we're looking to dip our toes back into the kiddie pool, not dive head first into the deep end," I said.

"David, this will give me a baseline of your likes and dislikes. From there, I'll be better able to find women who are right for you guys. Think of it as a litmus test."

"Sounds more like a science experiment . . . with us serving as the guinea pigs," Nubby said.

"Professors Sanchez and Jensen are great women. Just give them a chance," Dixie said.

"Do we have to call them professor?" Nubby asked.

"Of course not. You can call them by their first names — Maria and Anna."

"They're not fat, are they?" Nubby asked.

"No, they're not fat, slim," Dixie said, glancing down at Nubby's ever-expanding waistline.

"What are you going to tell them about us?" Nubby asked.

"Nothing. I think this is a case of less is more."

"Thanks a lot," Nubby said.

"Yeah. That's a real shot of confidence," I said.

"You're both unemployed, right?" Dixie asked.

"For your information, I happen to be one of the best bathroom deodorant spray salesmen in the city. I'm just on a temporary hiatus," Nubby said.

"And I'm teaching tennis several days a week and just landed a gig as a mentor."

"Okay. I'm going to take that as a yes from both of you," Dixie said. "Look, this isn't about comparing your curriculum vitaes."

"You think they'll go that far on a first date?" Nubby asked.

"I'm talking about your credentials. Don't be intimidated by the fact these women have Ph.D's. Just be yourselves."

"Easy for you to say. You don't hate yourself," Nubby said.

"All right. We'll give it a try, Dixie. But they better not be a couple of ball-busters," I said.

"They're not. They're just ordinary, average modern women."

"This has doom written all over it," Nubby said.

I shook my head at Nubby.

"Are you two ready to talk about bombing my father's factory?" Dixie asked bluntly.

"Sshhh!" I said. "Are you crazy? Not in public," I whispered.

Dixie was so convinced of the morality of her position, she didn't bother to consider its legality.

"How's your butter sculpture coming, Dixie?" I asked loudly, looking to quickly cover her gaffe.

"Not bad actually," Dixie said, nonplussed by my admonition.

"When is the New York State Fair entry deadline?"

"I'm already entered."

"Cool."

"I know, but they only pick one sculpture to display during the fair so I'm not getting my hopes up."

"Hey, you've got as much of a chance as anyone else, right? What's your subject?"

"I can't tell you. It's a surprise. The college has given me a large, refrigerated sculpting space, so I'm working away. It's kind of spiritual, actually. Did you know that Buddhists originated the art form in the Fourteenth Century?"

"No," I said.

"To this day, they make them with wax and yak butter."

"That's disgusting," Nubby said.

"No, it's not," Dixie said. "They build them for every Tibetan New Year, which they call Losar."

"Don't you mean *loser*?" Nubby asked.

"No, I don't. It's a big deal there. The sculptures are placed on alters in monasteries and homes as an offering to Buddha," Dixie said.

"Sounds stupid," Nubby said.

"It's not stupid, Nubby, you dinkus," Dixie said. "The Buddhists believe the sculptures help to create positive, collective karma and bring harmony and peace to the world. I think it's kind of cool."

"Positive karma, eh?" I asked. "Hurry up and finish, okay? I could use some of that."

"Sure, David. In the meantime, here's Maria's number. Give her a call," Dixie said, handing me a napkin with the digits scrawled on it.

"Okay, but I know I'll regret it," I said, excusing myself and sticking Dixie with the bill.

Back on Mt. Hope Avenue, I entered the house and found Beatie in the kitchen performing her usual magic with the eight-calorie pudding substitute she served Biff every evening.

"David, yer *home*," she said.

"Hey, Beatie."

"Where ya been?" Beatie asked.

"Oh, you know. Here and there. How are you feeling?"

"The usual."

"Don't forget the Reddi-wip, Beatie," Biff shouted from his recliner in the family room. "Your pudding tastes like shoe leather without it."

"Don't worry. You'll get yer Reddi-wip, ya old, ball-less bastard," Beatie barked. "That and a major case of the craps," she said under her breath, knowing full well the product had Olestra in it. "He'll be on the can all night," she said, winking at me as she went to deliver Biff's dessert.

When she returned, we took seats at the pine table.

"Ya hear Joan died?" Beatie asked.

"Joan who?"

Sometimes even Beatie didn't know their last names.

"Ya know — Joan from the Yarn Barn."

"I hadn't heard that."

"Yeah, it was a real shame. She got the croup and was gone in a month."

"That's too bad. . . . Listen, we need to talk."

"Are ya ready to help me die?"

"Actually, I need to talk to you about something else first."

"Ar- right," she said.

"Now I know you may not want to answer this question, but it's important to me, okay?"

"Ga-head."

"Okay. I need to know why mom called me Dragon."

"Oh, geez, I haven't hoyed that name in years."

"Why did she call me that?"

"That was so long ago, David."

Beatie lit a Carlton, a sure sign she was trying to buy time.

"I don't remembah. It was just a nickname," she said.

"There had to be more to it. Please. I need you to tell me everything you recall."

"I really don't remembah much."

"Tell me what you know. Anything," I said.

Beatie took a long look at me. Behind her wraparound sunglasses, she was deciding whether or not to tell me the truth and I could only hope she would see that I needed to hear it.

"Yer mother said ya were born in the year of the dragon. She read somewhere this meant ya'd have a good life, ya know, good things, good health, this and that."

"What else?"

"She said she had dreams about dragons during her pregnancy."

"Really?"

"She just had this crazy idear ya were a dragon in a prior life."

"A prior life? So she believed in reincarnation?"

"I don't know. I suppose."

"But you didn't believe her story?"

Beatie paused before answering.

"David, I'm not gonna lie to ya. I didn't encourage her. I thought she was cuckoo."

"Was there anything else? Besides the dreams?"

Beatie paused again.

"I suppose I can tell ya now. Ya know that scar on yer side?"

For as long as I could remember, I had a five-inch scar on the left side of my torso just below my ribcage.

"Sure, the one from the splenectomy when I was a baby."

"Ya nevah had a splenectomy."

"What?"

"We made it up."

"Why? What are you talking about?"

"Ya came out with that scar and the doctors couldn't explain it."

"Yer mother said she had a recurring dream during pregnancy about a dragon cut by a sword in battle. She thought ya were that dragon. I told you it was cuckoo, David."

"I don't understand. Why didn't she tell me about the scar?"

"I told her not to. It's one thing to talk about dragons. It's another to lay some cock and bull story on a child. I didn't think it was fair. She and I used to fight about it. She even claimed that ya talked about these battles when ya were two or three, but I nevah heard ya say a thing. I'm tellin' ya she was crazy, David. That's why I nevah called you Dragon."

"What about achieving greatness? Did she ever say anything about that?"

"Yer mother had high hopes for ya. Ya know that, though."

"Beatie, I need more Reddi-wip," Biff hollered through the wall.

"I'll be right back," Beatie said, grabbing the can of dessert topping and quickly leaving the kitchen, obviously relieved to get a break from our conversation.

For a moment, I felt elated. The mere possibility that I was more than just a paper dragon held up by my mother's hands excited me. When Beatie returned, however, it was clear she wanted to change the topic.

"I can't believe you didn't tell me about my scar," I said.

"David, I want to talk about my death."

"I'd rather not."

"Ya promised me we'd talk."

"No time for that. I've got good news," I said.

"What's that? Ya gonna shave?"

"No. Remember how you said you always wanted to go to the Oscars?"

"What about it? Did ya get tickets?"

"Not exactly."

"Then what's the good news?"

Even though our meeting with the Mayor had been a disaster, I was desperate to discuss anything but Beatie's desire to die. And I was more than willing to lie a little bit to do so.

"What if I told you I was going to bring the Oscars to you?"

"I'd say yer mental and ya need help."

"Now, it's not final or anything so you can't tell your friends, but it's looking pretty good that the Academy Awards are going to be held in Rochester."

"In two months?"

"No. Next year."

"I won't be here next year."

"Yes, you will."

"David, ya made me a promise. Ya said you'd help me die if ya didn't get tickets this year."

"I know. I was hoping you'd forgotten about that."

"Well, I haven't."

Given Beatie's iron-clad memory, my only hope was a diversion.

"How would you like to go on a road trip next week?"

"I wouldn't. I just want to die."

"C'mon. When was the last time you left Rochester?"

"1982. I went to Syracuse for an arts and crafts show at Pyramid Mall. Complete waste of time. Those people didn't know a pipe cleaner from a popsicle-stick."

"So it's been 30 years. I'd say you're due."

"David, I don't wanna go anywhere."

"What if I said I needed you?"

It may sound flakier than a Lebanese pastry, but I had a nagging sense that the answers I sought about who I was and where I came from, and what I needed to do to help revive Rochester, were somewhere out in America waiting for me to come and find them. Maybe it was because of my mother: her dreams; my scar; her claim that I spoke about a past life as a dragon when I was a toddler. Maybe it was the lifelong absence of my father, which made me prone to irrational searching. Whatever its origin, the feeling was undeniable and I needed Beatie to witness whatever I found. The question was where to look.

My mind kept returning to the article I'd read at the dentist's office about Chester Carlson and his late-in-life obsession with Buddhism and reincarnation. Shortly before he died, he funded a professor's work at the University of Virginia and my intuition told me I needed to start there.

EIGHT

Given my bumper crop of worries, the last thing I felt like doing was teaching tennis or spending time with Willa Nash, who I was scheduled to mentor for the third time after my group lesson. Without a choice in the matter, however, I made my way to Royal Flush and braced myself for an encounter with the usual suspects.

"Willa's all ready for your outing," Kit Nash called out as he approached me in the clubhouse.

"Great," I said. "I'm really looking forward to it."

"Dad, don't call me Willa. My name is Cheese," Willa said.

"Now, we talked about this, remember? Mom and I are not going to call you Cheese. After all, we just got used to Tony. Fair is fair."

"Fine," Willa huffed, storming away with her racket in one hand and Plank in the other, leaving me alone with Kit.

"Cheese?" I asked.

"Yes, for some reason the kids started calling her that at school and she likes it. I swear I'm going to lose my mind. . . . So where are you taking her after class?"

I had made no plans whatsoever.

"Uh . . . I thought we'd go someplace educational."

"Good. Take her to Strong Children's Museum. I hear it's excellent."

I nodded, knowing nothing of the place.

"David, let me ask you a question. What do you think about steroids?" Kit asked.

"Steroids? For who?"

"For Cheese — I mean Willa."

"Kit, she's a head taller and 50 pounds heavier than every kid in the class already."

"I don't think you understand. Do you have any idea how difficult it is to get your child into the right college these days? Our admissions consultant told us that if Willa's going to go Ivy, she'll need every edge she can get. Academics alone won't cut it."

"You've got a college admissions consultant?"

"Of course."

"But Willa's ten years old."

"I know. I hope we're not too late. The game starts early, David. By the time Willa applies, legacy admissions could be nothing but a pleasant memory. Stupid Supreme Court," Kit muttered. "The bottom line is she needs to be hooked."

"Hooked? What the hell does that mean?"

"It means she needs to be a star athlete or musician or star something to ensure admission and, from what I hear, that means steroids."

"Maybe you mean supplements, not steroids," I said.

"Supplements. Steroids. Whatever. I hear Focus Factor is pretty good."

"I promise I'll look into it, Kit."

I excused myself and entered the revolving door leading to the club's indoor bubble. Out on court six, my kids were inquisitive as ever. Just my luck.

"Why are you limping, David?" Becky Pardi, my most compassionate student, asked.

"General aches and pains," I said.

Indeterminate twinges in my hips, calves and knees had multiplied of late.

"I've got those, too," Becky said.

"You do, huh?"

"How old are you, David?" Becky asked.

"Old enough to know better."

"What does that mean?" Becky asked.

"Yeah, what does that mean?" Danny Cohen asked.

"It's just an expression," I said.

"Shouldn't you be married by now?" Becky asked.

"That's none of your business," I said.

"He should be married with kids by now . . . maybe even divorced," Danny said.

"That's enough. Start hitting," I said.

Like every person before me, I had learned that time's winged chariot would not ride past and leave me unmaligned. I would not be the miraculous exception to the rule. My waistline would thicken. My hair would recede. Gravity would pull me in one direction and it was futile to fight it. The changes would come, imperceptibly at first then steadily onward. I might 'make the sun run' as one poem my mother read to me many times suggested, but I could never win the race, a reality that should have been obvious to me from the start given my degenerated eye. There was a lesson in all this to teach my students. I just wasn't sure how.

After watching them warm-up for ten minutes, I called them in for a pep talk.

"Everybody gather around," I said. "I want to ask you guys a question."

My students met me at the net.

"How many of you want to be great tennis players?"

Every child, besides Willa, raised his or her hand.

"Okay, good. Blaise, tell me why you want to be a great tennis player."

"'Cause my dad says it'll help me get into Yale."

"All right. That's a rational explanation. What about you, Zandra?"

"I don't want to get fat. My mom says nobody likes a fat girl."

"What about you, Becky?" I asked.

"Well . . . I just think it's really, really cool to see how great you can get at something. Does that make sense?"

"Yes. I think that makes a lot of sense," I said. "But why is it cool?"

"It makes you feel good," Becky said.

"Exactly. That's exactly right. Challenging yourself to see how great you can be at tennis or anything else in life feels good."

"Are we going to sing *Cumbayah*, now?

"No, we're not. I'm just trying to teach you something, Willa."

"The name is Cheese."

"Just cool it for a minute, Cheese. Let me ask you guys something else. What would you be willing to give up in order to be great at tennis? Would you be willing to give up television? The Internet? Video games? Would you be willing to give up your weekend time with friends? Because that's what it takes."

"You have to give up all that?" Danny asked.

"Sounds boring," said Boyle.

"Trust me. It's not boring. But it does take sacrifice and practice; lots and lots of practice."

"What if you hate practice?" Willa asked.

"It doesn't matter. You have to practice anyway," I said.

"I'm not that that crazy about practice," Danny said. "Does that mean I can't go to Yale?"

I was losing the class with my tough talk of sacrifice. Time to switch to scare tactics.

"Look, there are some harsh realities you're going to have to face in life," I said.

"Like what?" Willa asked, defiantly.

"Like ear hair," I said.

"Ear hair?"

I could have picked pot bellies, toe mold, back fat or any number of other indignities of advancing age, but I knew this would get their attention.

"What's ear hair?" Becky asked.

"It's God's warning shot," I said.

"My dad has it," Blaise said.

"We don't believe in God at my house," Zandra said.

"Then think of it as your body's warning shot."

"What do you mean 'warning shot'?" Danny asked.

"Everybody be quiet for a minute," I said. "Let me try to explain. Think of it this way. When you get a little bit older, you'll start getting ear hair."

"You mean hair that grows out of your ears?" Becky asked.

"Yes."

"Ear hair is a signal — a reminder if you will — that you're approaching middle age. It's your body's way of telling you that life is short and that you need to make the most of your time while you're still here."

"So what the hell does this have to do with us?" Willa asked.

"Everything. What I'm telling you is that your ear hair will be here before you know it. One day, your ears are smooth as a baby's bottom and the next thing you know, they're covered in sprouts."

"David, that sounds awful," Becky said.

"It is. Take a look at mine."

Becky came closer to inspect my lobes.

"Ooooh, gross," she shrieked.

"So if you want to make some kind of mark in this world with your tennis or anything else, you need to start now."

"That's a load of crap," Willa said.

"Hey, go ahead and take your chances, Cheese," I said. "But when the ear hair arrives, it's pretty much over."

"Can you sue someone when you get it?" Danny asked.

"I'm afraid not."

Sure, my teaching methods could be unconventional at times but I needed to impart to them the fleeting nature of youth. What no one tells you when you're a child is that the inevitable deterioration of your physical state will be accompanied by a corresponding corrosion of your dreams and that you'll have to wrestle both body and mind to keep yourself and your aspirations alive. By telling my students the truth, I might convince them to make the most of their time.

"How's my serve look, David?" Boyle asked.

By now, all of the kids except Willa, who was sprawled out on her back hyperventilating, had returned to the baseline and were frantically hitting serves, terrified by my tale of ear hair.

"Keep practicing," I shouted. "Make something of yourselves."

Following the lesson, Willa followed me to the club's parking lot where her lack of enthusiasm for our prearranged mentoring excursion became readily apparent.

"I'm not riding in that hunk of junk," she said.

"Just get in the car," I said.

My Mustang, covered with the salt and dirty snow of Rochester's roads, didn't exactly glisten in the sun.

"My mom's got a new Mercedes — the S-class."

"Good for her."

"It parks itself."

"That's great."

"I can't wait 'til they make something better than that."

"Like what? A space shuttle? Listen, I'm going to take you to see Santa. What do you think about that?"

"Santa's a tool."

"Santa is not a tool. He's a symbol of goodness."

"Take me to the track. We can play the ponies."

"Don't be a wise-ass. We're going to see Santa and that's that."

"Fine," Willa said, pulling out a pack of Marlboros. "You got a lighter in this pile?"

"No. Are those cigarettes? Give me those. Since when do you smoke?"

"Since I do."

"Well, you *shouldn't*. It's not good for your tennis game."

"I hate tennis. I want to be is a pro-skateboarder like Tony Hawk. That guy rips."

"Yeah, your dad mentioned you like skateboarding."

"Not just skateboarding; all extreme sports. Someday, I'm going to win a gold medal at the X Games. They're totally rad."

"Tennis is rad."

"Give it up, all right? Do you know who Mat Hoffman is?" Willa asked.

"No."

"Are you joking? He's the godfather of BMX. He's broken just about every bone in his body."

"And that's rad?" I asked.

"Of course it is," Willa said, self-consciously pulling the top of her white Fila sweatsuit down to cover a bit of exposed belly.

"May I ask you a question?"

"It's a free country," Willa said.

"Does it bother you when the other kids tease you about your weight?"

Willa paused as vulnerability flashed across her eyes for the briefest of seconds.

"Hell, no. I don't care what those gomers think."

"That's good. 'Cause you shouldn't."

"Does it bother you when people make fun of your eye patch?" Willa asked.

"Sometimes," I said.

Our destination, a downtown indoor mall called Midtown Plaza, was a source of happy, childhood memories for me. Every holiday season, Beatie and my mom took me there to ride a motorized monorail and see Santa. Besides the monorail, Midtown's two-story atrium held a large authentic Indian totem pole and a tree-sized cuckoo clock, where you could hear the national anthem of a different country played every hour while one of twelve egg-shaped automatic doors, perched up high, slid open to reveal mechanical dancers dressed in native attire. Although I hadn't been there in years, I hoped the old mall's magic, which had captured my imagination so many years before, would have the same effect on Willa. Unfortunately, my hopes were immediately jolted by the armed guard who stood by the main entryway and directed us to pass through a metal detector.

"A little extra security never hurt anyone," I said, attempting to remain upbeat. "When I was a kid, I couldn't wait to come down here every Christmas."

"Why? This place is lame," Willa said.

"It is not lame. It's fun. You'll see."

"Sir, please take off your jacket and shoes and place them on the conveyor belt. We're gonna hafta wand you and the girl."

"This blows," Willa said.

"Just give it a chance," I said, nervously eyeballing a second armed guard who stood ten feet away ready to shoot anyone who made a break for it.

"Is the monorail running?" I asked as the guard maneuvered his electronic wand from my ankles to my head.

"Monorail?"

"The monorail. The one they always have here for Christmas. It's up, right?"

"Ain't no monorail here, sir."

Our expedition had taken its first broadside. Walking into the mall, I couldn't believe the change in atmosphere. Midtown had been a vibrant and bustling place of commerce, but now half the stores were shuttered, the crowd, comprised mostly of menacing teens, was sparse and all the major tenants I remembered were gone. Far be it from me to tell management its business, but when your busiest outlet is a weapons and ammunition shop called Up Against The Wall, it can't be a good sign. I thought Willa might be scared so I offered her my hand.

"Get away from me, creep," she said.

"All right. Just settle down. You want a pretzel from Hot Sam's?"

"Not really."

The line to see Santa was long, snaking out from Magic Mountain, the hollow, white fiberglass monstrosity where he dwelled.

"What are you going to ask Santa for?"

"I don't believe in Santa."

"Don't say that or you won't get any presents."

"I've already seen everything I'm getting. My mom hides the gifts in her bedroom closet every year. My dad doesn't even bother. He just dumps them on the ping pong table in our basement."

"Hasn't anyone ever told you? There are gifts you get from your parents and gifts you get from the North Pole."

"Yeah, right, and I'm Herbie the dentist."

"Jeez. How did you get so cynical?"

"M-TV mostly."

Minutes later, when we got toward the head of the line and stepped inside Magic Mountain, I felt my heartbeat quicken and my face turn cherry-red. I couldn't believe my eyes. Dressed as Santa and sitting on a festooned throne surrounded by elves was Guru Ganges, the lecherous yoga instructor who'd blown up my relationship with Miranda the way an IED destroys a tank. And by his side, working as his head elf, was you know who.

For the last month, I'd been reasonably successful at putting *her* out of my mind. I'd returned the engagement ring, put away all my pictures of us, and came within inches of throwing out my shoebox of mementos, including a napkin from our first date at Ponderosa, a pair of Motley Crue ticket stubs and a Sweetest Day card she gave me but forgot to sign. Seeing the two of them now, smugly besmirching innocent children with fake smiles and empty promises, however, I felt all the humiliation of discovering them together in bed again.

"Are you okay?" Willa asked.

I nodded robotically. Set a good example for the girl and be civilized, I thought as we shuffled closer. You're a mentor now, I reminded myself. I wanted to turn and leave, but I didn't. Something kept me moving forward until we reached the front.

"Vell, lookee, lookee, lookee. Vut do vee have here?" Guru Ganges asked.

"Looks like Cyclops has a protégé," Miranda said, eliciting a laugh from Santa.

"Yes. And sheez a chun-kee one, isn't she?" Ganges said, pointing at Willa.

"Maybe you should put some Slim-Fast in her stocking," Miranda said.

"Shut-up, Miranda," I said. "Don't make fun of the kid."

"*You* shut-up, David. You owe me fifteen hundred bucks for smashing my car."

"What?" I asked.

"Oh, you don't remember the night you smashed your Mustang into my car? Let me refresh your recollection."

Miranda, whose breasts peeked out from a plunging neckline trimmed with white fur, leaned over and planted a suggestive kiss on Guru Ganges.

"Is this ringing any bells?" She asked while continuing to caress Santa's shoulder.

"Screw you, Miranda," I said. "You really are a world-class tramp."

"Vut did you say?" Ganges asked.

"You heard me. And, by the way, *you* can't play Santa," I said. "You're a Hindu."

"I'm a secular Son-ta. Deal vith it."

"There's no such thing as a secular Santa. He's a symbol of Christian faith."

"Son-ta is only a symbol of consumer faith. Tell me vut you vant, little girl," Ganges said, gesturing for Willa to climb on his lap. "Vould you like a book of yoga gift certificates?"

"No. She doesn't want a stupid book of yoga gift certificates. Don't you dare climb up there, Willa. C'mon, we're going."

We began making our way out of Magic Mountain, and had nearly escaped the scene when Ganges called out after me.

"That's right. Run away you loozer!"

"Yeah, run away you big loser," Miranda said.

A reasonable person would have let it go. A rational person would have set a good example for Willa. Unfortunately, I wasn't feeling reasonable *or* rational. Instead, I turned and ran toward Guru Ganges, tackling him into a pile of fake presents. Rolling around on the floor, trying to tear each other's eyes out, we were soon encircled by parents, children and a dozen dwarves in elf costumes who began dancing around us and shouting epithets at me until the police arrived. Billy-clubbed, handcuffed and bleeding, I was arrested on criminal assault charges, something that seemed to genuinely delight Willa.

As for Miranda, I couldn't deny that seeing her hurt. It forced me to admit that I'd been in denial about my emotional wounds since our break-up. For two years we were inseparable and however horrible a beast she had become, there was an absence, some sort of perverse void, I felt acutely now. Like every life, every relationship is defined by certain moments and, although we'd had some good ones, there were too many times she left me feeling like I wasn't enough for her in all the important ways. As I rode in the back of a squad car toward the police station, I realized that good mentoring, like good love, is a lot harder than it looks.

My violent outburst frightened me. Why was I so angry? Miranda was the proximate cause but my accumulated frustrations were the more likely culprit. Locked in my jail cell, I felt like a boxer; not a champion but a palooka; a has-been who was one punch away from hitting the canvas and never getting up.

NINE

Biff bailed me out of the Monroe County jail, one of the few places he could go in his robe without drawing stares.

"What's your problem, Buster Brown?" Biff asked, starting up the engine of his Crown Vic.

"I don't have a problem," I said.

"Oh, no? You take a 10-year old to see Santa and you end up beating Kris Kringle within an inch of his life."

"He was taunting me."

"Right. And next you're going to tell me that his elves were dancing around you in a circle and calling you names."

"Yes, that's exactly right."

"David, you've stooped to a new low."

"You weren't there, so do me a favor and don't judge me. Just drop me off at Nubby's place, please. He and I have a double date in an hour."

An evening with Professors Sanchez and Jensen had been arranged.

"A woman agreed to go out with *you*?"

"You sound shocked."

"I just feel sorry for her."

"Thanks a lot, Biff. You're doing wonders for my self-confidence."

Arriving at the Golden Acres trailer park where Nubby lived, I got out of the car without a word and staggered toward the next hurdle on the track.

"What happened to you?" Nubby asked, referring to the prominent scratches and bruises on my face, as he let me inside.

"Don't ask. You'll hear about it on the news tomorrow."

"Well, get yourself cleaned up. You look like Rocky Balboa," he said, pointing toward the black eye that now matched my eye patch. You do remember we've got this date thing, right?"

"Why do you think I'm here? You're not wearing that T-shirt, are you?" I asked.

"Why not?"

"Dixie told you to lose the T-shirts."

"This isn't the same one."

"Nub, I don't think a T-shirt that says 'Toadily Horny' with a picture of two toads is any better than one that says 'See That My Grave's Kept Clean.'"

"Okay. How about this one?" Nubby asked, holding up a shirt with a panda bear and the phrase 'Quit Yer Bitchin' on it.

"You realize that it's December? Don't you have any long-sleeved shirts? Something flannel?"

"None that are clean."

"This is hopeless," I said. "Just wear what you want."

"Works for me. I'm not going to pretend to be someone I'm not."

Nubby returned to his bedroom, a few feet away, to change.

"I thought we'd take my car," I said, grabbing a Coke out of his refrigerator.

"No, we can't do that. It's too small. Those bucket seats

in the back barely fit one person let alone two. Let's take Vanilla Thunder."

Vanilla Thunder, Nubby's beloved off-white 1957 Ford Thunderbird with black vinyl interior and no seatbelts or other safety features, reliably broke down every 75 miles.

"No way. Your car won't make it through the night."

"Of course it will. I just lubed her up. She's running like a deer."

"Right. A deer that's been shot."

"Shut-up. She's running good."

"All right, fine, but you've got to take the NASCAR flags off."

In honor of Dale Earnhardt and Dale Earnhardt, Jr., Nubby had mounted two small flags, one bearing the number three, the other bearing number eight, on opposite sides of Vanilla Thunder.

"You want me to take off my flags?"

"I don't mean forever; just for tonight."

"I already told you. I'm not gonna try to be someone I'm not. If these chicks don't like NASCAR, then the hell with 'em."

Against my better judgment, I climbed aboard Vanilla Thunder with Nubby, now clad in a T-shirt that read 'My Karma Ran Over My Dogma!' behind the wheel.

"Where should we take them?" Nubby asked.

"How about the Rio Bamba?"

"Are you crazy? That's way too expensive. We can't swing that," Nubby said.

"Okay. How about the Olive Garden?"

"Did you just rob a bank? I hope so, 'cause you're gonna need a lot of scratch if you want to go to the O.G.," Nubby said.

"The Olive Garden is cheap. You get free breadsticks and a bottomless salad bowl. That's a meal right there."

"Sure, if these chicks only eat salad and bread. But what if they want a piece of meat or a glass of wine? That can add up. Listen, David, we shouldn't create pie in the sky expectations. You take a woman someplace nice on the first date and she'll want that every time."

"I never thought of it that way," I said.

"You have to build up to a place like the O.G. We're talking year two of a relationship."

"But you've never gotten to year two of a relationship."

"I know. I can't afford it."

"So where do you want to take them?" I asked.

"Just leave it to me, okay? I've got the ideal spot. And I've got the ideal music to set the mood."

"Good. We need to have the perfect song playing when they climb into the car. And none of that blues crap," I said.

"Crap? That crap is the ultimate aphrodisiac."

"Oh really? How many women do you know who get hot while listening to songs called *Prison Cell Blues* or *I'm Your Hoochie Coochie Man*?"

"Lots of them."

"We need something more contemporary."

"All right, I've got an idea. They're professors, right?"

"Right."

"So we go with an education theme — I'm thinking *School's Out* by Alice Cooper or *Hot for Teacher* by Van Halen."

"I said contemporary."

"I think I've got a cassette of *Upstairs at Eric's* by Yaz," Nubby said, reaching over and rummaging through Vanilla Thunder's glove compartment.

"Yaz?"

"Look, I stopped listening to new music after 1987 so it'll have to do."

"Don't you have anything else?" I asked.

"Oh, wait. If you dig down under your seat, I think I've got a cassingle of *99 Luft Balloons*."

"Good lord," I murmured.

"Asia's greatest hits might be under there, too."

The first time I went to Nick Tahou's, there was a pimp on the restaurant's pay phone and I ate the house specialty, the garbage plate; a heaping mound of macaroni salad, potatoes, onions, mustard, hamburger patties and other unidentifiable objects, before going home and throwing up on Beatie's pet pig, Woofie. Every time since then has been the same minus the regurgitation. Located downtown on West Main Street in an urban DMZ, Tahou's is a place where the food is so good you're willing to risk your life to get it. Arriving before midnight decreases but does not eliminate the possibility that you'll be shot so you learn to eat fast and keep conversation to a minimum amidst chipped paint and peeling wallpaper. The owner likes to turn the tables over quickly and tacitly understands that the threat of impending death keeps things moving, particularly when it comes to the bratty, teens that drive to the restaurant late at night to convince themselves that their lives have some edge. Twenty plus years ago, that was Nubby and me.

After picking up the two professors; Anna, a tallish trim blond, and Maria, a shorter and rounder brunette, a creepy quiet pervaded until Anna surprised us at the restaurant.

"I love your T-shirt, Nubby," Anna said.

"Really?" Nubby asked, arching his eyebrows and casting a smug glance my way.

"Yes. I think it's an incredible statement about today's society. The world's at war over competing beliefs and the alleged differences between people, but we all have much more in common than we realize. I don't know about you, but I often feel the world would be a better place if we all let our karma run over our dogma. The irony of the message is brilliant."

"Uh, yeah. It's pretty uh . . . brilliant, I guess," Nubby said. "You know what else is brilliant? The Garbage Plate here. I recommend it highly."

"I love this whole concept of slumming it on the first date," Anna said. "Don't you, Maria?"

"It's different. I'll give you that."

"Slumming it?" Nubby asked.

"Oh, don't play coy with us. This whole down-market date idea is great. I expected you to try and impress us by going someplace expensive like the Rio Bamba, but that would have been so predictable. I really admire a man who's not afraid to flaunt convention," Anna said.

"Hey, you show me a convention and I'll flaunt it," Nubby said, unconvincingly; suddenly aware that his date thought his suspect taste in restaurants was part of an intentional joke.

"I mean, really. The car? The retro eighties music? Tahou's? You guys went all out," Anna said. "What a riot."

"Hey, that's us," I said, catching eyes with Nubby. "Anything for a laugh."

"Don't you think it's funny, Maria?" Anna asked.

"I suppose, although there's nothing funny about those awful flags with the numbers on them," Maria said, drawing a frosty stare from Nubby that she failed to notice. "I feel like I'm in some kind of funeral procession."

As Nubby and Anna coupled up and made their way through the food line, I tried to make my time with Maria as pleasant as possible.

"So, Maria, I take it this is your first trip to Nick Tahou's."

"Yes, it is. I thought the police shut down this part of the city."

"Actually, they cordoned it off briefly a few months ago, but since then, they've washed up all the blood and it's been wide open to the public. Come one, come all."

"Charming," Maria said, smiling politely.

"I understand from Dixie that you're in the Women's Studies Department at Monroe Community. What do you teach?" I asked.

"A number of different classes: Advanced Feminist Thought, Twentieth Century Lesbian Novels, Transgendered Anthropology, Androgyny and Gender Dialectics and, of course, my seminar on Utopian Castration Theory."

"Utopian Castration Theory? What's that all about?"

"It posits that the uncontrolled sexual urges of men can only be cured by radical surgery to their genitalia, and that women will only truly be free when man is eliminated from the Earth."

"Wow. Does that mean no goodnight kiss?"

"That's not funny. I've been studying the biological redundancy of the American white male as depicted in television commercials and sitcoms for quite some time now and I truly believe that, in 20 years, people like you will be the equivalent of poor black women today."

"I see. So you have any hobbies?"

"I enjoy Nordic Track and scrapbooking. I also run several feminist task forces."

"Hey, gotta love a good task force."

The opposites attract energy pulling Nubby and Anna together wasn't working for Maria and me, but I knew Nubby's foot would find his mouth once we sat down with our Garbage Plates. With him, it was inevitable.

"So, Maria, your last name is Sanchez. Are you Mexican?" Nubby asked.

"That's right."

"Then you must like tacos a lot."

"No, not really. To be honest, I detest Mexican food," Maria said.

"Anyone ever call you Speedy Gonzales?"

"No."

"Nubby, you're hysterical," Anna said. "Don't you get it, Maria? It's all part of the evening — the flags, the Garbage Plates, the racist humor. They haven't missed a trick. No wonder Dixie wouldn't tell us anything about you guys. She didn't want to ruin the joke. She was in on this, wasn't she?"

"She was in on it all right," I said. "More than you can imagine."

By the end of the evening, Anna had come down with a case of Nubby fever. Unfortunately, Maria was only suffering from Daviditis. I walked her to the door fearing for my life and felt lucky to return to the car unscathed. Nubby, on the other hand, made out with Anna on her doorstep for ten minutes while I watched through the dirty windshield of Vanilla Thunder.

"I'm in love, man," Nubby said, climbing behind the wheel. "I'm in love."

"Good for you. You two really seemed to click."

"I know. That never happens to me. What about you?"

"Not so much. I think Maria wanted to castrate me," I said.

"Geez, that's rough. Maybe you should've borrowed one of my T-shirts. I've got a new one that says 'Free Petting Zoo' with a big arrow pointing down to you know what."

"I don't think that would've helped," I said.

"Maybe next time. How about 'Give Me Head 'Til I'm Dead'?"

"No, but thanks for offering."

As we drove on, Nubby's mood changed as he reflected on the evening's events.

"You know how, earlier, I said I wasn't going to pretend to be someone that I'm not?"

"Yeah, I remember," I said.

Nubby paused before speaking with seriousness.

"If I want to keep this going with Anna, I may have to."

"I don't think that's true."

"Yes, it is. If Anna finds out who I really am — that I'm unemployed and live in a trailer; that I can barely pay my bills and have no family — it'll be over quick."

"She's not going to care about those things."

"David, everybody cares about those things."

"Just be yourself."

"You know what? That's probably the worst advice you've ever given me."

"I mean it."

"I know. That's what scares me. You've been around me so long you actually think I'm normal."

"I didn't say that."

"Oh. So you don't think I'm normal?"

"Of course, you're normal. But I agree with what you said at the start of the night. You can't try to be someone you're not."

Nubby was normal. Perhaps not by conventional standards having to do with employment, finances or attire, but certainly by those having to do with human emotions. He was plagued with all the same fears, doubts and needs as the rest of us which made it wonderful to watch all his thoughts of Lilly Bee fade from sight as soon as he met Anna. It gave me hope that the same thing would happen to me and that Miranda would be nothing but a memory soon. Still, I couldn't help but observe and wonder about the way his old problems were replaced by new ones, nearly all of them existing in his head. I knew this was normal, too, though regrettable. We wish for things and when they arrive, we dissect them, catalog our new problems and immediately start wishing for something else. To be satisfied would save us so much pain, but we can't do it without concentrated effort. It is against human nature.

ten

Three days later, I gassed up the Mustang, strapped Beatie into the passenger seat, bought a sack of Tailburgers, and recruited Nubby for our road trip; promising him that he could deejay in the car. Although I knew I was subjecting myself to his extensive collection of blues music including a slew of bootleg tapes he'd picked up from a witch doctor at a Memphis flea market, I wanted Nubby to experience everything that was about to transpire.

"Are those Dockers you're wearing?" I asked as Nubby climbed into the backseat.

"Yeah, so what? Hey, Beatie."

"Hiya, Nub," Beatie said.

"So I've never seen you in anything but torn jeans."

"What's the big deal? They're seconds."

"Seconds?"

"Yes. Look at the stitching. It's all effed up. The saleswoman said they were irregular."

"You're irregular."

"Why are you on my back? A man's taste *can* mature. Plus, they have stain-defender."

"*And* you're wearing a shirt with a collar? This is about Anna, isn't it?" I asked.

"No," Nubby said.

"David tells me ya have a new lady friend," Beatie said.

"She and I just met, Beatie," Nubby said.

"You're changing for her, aren't you, Dapper Dan?" I asked.

"Go to hell. I'm not changing."

"Are you wearing a belt?"

"Yeah, what about it?"

"You don't own a belt."

"Well, I do now. Lay off."

As much as I enjoyed hassling Nubby, I envied the fact he had someone to try and please. For a man with a lifetime fealty to T-shirts, my friend's makeover spoke volumes about how much he liked his new girlfriend.

"Sorry, Nub. I didn't mean to be such a jerk. I guess I'm just jealous."

"It's okay, man. Don't sweat it. So where are we going?" Nubby asked, slipping Robert Johnson's *King of the Delta Blues* into his portable cassette player and firing up *Hell Hound On My Trail*.

"Can ya turn it down?" Beatie asked.

"Sure," Nubby said.

"We're going to Virginia," I said.

"What the hell's that?" Nubby asked.

"It's a state, you idiot."

"You're putting me in an asylum, aren't you? You're committing me to the nut house and you don't have the balls to say so."

Having spent much of his childhood inside institutions, Nubby was easily spooked.

"No. I'm not putting you in the nut house. I swear."

"Don't lie to me, David."

"I promise I'm not putting you in the nut house."

"Then why are we going to Virginia?"

"Nub, do you ever ponder life's big questions?"

"What? Like who's going to win the Daytona 500 next year?"

"Not exactly. I mean questions about the meaning of life — where you came from, where you're going, who you are — the biggies."

"Nah, I don't think about that shit. I think about what's on TV and whether or not I've got enough beer in the frige. Those are the big questions to me."

"But do you ever wonder where you came from?"

"I guess. I mean I never really knew my parents so there's part of me that wonders what they were like. You know, other than people who abandon their child."

"Well, that's what this trip is all about — thinking deeply about life's big questions."

"Sheeesh. I've got a headache already. Why do we need to go all the way to Virginia to do that?"

"That's what I asked, too," Beatie said, thumbing through her *Reader's Digest*.

"Because Chester Carlson, the inventor of the Xerox machine, gave money to a professor at the University of Virginia to study reincarnation and things like that."

"Oh, no — not this Carlson guy again. So what if he gave some dude money?"

"So he believed in reincarnation and the immortality of the soul."

"David, I don't know what the hell you're talking about."

"Look, I've got something to tell you that might sound a little strange, but I want you to hear me out."

"You *are* putting me in a nut house. I knew it."

"No."

"Then what is it? Just tell me."

"All right, I'm just going to say it. The long and short of it is that I think I may have been a dragon in a prior life and I'm going to Virginia to find out if it's true."

"You think you were a dragon in a prior life? Wait a minute. Is this a prank?" Nubby asked.

"Tell him, Beatie," I said.

"He thinks he's a dragon. I think he's bonkers."

"Are we on one of those hidden camera shows?" Nubby asked, looking around the car for a lens. "Is this a new reality show? Are you punking me?"

"No, we're not on television and I am not punking you. You remember how my mom called me Dragon, right?"

"Sure. But it was just a nickname, David. Maybe I should put *you* in a nut house."

"Nubby, I'm telling you that I've got evidence that shows I may have been a dragon. I know it sounds crazy, but I've got to find out who I am."

"You're David Horvath. You're not a dragon. Trust me. I've known you my whole life. You're losing it, man. Tell him, Beatie."

"I've tried," Beatie said.

"I'm not losing it. You have to believe me. My mother told me that I was a dragon and that I was destined for greatness, but I didn't understand that she was serious until recently."

"Hey, we all want to believe that. Shit, I thought I was destined for something great when I was young, too. I was going to be a roadie for Led Zeppelin. But that's not how it works out, David. You grow up and you turn out just like everybody else. You just have to accept it. That's all."

"No, I don't have to accept it. And neither should you."

"Going to Virginia isn't going to change anything," Nubby said.

"Maybe not, but I'm trying to find out who I am so that I can move forward. I want to unlock whatever's inside of me."

"God, you think too much," Nubby said.

"I'm serious. I want to break free from the things that have been holding me down. Don't you ever feel the need to break free?"

"From what?"

"From everything. From the whole mentality that your opportunities in life are limited; from the voice in your head that tells you to stop trying because this is the very best you're ever going to be and the most you're ever going to accomplish; from all the negative energy that saps you and your dreams . . . I don't know . . . from an ordinary life I suppose. Don't you ever feel that way?"

"Sometimes, sure. But I don't understand why you're so afraid of an ordinary life. What makes you think you're entitled to more? If you think you're better than other people, I've got news for you. You're not."

"Screw you, Nubby. I never said I was better than anybody. I just have high expectations for myself, and it's killing me that I'm not meeting them. What's wrong with that? What's wrong with wanting something more? What's wrong with wanting to matter? Maybe you just can't understand it."

"Boys, don't argue," Beatie said. "Yer givin' me gas."

"I can understand it fine," Nubby said. "Do you think I'm thrilled with how my life is turning out? Do you think you're the only one who's not meeting his own expectations? Jesus, man."

"So if you feel that way, why don't you do something about it?"

"Because I've adjusted my expectations. If you want to know the truth, I'm three months behind on my trailer payments. If I don't get a job soon, I'll be sleeping on your couch. Now all I really want is a steady paycheck and a family. If things work out with Anna, that'll be enough for me. She makes me happy."

"You can't rely on someone else to make you happy. That's a recipe for disaster. You have to make yourself happy," I said.

"Who told you that? Dr. Phil?"

"I can't remember who said it, but I believe it's true."

"And you think making some kind of mark will make you happy? You think if the Oscars come to Rochester your life is suddenly going to be perfect?"

"I don't know, but wouldn't you like shock the world?"

"Stop using that phrase! You sound like the basketball coach at Idaho Teachers College just before the team gets blown out 126 to 12 by Duke. You're not going to *shock* the world."

"That's *your* opinion."

"That's right. That is my opinion. And it's not going to change. You've gone goofy. I mean, really; all this Oscar talk and now you think you're a dragon. What the hell's gotten into you?"

"I don't want to talk about it anymore."

"Well, I do. You're a dreamer, David. Not a dragon; just a dreamer. Even your own grandmother knows it. Just accept it"

"Keep me out of this," Beatie said.

"David, you're the type of guy who's always going on about Gatorade commercials and Nike slogans and how they speak to you, but you never actually get in the game."

"Maybe that's what I'm trying to change."

"I'll believe it when I see it."

"Look, this whole thing is about a lot more than marketing platitudes," I said.

"Platiwhats?"

"Nevermind."

The only person who spoke for the next hour was Robert Johnson. *I Believe I'll Dust My Broom. Ramblin On My Mind. Love In Vain. When You Got A Good Friend. Dead Shrimp Blues.* "I woke up this mornin' . . . and all my shrimp was dead and gone. I woke up this mornin' . . . and all my shrimp was dead and gone." With Beatie sound asleep and snoring in the front seat, Nubby finally broke the verbal silence.

"David, listen. I want to apologize. I didn't mean all those things I said before."

"Did you mean *some* of them?"

"Maybe a few," Nubby said. "Seriously, I think I understand how you feel."

"Lately, I find myself questioning everything about my life. It's like I'm off-balance and . . . I don't know . . . ."

"You feel like you're about to fall over?"

"Yes. Sometimes I get so down, Nub. Late at night, after Beatie and Biff have gone to bed, I sit by myself in the family room flipping from one channel to the next. I just sit there in the dark, staying up for hours watching sports or worse, some celebrity profile about how great it is to be this person or that person; about how much they love what they do."

"I hate those shows."

"So do I . . . but it's hard to turn off the TV. You know what you said about me loving Nike commercials but never getting in the game? Well, you're right. But it's not because I don't want to. That's not it at all. I'd love to get in the game, but I feel like I can't find the stupid field."

"I know what you mean. I really do."

"When I watch those shows, I always get the same horrible sinking feeling that I never *will* get in the game and that I'll spend my entire life watching others experience all the things that should be a part of my daily existence but for some inexplicable reason aren't. It's awful. And even though

I know it's bringing me down — this knowledge that I'm wasting the hours of my life peering in at these strangers who I've been convinced I care about by the media — I feel powerless to stop myself."

"I'm the same way with NASCAR. Sometimes, I find myself watching *Speed Week* at three in the morning."

"And when I finally do turn off the TV, pretty soon I've got a *People* or an *US* magazine in my hands and I'm escaping again; not to anyplace good, but to a place where I can temporarily anesthetize myself from the pain I feel about being a failure."

"I can relate. I really can, but haven't you ever heard of a guilty pleasure?" Nubby asked.

"That's how it all started but, at some point, I crossed a line."

"I think you're being too hard on yourself," Nubby said. "You're going to find the field. It may take some time, but you'll find it."

"Thanks," I said.

I looked at Nubby for a moment; surprised by his uplifting words. I'd grown accustomed to his sour attitude and permanent frown.

"How come you never smile?" I asked.

"What do you mean?"

"You never smile."

"Yes, I do."

"No, you really don't. I can't remember the last time I saw you smile."

Nubby paused and put his hand up to his mouth reflexively.

"Have you ever taken a good look at my teeth?" Nubby asked, opening his mouth wide so that I could glance away from the on-rushing road and take a peek.

All of his teeth were deeply stained; an ugly array of yellow, brown and gray enamel.

"Would you smile if your teeth looked like that?" He asked.

"They're not so bad," I said, trying to minimize what I'd seen.

"C'mon, David. I know they're awful. You don't have to pretend otherwise. I've been staring at them my whole life."

"What happened?"

"My mom. She took something when she was pregnant with me. Tetra-something. Some kind of drug that causes a baby's teeth to stain. It wasn't her fault. I'm sure she didn't know any better."

"I'm sure she didn't," I said.

"I learned to keep my mouth shut early. I didn't want to get teased. I've come to live with them but I'd be a liar if I said I didn't think about them every time I look in the mirror."

"I'm sorry, Nub."

"It's okay. There are worse things. Anna makes me smile."

The next morning, having spent an uncomfortable night at a Comfort Inn and dined on mini-muffins and melon at the free continental breakfast, we headed for the University of Virginia and the offices of Professor Ian Stevenson. According to the article I'd read at the dentist's office, Stevenson published a paper in 1960 called "The Evidence for Survival from Claimed Memories of Former Incarnations," in which he theorized that a person's character and physical attributes developed not only from heredity and environmental influences, but also from the forces of reincarnation. Carlson was so taken with Dr. Stevenson's ideas about rebirth; he gave the professor money to travel to India and study cases of children who claimed to recall prior lives and eventually endowed a chair for him at the University of Virginia.

"Let me guess. He's an expert on dragons," Nubby said.

"No. He's an expert on reincarnation."

"Oh, no," Nubby said.

"David, I wanna go home," Beatie said.

"Look, are you guys with me or not?" I asked. "Don't you see? This is one of the biggest moments of my life?"

"Puller over, David," Beatie said.

"Why?"

"'Cause I got the craps."

Driving down I-95, following Beatie's hurry call, we were three insignificant ants on a log. Nubby put on some Blind Lemon Jefferson and we settled in for the long drive ahead. Located off Route 64 near the center of the state, the University of Virginia seemed an unlikely home for Dr. Stevenson. Given the conservative environs of the institution and its core curriculum of liberal arts subjects, languages and other earthbound disciplines, one would expect Stevenson's paranormal subjects of study to be as welcome in Charlottesville as a *Star Trek* convention. The only possible explanation for their existence lay in the maxim of school founder, Thomas Jefferson, who said, "Here we are not afraid to follow truth wherever it may lead, nor to tolerate any error so long as reason is left free to combat it."

"Should we stop by and see Monticello?" I asked.

"What's that?" Nubby asked.

"It was Jefferson's house. It's famous."

"I thought he lived in a dee-luxe apartment in the sky," Nubby said.

"Thomas Jefferson?"

"No. George Jefferson."

"I'm not talking about George Jefferson. I'm talking about Thomas Jefferson."

"Are you sure?" Nubby asked.

"Yes, I'm positive. Just nevermind, all right?"

"God, you're huffy."

The aging two-story structure housing the Division of Perceptual Studies, as the dirty, brass plaque outside read, was far from lavish. We found Dr. Stevenson in his office eating a sandwich at his desk amidst a pile of papers and books; just the way one likes to picture a professor. Well into his eighties, he was dressed neatly in brown, herringbone pants, a white dress shirt and maroon bowtie.

"May I help you?" He asked.

"Are you Dr. Stevenson?"

"I am indeed. Who are you?"

"I'm David Horvath. This is my grandmother, Beatie. And this is my friend, Nubby Jones," I said, as we stepped further into the room. "We're from Rochester, New York."

"I think I know why you're here," Dr. Stevenson said.

"You do?" I asked.

"Yes, I believe I do. Young man, were you born without your thumb?" He asked Nubby.

Nubby, ill-prepared to field questions, stared down at his own hand.

"Oh, this? No. It was bitten off by a goat when I was a kid."

"And your eye?" Dr. Stevenson asked me, pointing to my black patch. "Was that damaged at birth?"

"Well, it didn't really go bad until I was two."

"Oh. Then, perhaps, I don't know why you're here," Dr. Stevenson said.

I proceeded to tell Dr. Stevenson about all the reasons I thought I was a dragon in a prior life.

"Let me see the scar on your torso," Dr. Stevenson said.

What I didn't know was that Dr. Stevenson's work involved the study of birthmarks, birth defects and scars, with no genetic rationale, as possible evidence of prior lives. He told us, however, that he published a book called *Reincarnation and Biology* that focused on this very subject in 1997.

"And you say the doctors could provide no medical explanation for the existence of this scar?"

"That's true," I said.

"He's right," Beatie said. "I was there."

"Do you have your medical records?"

"No," I said. "Not with me."

"But you're certain this scar was not created by a childhood accident or injury?"

"Yes, I'm certain."

"He was born with it," Beatie said.

"David. It's David, correct?" Dr. Stevenson asked.

"Yes."

"David, my work in this area focuses on cases where I believe that a birthmark or congenital deformity may have derived from a prior life. Often times a family will provide anecdotal evidence about wounds or marks on a deceased relative that correspond to those present on a young child who is thought to embody the dearly departed's reincarnated soul. I've documented many children who've talked about a prior life, just like your mother claimed you did, but it is the autopsy reports and medical records of the person who has died that gives my research an added element of objectivity. Unfortunately, it seems unlikely that you could produce the medical records of a dragon — Komodo or otherwise — for me."

"Are you saying it's not possible that I was reincarnated?"

"I've learned not to say that. You strike me as an honest person and I have no reason to think that what you say about your mother and the circumstances surrounding your birth are not true. Like all cases that I have studied, there is no definitive proof to be found. There are only degrees of believing."

From my research, I knew Dr. Stevenson's stance on proof. Other than in the field of mathematics, it did not exist in his estimation, and I realized, only after I left, that this was probably the reason he didn't dismiss the possibility that dragons of the variety I spoke had ever existed. Even in the presence of compelling evidence, such as that he'd gathered on reincarnation, all such matters were ultimately ones of faith.

What I needed to know was suddenly clear. Stevenson offered me and others a choice to disengage from the fear of death that consumes us during life — a choice to believe that our personality or soul is something separate and apart from both our body and brain — a choice to believe in the possibility of reincarnation. And though I had no absolute proof to call on, when it came to believing whether or not I was a dragon, reborn in this lifetime as a man with all the same powers, abilities and inclinations to succeed and fly, I chose to believe. I chose to believe I was a dragon.

"Thank you, Dr. Stevenson," I said.

"Good luck to you."

Back in the Mustang, I prepared to drive north, satisfied that our trip had been worthwhile.

•

eleven

I woke up feeling invigorated and alive; determined to bring the Academy Awards to Rochester *without* the help of Mayor Candee.

"Today is the day our quest for greatness takes wings," I announced to my friends at the Patch. "Today is the day we throw this city on our back and carry it to unprecedented heights."

"Sounds kind of heavy," Nubby said.

"Nub, don't bring us down. We need a plan," Dixie said.

"We need a miracle," Big Nasty said.

"How's our celebrity petition coming?" I asked.

"It's not. We can't find anyone to sign it."

"What about Foster Brooks?"

"The lovable lush? He's dead," Big Nasty said.

"What about Cab Calloway? He's from Rochester," I said.

"He's also dead."

"Oh . . . too bad. Who else? Let's see . . ."

"What about Philip Seymour Hoffman?" Dixie asked.

"Phillip Sigmund who?" Nubby asked.

"Hang on. I've heard of that guy," I said.

"Of course you have. He won the Oscar for *Capote*. He's been in everything; *Boogie Nights*, *Talented Mr. Ripley*,

Magnolia, Almost Famous, Love Liza. The guy rocks," Dixie said. "He's one of the best actors out there."

"And he's from Rochester?"

"Yes, he grew up in Fairport."

"And he's still alive?" I asked.

"Yes," Dixie said. "He's also a big supporter of the High Falls Film Festival."

"You're kidding? Now we're getting somewhere. This is very cool."

"He'll never sign the petition," Nubby said.

"Forget the petition. Maybe he'd be our spokesman; sort of like the city's goodwill ambassador to the Academy."

"What about Wendy O. Williams?" Nubby asked.

"Who's that?" I asked.

"You remember her -lead singer for the punk rock band the Plasmatics. She used to live here growing up. She liked to cover her tits with electrical tape and then just run around wildly on stage during concerts."

"And you see her in the goodwill ambassador role?" I asked.

"I don't know. She was pretty much a badass. I heard she got kicked out of the Brownies as a kid."

"Tell you what, Nub. She's probably not a great candidate for the goodwill ambassador role, but that's just my gut talking. I'm not quite sure how the whole electrical tape thing would play, but we'll put her on the list as a back-up."

"Don't bother. She's dead," Big Nasty said. "She killed herself in 1998."

"Dammit, that's right," Nubby said. "What about Tom Cruise?"

"What about him?" I asked.

"He's originally from Syracuse," Nubby said.

"So?" I asked.

"So it's close enough. I say we contact him. He's always saving people. Maybe he'd save us," Nubby said.

"Syracuse is an hour away. Let's try and exhaust our own city before we move on to others, all right?"

"But they've got Richard Gere and Bobcat Goldthwait, too," Nubby said.

"Just Rochester, okay?"

"How about Rick James?" Big Nasty asked.

"The Superfreak?" I asked.

"Yes. He could bring the funk to our cause," Big Nasty said.

"Is he from Rochester?"

"No, he's from Buffalo," Nubby said.

"He's also dead," Dixie said.

"Oh, I didn't know that," Big Nasty said. "Farewell, sweet Superfreak."

"David, can I be candid?" Dixie asked.

"Of course."

"Listen, don't get me wrong. I'm very excited about this whole idea but even if we got Phillip Seymour Hoffman or Tom Cruise to be our spokesman, I don't think that's going to be enough to get the Academy to move the Oscars here. We need something bigger. I don't know what, but I know it's got to be something that involves the whole community."

"I still say we should kidnap Billy Crystal," Big Nasty said.

"That's not going to help," I said.

"What about Ellen DeGeneres?"

"Big Nasty, for the last time, kidnapping is not an option."

Dixie was right. I had to think differently. What would a dragon do? Deservedly or not, I was the leader of the group and it was time I started acting like it.

"So what are we going to do, David?"

I looked around the Patch hoping for a sign. People who fail to distinguish themselves with speed or strength often turn to endurance or daring to make their mark. Marathoners, bicyclists and rock climbers are usually average childhood athletes who learn to push past human limits as a way of showing the world they're worthy. We needed to do the same. But how?

It didn't come to me in a dream, by lightning strike or via deathbed epiphany. Instead, it was staring at me from the wall. I locked eyes with the pen and ink rendering of Sam Patch, the bar's namesake daredevil, and I knew the answer. Legend has it that dragons carry the essence of life in what's known as their sheng chi or celestial breath. I took a lungful of air and let it out slowly.

"We're going over the falls," I said.

"We're what?"

"On Friday November 13, the opening night of the High Falls Film Festival, and the very same day Sam Patch leapt to his death in 1829, we're going to jump into the Genesee River and ride over the High Falls."

"What for, you lunatic?" Nubby asked.

"To stop the Mayor from destroying our past *and* our future."

"David, what are you talking about?" Big Nasty asked.

"I'm talking about the historic heart of this city; the High Falls, which the Mayor wants to turn into a waterslide park and casino."

"You're insane. The falls are a hundred feet high. We'll all be killed," Big Nasty said.

"No, we won't."

"David, this is a great idea," Dixie said.

"I thought you might like it," I said.

"We can't go over the falls," Nubby said.

"Why not?" I asked.

"I'm sure it's illegal," Nubby said.

"Maybe it is, but so what? Sometimes greatness requires

breaking the law. Look at all the famous, non-violent protest movements."

"But we wouldn't be protesting, we'd be trespassing."

"How do you figure?" I asked.

"The falls are city property."

"Nobody owns those falls. They're the property of the people of Rochester."

"Well, I think this is stupid and I'm not doing it, David," Nubby said.

"From now on, don't call me David. My name is Dragon. Dragon Horvath."

"Dragon?" Big Nasty asked, a bit confused.

"He thinks he's a dragon," Nubby said.

"We better call a doctor," Big Nasty said.

"A reincarnated one," I said. "And I don't need a doctor."

"Have you guys been doing whippets in the dairy aisle again?" Big Nasty asked.

"No," I said.

"Then what's all this going over the falls and dragon business about?" Big Nasty asked. "Is this about Miranda?"

"Negative," I said.

"Is this about your upcoming trial? You're going to beat the charges."

"No."

"Is it about losing your job at the Eggroll Ranch? 'Cause you can find another job," Big Nasty said.

"No. It's not about losing my job," I said.

"Well, whatever it is, David, it's not worth committing suicide over," Big Nasty said.

"The name is Dragon and this is not about committing suicide. It's about stopping the Mayor and the city from developing the High Falls into Candee Land. It's about our quest for greatness. Tell him, Nub."

"*Look*, Dragon. *We* may be on a quest for greatness but *you* are the only one who's going over those falls," Nubby said.

"No, he's not. I'm going, too," Dixie said.

I smiled at Dixie. "C'mon, Big Nasty. Whattya say?"

"No way. I'm terrified of heights and water."

"Are you doing this to bring the Oscars here?" Nubby asked.

"No. If Oscar wants to come to us, let him come. But dragons don't beg, and neither does Rochester."

"It's not too late to build that two thousand foot dick we talked about," Big Nasty said.

"David, I don't want you to go over the falls," Nubby said.

"It's Dragon, and I appreciate the sentiment, but I'm going over. And I hope you'll go with me."

"Man, I've heard some crazy shit, but this is the craziest," Big Nasty said. "I feel a poem coming on. *'Dragon Horvath's gonna ride the falls. A reinforced jock couldn't hold his balls. If he hits a rock and smashes his head, the odds are good he will be dead.'*"

"Thanks, Big Nasty. That's really moving," I said.

"It needs a little work, but it's most of the way there."

"Dixie, what do you know about protest rallies?" I asked.

"Are you kidding? I know a lot. I've protested everything from WTO meetings to Augusta National to last year's Boy Scout Jamboree. Why?"

"Because I'm going to need your help setting one up."

"Whatever you need, you've got it."

"Does this mean blowing up your father's factory is off for now, Dixie?" Nubby asked.

"Yes. For now, that's off," she said.

"Damn. I was looking forward to that."

It may have been the chili cheese dog I ate but, whatever the reason, I believed I was seeing the signs that life provides to point the way when you're paying attention; although it's possible that I was making too much of the facts. After all, I'd known for years that Sam Patch rode over the High Falls in 1829 on November 13, my birthday, but I'd never ascribed any significance to it. Likewise, the other ghosts I'd been revisiting, from George Eastman and Susan B. Anthony to Frederick Douglass and Chester Carlson, were not foreign to me, having grown up with a reasonable understanding of who they were and the roles they'd played in Rochester's history. So what, if anything, had changed? What made them more important now?

When I got home, I walked across the street and entered Mt. Hope Cemetery. Frederick Douglass and Susan B. Anthony were buried there, and though outsiders might presuppose that it was just bad luck — like President McKinley getting shot in Buffalo — both Douglass and Anthony, along with many others, some 350,000 at Mt. Hope alone, chose to live and die as well as rest in peace in Rochester. Alongside the two of them lay optical giants, John Jacob Bausch and David Lomb, newspaper man, Frank Gannett, and the founder of Western Union, Hiram Sibley — legendary figures all in the city's history. Any one of them would have made a perfectly good sounding board, but I had come to commune with Douglass and Anthony.

Douglass and Anthony were towering agents of change and yet, somehow, Rochester's role in enabling their achievements was lost on the public, both locally and nationally. Was it mere happenstance that the racial and gender equality civil rights movements found homes in Rochester and flourished, despite strong opposition forces, while a world of entrepreneurial innovation sprung up around them? Or was it a credit to the city and the character of the people who lived there and changed the world with their cameras, copiers, lenses and protests, helping people see things and each other differently, more clearly and in many cases, for the first time?

There was some elusive connection between the monumental events that occurred here in the past and the people who lived through them, but I couldn't quite put it together. Like a sea of cosmic threads I longed to weave into a beautiful, karmic blanket, the images of the past floated everywhere around me yet I was unable to grab hold of more than one or two of them at a time. All I knew for sure was that there'd been greatness in Rochester and its citizens many years before and as I left Mt. Hope Cemetery, I felt certain it would return again.

―――― twelve ――――

Kit Nash insisted Willa accompany me to the first preliminary hearing following my arrest for criminal assault. "This'll be her *Scared Straight* experience. I want her to see what happens when you go down the wrong path in life," he said over the telephone. "Plus it's good training if she goes pre-law."

I picked her up at the house that plastic surgery for pets built, a palatial spread posing as a medieval castle complete with gated entrance, drawbridge and separate zip code. How many poodles had suffered for its ostentatious exterior one could only imagine. Willa emerged slowly, haggling with a gaggle of nannies who bundled her up for the wintry weather. In her right hand, she carried Plank.

"What's up, Willa?"

"My name is Cheese."

"Right."

"You're still driving this junker?"

"No, it's an optical illusion. You're actually climbing into a Jaguar."

"This is embarrassing. I hope nobody sees us."

"If you knew anything about cars you'd know that the '75 Mustang is an automotive legend," I said.

"Yeah, right. A legend of dog crap."
"Do you have to bring that piece of wood with you?"
"Anywhere I go, Plank goes."

Willa put her feet up on the dash as I backed out of the driveway.

"Hey, put your damn feet down. Show a little respect."
"I was just getting comfortable."
"Well, don't."
"Geez, what bug crawled up your butt?"
"The going-to-court bug."
"You're uptight about going to court?" Willa asked.
"Maybe a little."
"Why? Are they going to put you away? That would be sweet."
"That would *not* be sweet," I said.
"I think it would be cool to do some time. What kind of stretch you think you'll do for jacking up Santa?"
"I did not jack up Santa, and I will not be doing a stretch. Where'd you pick up that term anyway?"
"*The Shawshank Redemption*; probably seen it 50 times on our 80-inch plasma."
"It's a good movie, but it's fiction. Remember that."
"Maybe they'll put you in the hole."
"Shut-up, Cheese."

Because of my limited financial resources, I was assigned a public defender to handle the charges leveled against me. Fitzpatrick "Bug" Boone, who moonlighted as a stand-up comedian, worked by day as a government lawyer in a converted warehouse along the Genesee River. The fact he became an attorney was both miraculous and confusing to all of us who knew him growing up since he spent most of his time rolling doobies and sleeping out for concert tickets. Back then, he was the guy to see if you wanted front row seats to Rush and a bag of Maui Wowie, but he always talked about his dream of heading to Hollywood to become a famous comedian and actor. "As soon as I save up enough money, I'm going to Los Angeles, David. I'm gonna be a huge star and, if you're nice to me, I'll let you ride in my limo."

Unfortunately, Bug, like so many others do, drifted into law school and married too soon, saddling himself with loan debt and eventually alimony when his marriage predictably unraveled. He was a sad and lonely figure — working for low pay, chasing after paralegals and sending unimpressive articles about himself to DePauw's alumni magazine — but he didn't want you to know it. To anyone who'd listen, Bug continued to trumpet his tinsel town ambitions, trying to project the confidence of the seventeen-year old he still saw in the mirror, a reflection growing fainter by the day. As a public defender, he couldn't charge me any legal fees and I was getting exactly what I paid for.

"David, over here."

Bug spotted me and bounded over like a puppy. His face had grown fuller and looked flush, like the tie he was wearing was too tight.

"Hi, Bug," I said, shaking his extended hand.

"God, it's good to see you. How long's it been?"

"Quite awhile. I think I saw you at Thirsty's last winter."

"That's right. I remember that. Can you believe we're going to be working together?"

"That's one way to put it."

"Yeah, right. . . . Who's this young lady? Your daughter?" Bug asked.

"No, this is Willa. She's my mentee believe it or not."

"Sure. Gotta show the young people the way, right? If we don't do it, who else will? Come with me to my office and we'll talk for a few minutes before heading over to the courthouse for the hearing."

The three of us began making our way down a crowded corridor.

"Make way for the bad guy. Bad guy coming through," said Willa, repeatedly shouting her favorite lines from *Scarface*. "Make way for the bad guy. 'Cause you're never gonna see a bad guy like this again."

"Will you please stop that? I am not the bad guy. Knock it off."

"Hey, you're the one who jacked up Santa Claus. You've earned your props," Willa said.

"I *didn't* jack up Santa Claus and I *don't* want my props, okay? I just want to get this over with and go home," I said.

"You're a Pacino fan," Bug said, recognizing Willa's words. "Someday, I'm going to work with him."

"Whatever."

"What's with the two-by-four, Willa?" Bug asked.

Willa was silent.

"That's Plank," I said. "He's a friend."

"Is this a non-smoking building?" Willa asked.

"Yes. Especially for you," I said.

"Willa, have you heard the one about the rabbi, the priest and the prostitute?" Bug asked. "Get this. The three of them are walking into a Russian Bath House when the rabbi says..."

"I gotta pee," Willa said, peeling off into a women's room.

"They're great at this age, aren't they?" Bug observed.

In his office, Bug had sobering words for me.

"Listen, David, I think you should change your plea to guilty and let me try to cut a deal with the prosecutor."

"But you told me to plead *not* guilty at the arraignment."

"I know, but I hadn't seen the video yet."

"There's video?"

"Yes. They've got the whole thing recorded. From what I can see, you really took it to Santa."

"I did *not* take it to him. He slept with my girlfriend. He called me a loser. Doesn't that count for anything?"

"The problem is that everybody loves Santa Claus. We get in front of a jury and all of a sudden it's St. Nick, the man who brings presents to ghetto kids, versus you, the unstable monster who beat the hell out of him. Know what I mean?"

"This guy is *not* Santa. He's a yoga instructor who goes around shtupping other people's girlfriends. Mine included. Don't you believe me?"

"Of course I believe you. I really do. But all the jury is going to see is the red suit and the white beard. Add a couple of reindeer and a sleigh and we're sunk."

"Bug, he's not going to have a sleigh with him in court. The guy's a Hindu. If you ask the right questions on cross-examination, the jury will see right through him."

"First of all, that's a big if. To be honest, I'm not that good at cross."

"You're not?"

"No."

"Then what the hell are you good at?"

"I'm pretty good at opening statements."

"Great. So after the first day it'll be all downhill?"

"David, I'm not recommending you plead guilty just because of the video. There are also witnesses. Santa's assistant has already said she'll testify against you."

"*She* said that?"

"Yeah, why? Do you know her?"

"Know her? That *assistant* is my ex-girlfriend, Miranda."

For a moment, Bug was speechless.

"I'm going to try to get the charges thrown out today, but don't get your hopes up."

"I don't want to plead guilty. I know I can beat this."

"Sure you can. And I can go off my medication anytime I want."

"I'm serious. I don't understand why you're being so negative. Is this what they teach you in law school?"

"To be honest, I don't know. I didn't actually *go* to law school. I got my degree on-line."

"Wait. You didn't go to law school?"

"Just relax. I've got my J.D. But why pay for the bricks and mortar when you can do the whole thing from the comfortable surroundings of your own mother's basement?"

"Great. I've got an on-line attorney with a law degree from YouTube."

"You worry too much."

"That's for sure," Willa said, having rejoined us and now sitting with her feet propped up on Bug's coffee table.

"Look, let's go into court and see what we can do. We need to hustle though. I'm performing a set at the Chuckle Hut in an hour. Rumor has it a pretty well-known promoter may be in the audience. This could be my big break," Bug said.

Bug was right. Not about the promoter, but about the judge, who refused to dismiss the charges and gave me a week to decide whether to change my plea to guilty and cut a deal or take my chances with Bug and proceed to trial.

"I think a trial would be rad," Willa said, as we drove toward her parent's home.

"No, it wouldn't. There is nothing *rad* about trials."

As I dropped Willa off, I expected at least one more smart-ass remark and was stunned when she made a simple admission instead.

"My parents are separating."

"What?"

She looked at me and nodded.

"Yeah, they told me yesterday. My mom's moving out. They say it's just temporary."

"I'm sorry. I had no idea."

"She's not around a lot anyway so it won't make much difference."

"I'm really sorry."

"I don't care. I really don't."

Willa sounded unpersuasive so it seemed appropriate, as her mentor, to put an arm around her shoulder and try to comfort her.

"Get off me, man, before I call the police."

"Sorry!"

Turns out she was holding up pretty well, but her brave face couldn't last forever. Willa opened the dirt-crusted door of my Mustang and climbed out of the bucket seat.

"Listen, Willa, if you need someone to talk to about all this, just say the word."

"How many times do I have to tell you? My name is Cheese."

With Plank in tow, Willa slammed the car door and began trudging up the snow-covered driveway toward her house. As I watched her go, I knew she was in for a very long walk.

thirteen

"Okay, bring it in, guys. We're going to start off with something called the kamikaze drill," I said, after my students had warmed up for a few minutes.

"Sounds boring," Blaise said.

"Blaise, I don't want you to use that word anymore. Do you understand me? I want you to banish it from your vocabulary."

"Boring?" Blaise asked, seemingly unaware of his offense.

"That word is politically incorrect," Zandra said, twirling her dark locks around a finger.

"Which word? Boring?" Blaise asked.

"No. Kamikaze."

"Why is it politically incorrect?" I asked.

"My teacher says it conjures up images of World War II and demeans the Japanese. FDR put them in prison camps. Did you know that?"

"Yes, I knew that, but I assure you the word 'kamikaze' in no way demeans anyone. The kamikaze drill is all about running and endurance. It's about playing with controlled abandon."

"Isn't that an oxymoron?" Danny asked.

"No, it's not. Cheese, why don't you start us off?"

"Hell, no."

"Just do it!" I barked.

Willa reluctantly did as told and moved to the baseline.

"Please put down Plank and use your racket," I said.

"Fine," Willa moaned.

"All right, I'm going to feed a ball to your backhand," I said, hitting the first ball off to Willa's left. "Then I'm going to feed one to your forehand off to your right. Then I go back to the backhand and so on."

"Hey, not so far away."

"I told you this was about running and endurance. Now, get moving!"

Feeding balls left and right, I ran Willa back and forth until her breathing became heavy and labored.

"I need my Pimp Juice," she gasped.

"Not yet, Cheese. Fifty more balls to go."

"Fifty? Aw, man. This drill blows."

Each student took three turns in the torture chamber until all seven of them were sprawled out, supine on the har-tru, exhausted from more exercise than they'd probably ever experienced.

"Who wants to go again?" I asked.

"Are you insane, David? I'm having a heart attack over here," Zandra said.

"I gotta stop smoking," Willa said, between gasps.

"This is child abuse, I think," Boyle said.

"My dad could sue you for this, David," Danny said.

I was poised to pass on lesson number three: the old tennis is life, life is tennis metaphor. A real chestnut.

"Who can tell me what we learned today?"

"We learned that the kamikaze drill is hard."

"That's good, Becky. What else?"

"You have to keep going, even when you're tired."

"That's right, Danny. What else?"

"You're not going to make all of your shots, but you have to try."

"Another very good point, Blaise. Anyone else?"

"Sometimes you just have to go for it."

"That's exactly right. Sometimes you just have to go for it."

"Good, Boyle. Cheese, what did you learn today?"

Some of these brilliant life lessons had to be getting through to Willa who, having finally caught her breath, contemplated the question for a few seconds before answering.

"What are you going for?" Willa asked, ignoring my inquiry.

"What?" I asked.

"You just said, 'sometimes you have to go for it.' What are *you* going for?"

Ordinarily, Willa's thinly veiled assertion that I wasn't *going* for anything worth noting in my life would have nicked me like a paper cut between my toes. To date, I'd been someone who spoke openly of my aspirations but did very little to achieve them; a fault worse than never speaking of them at all in my opinion. This time, however, the insinuation that I was a hypocrite didn't bother me.

"That's personal, Cheese," I said. "I get to keep it to myself just like you do."

As I deflected Willa's pointed question about what I was *going* for, I realized I had a good answer for the first time.

At home, Beatie and Biff were seated in their matching La-Z-Boys having dessert when I walked into the family room.

"O'Reilly's right. These asshole liberals want to destroy Christmas," Biff hollered at the TV.

"Calm down, Biff," Beatie said.

"Don't tell me to calm down. Kids can't even decorate a damn tree in their classrooms anymore because of the gay agenda. Some jackass judge in Seattle even banned the pledge of allegiance because it has the word God in it. These people are destroying the country I fought for."

"Ar-right. Taker easy," Beatie said. "How 'bout some more Reddi-wip fer yer Jell-O?"

"Hey guys," I said, taking off my coat and hanging it up in the front hall closet.

"Hiya, David," Beatie said.

"Watching *The Factor* I see."

"Damn right. Only show worth watching," Biff said.

"Can I talk to you?" I asked Beatie.

"Of coyse," Beatie said.

"Your grandmother tells me you think you're a dragon. What the hell's that all about?" Biff asked.

"I don't want to get into that right now, Biff."

"Son, I'm worried about you. You've got an overactive imagination."

"Like your overactive bladder, Biff?" Beatie asked.

"No, Beatie! Not like that. Will you just go get the Reddi-wip? David, what you need is a wife and a steady job. A regular nine-to-five. That'll set you straight."

"Maybe someday, Biff, but right now I've got other plans."

"What other plans? There's no such thing as other plans," Biff said.

"Let him talk," Beatie said.

"Where's my topping?" Biff asked.

"In a minute," Beatie said. "Ga-head, David."

"I've made a decision," I said.

"Let me guess. You're no longer a dragon. Now you're a butterfly?" Biff asked.

"Hush, Biff," Beatie said.

"I'm going over the High Falls."

"Yer what?" Beatie asked.

"Call the loony bin, Beatie. Tell 'em they've got incoming," Biff said.

"In November, I'm going to jump into the Genesee River and let it take me over the High Falls just like Sam Patch did in 1829."

"Who the hell's Sam Patch?" Biff asked.

"I don't like that idear, David," Beatie said.

"It's suicide," Biff said

"No, it's not."

"Why would ya want to do that?" Beatie asked.

"The Mayor wants to turn the High Falls into a waterslide park and build a gambling casino there. She's got plans drawn up for this awful adult entertainment theme park called Candee Land. I'm trying to stop that."

"So yer doin' this to save the falls?"

"Yes, but it's more than that. I want to rally the people of Rochester. I want to remind them of everything that's great about this city. I want to shock the world."

"You're sure as hell shocking me," Biff said.

"Look, I haven't figured out all the details yet, and it may not make sense, but something good is going to come from it."

"Forget what I said about a wife and job. What you need is a good 12-step program for wackos," Biff said.

"I'm not a wacko," I said.

"Oh, no? How many dragons do you know whose primary occupation is riding waterfalls?"

"Shut-up, Biff," I said.

"You need help," Biff said.

"Would ya do it alone?" Beatie asked.

"No. I think some others down at the Patch might join me. I'm not sure."

I glanced at the TV as Biff flipped around on the Fox commercial break.

"Wait, Biff, turn this up please," I said.

Mayor Candee was holding a news conference. Dressed in her trademark white pantsuit and black string tie, she stood behind a lectern inside City Hall while reporters and cameramen, representing every local media outlet, packed the building's open atrium.

"Ladies and gentlemen, I want to speak to you and all the citizens of Rochester. But first, I want to tell you that this press conference is being brought to you by the good people at Cockeye's chicken wings. As our slogan says, 'if you haven't had our wings, then you don't know cockeye.' Now, with that bit of business out of the way, let me say that I see a great opportunity for our fair city on the horizon. As you are all aware, Oscar week is approaching fast and all the morally compromised people in the world will be descending upon Los Angeles for their annual bacchanalian sin-fest. I don't know about you, but when I witness such decadence and hedonistic self-indulgence, I ask myself one question: why the hell should L.A. have all the fun? That's why I'm here today; to give notice to the world that Rochester is throwing her hat into the Oscar ring for next year."

"Whaddya know," Beatie said. "You and the Mayor came up with the same idear."

"She didn't come up with anything. She stole the idea from me. I should have known," I said, as Mayor Candee continued.

"I am currently putting together a distinguished blue ribbon panel of local liquor distributors, oddsmakers, and fellow strip club owners, who will help craft a winning proposal for submission to the Academy of Motion Picture Arts and Sciences. With that said, the floor is now open."

"Mayor Candee, are you saying you're going to try and bring the Academy Awards ceremony itself to Rochester?" Channel 10's Ginny Ryan, a sunny presence, asked.

"That's right. We're going to hold it in the Eastman Theatre and it's going to be the greatest thing this city's ever seen," Mayor Candee said.

"Madame Mayor, how did you come up with this idea?" Ms. Ryan asked.

"Well, truth be told, I was hot-tubbin' with three waiters from Cockeye's last week. We were playing a game called hide the greased cucumber and . . . oh wait, I'm thinking of something completely different. What was the question again?"

"The idea. How did you come up with this idea?"

The Mayor paused.

"Let's just say it came to me."

"It came to her, all right. It came to her from me," I shouted at the TV.

"With all due respect, Mayor Candee, the Oscars have never been held anywhere other than Los Angeles. What makes you think the Academy would be willing to hold them here?" Dick Dougherty, a top columnist for the *Democrat and Chronicle*, asked.

"Dick, I'm glad you asked that question because I've got a lot to say on the subject. Everybody knows that Rochester is the birthplace of Eastman Kodak. And everybody knows that this is the home of the International Museum of Film and Photography. But I'm not sure that people across the country know what an important role Rochester has played in the civil rights movements for both women and blacks, two titanic struggles that have always been near and dear to my heart."

"What involvement with civil rights have you had, Mayor Candee?" Dougherty asked.

"Dick, I haven't had any *involvement* per se. But back in the forties, I dated a pair of conjoined twins named Pepper and Licorice who I met on the vaudeville circuit. Talk about two hot bars of chocolate. They liked to sing Negro spirituals after sex and believe me; those boys could do a number on ya. Now, that's gotta count for something, right?"

"What does that have to do with the Oscars coming to Rochester?"

"Everything. Hollywood has an abysmal record when it comes to women and minorities and I'm calling them out on it."

"Do you have any women or minorities working for you here at City Hall?"

Mayor Candee looked around at her all-white, male staff.

"You people are missing the big picture," Mayor Candee stammered. "Today I'm issuing a challenge to the heathens out West: bring the Academy Awards to Rochester next year and show the world that you respect all of the little people or be exposed as the hypocritical sexists, racists and ageists you appear to be."

"Are you calling women and minorities little people?" Jack Garner, a film critic, asked.

"Of course not, Jack, although I've never seen a Puerto Rican broad dunk a basketball. Have you? . . . I joke of course. Look, what I'm saying is that our city is where Susan B. Anthony, the ultimate suffragette and a former Charlie's Angel, and Frederick Douglass, a very famous black guy who invented peanut butter, fought their guts out for the highly integrated and racially harmonious society we live in today. Rochester is a beacon of hope and its historical contributions must be respected and acknowledged."

"George Washington Carver invented peanut butter, Madame Mayor," Dougherty corrected.

"Well, good for him. Tell him he's invited to the party and ask him to bring some. I prefer crunchy if he asks."

"Mayor Candee, many people would say that the level of

racial discord in Rochester is higher than ever with segregated neighborhoods, urban poverty, mutual distrust and a crumbling economic infrastructure in the African-American community."

"Not me. I'm not one of those people. I love my homies... or is it brothers? Whatever it is, I love 'em. People, if you'd pull the cotton balls out of your ears for a minute you'd see that we have a very compelling story to sell here about our beloved city. Birthplace of film and photography. Land of civil rights. Home of the annual Lilac Festival. We deserve to host the Oscars and I'm going to make sure we get the chance. Last question."

"Mayor Candee, your critics will say that this Oscar plan of yours is little more than a stunt and that your real goal is to bring legalized gambling and prostitution to the High Falls area. Is that true?"

"Stunt? Did you say stunt? You jaded, ungrateful bastard. I can't believe you'd even suggest that. I was elected by the citizens to do what's in their best interest and that's exactly what I'm going to do. I am the decider. Security, remove that stooge."

As the press conference ended, Channel 13's distinguished lead anchor, Don Alhart, was hauled away in cuffs by police personnel, and Biff flipped back to *The Factor*.

"She stole my idea. She just flat out stole it," I said.

"Candee's a no good thug," Beatie said. "Always has been. Always will be."

"She doesn't care about the Oscars. All she cares about is Candee Land," I said.

"Be quiet, you two. I can't hear O'Reilly," Biff said. "He's raking some commie flag-burner over the coals."

"David, come with me," Beatie said.

Beatie and I retreated to her lair and took seats at the kitchen table.

"David, I wanna ride the falls with ya," Beatie said.

"You do?"

Beatie nodded as she put a Carlton into the right corner of her mouth and lit up.

"It's too dangerous," I said.

"What difference does it make? I'm dying. This is somethin' I wanna do."

"Are you sure? You're 102 years old."

"So what? This is how you can help me."

"How about taking another trip instead? After Grandpa died, you said you'd like to travel a bit. What about Banff?" I asked.

"What about it?" Beatie asked.

"You once said you wanted to see it?"

"I once said I wanted to see Karl Malden's tuchus, but I never took a trip there."

"You could go with a tour group."

"To Karl Malden's tuchus?" Beatie asked.

"No. To Banff."

"And what? Ride around Canada on a Greyhound full of imbeciles and sex offenders wearing white baseball hats and orthopedic shoes? No thanks."

"I'm sure they weed out the imbeciles and sex offenders."

"Those box lunches they give ya are awful — soggy, miserable sandwiches and fun size Milky Ways."

"I'm sure the food has improved."

"Don't count on it. I wanna go over the falls with ya."

"I just don't know . . ."

"I've spent my whole life takin' care of others. Yer grandfather. Yer mother. You. Biff. And don't get me wrong, I've loved it. I really have. . . . But, David, this is my last chance fer an adventure and a great way to go out of this world. Ya wouldn't deny me *that*, wouldya?"

I couldn't say no to Beatie's face. Having been unable to secure tickets to this year's Academy Awards, a show about to come and go, I was in desperate need of something to replace the excitement Beatie felt when attendance in Los Angeles was still a tantalizing possibility. If the false promise of a trip over the High Falls could serve such a purpose, I was willing to let the illusion linger. Damn the guilt. I had other more pressing problems.

The Mayor's Oscar pledge was going to make her popular in many circles, and if people saw my new plan as an attempt to prevent her from succeeding, the backlash would be severe and my cause would be lost. A perverse chess match had begun and my next move would be critical. I had to explain to the public why I wanted to stop her. Sure, I wanted to save the High Falls. It was an amazing place and to see it turned into some kind of commercial carnival with nickel slots would be sad for the city. But there was much more behind my longing to leap.

Part of it was selfless; I wanted to bring attention to Rochester and put the spotlight on the city, its people and their accomplishments in a way that hadn't been done in years. Part of it was personal; I wanted to count and to feel like I made a difference. I wanted to have an impact and to know that, somehow, I mattered. Mostly, I wanted my one bold act to appeal to the braver and more daring heart in each person who witnessed it. I wanted to inspire imaginations and awaken the collective consciousness of the place I called home. By trying to bring out whatever greatness existed in me, I might help bring out the greatness in those who walked the streets and sidewalks of Rochester every day. If I could make this happen, the future of the city would be altered for the better, forever — a metropolis reborn and reincarnated — and I would be a hero, a legend and, in my own estimation, a dragon.

Fourteen

The process of saving the city would start with a protest rally and I knew the perfect place to stage it.

Brown's Race, an area located in downtown Rochester near the mouth of the High Falls, is a 110-acre, historic district listed on the National Register. There are restaurants and bars, including the Sam Patch Saloon, as well as an arts center, a brewery, a laser light show featuring the falls at night, and a host of other diversions.

In 1818, entrepreneurs Francis and Matthew Brown cut a quarter-mile raceway or power canal, as some called it, 500 feet south of the High Falls through the limestone, sandstone and shale riverbed of the Genesee. The water that was diverted into the raceway via a 25-foot, 12-ton wheel was then distributed into a series of spillways which, in turn, fed the long row of grist mills sitting between the raceway and the gorge, and gave birth to the Flour City. The Brown brothers were the first to recognize the power of the High Falls and find a way to use it, but they wouldn't be the last.

"Okay, let's go through our checklist," Dixie said.

Inside the Patch, our commando unit, comprised of

Nubby, Big Nasty, Dixie and me, prepared to go outside and meet the world. Putting Dixie in charge of organizing our protest seemed like a good idea at the time given her activist background, but I was starting to wonder if her desire to show up her father and Goliath Industries, the slated developer of Candee Land, was clouding her judgment. Although there were only four of us, Dixie was acting as if there were four hundred.

"Does everyone have their pepper spray and goggles?" Dixie asked, from behind a bandana that covered most of her face.

"Dixie, I don't think we're going to need goggles," I said.

"Oh, no? Tell that to Bikes Not Bombs or The Hemp Revolution. They both marched on Washington last month and half their members are still washing tear gas out of their eyes. Believe me, when the pigs start squealing, you'll be glad you've got them."

"Pigs?" Nubby asked me under his breath.

"I think she means the police," I said.

"What about your pee bottles?" Dixie asked. "Did everybody get one?"

"What's a P bottle?" Nubby asked.

"It's where you relieve yourself while you're marching, stupid," Dixie said.

"I'm all set there," Big Nasty said, motioning to his colostomy bag.

"I'm not peeing in a bottle," Nubby said. "We're only going to be a few hundred yards away from here. I'll just come inside when I have to go."

"You'll kill our momentum if you do that," Dixie said.

"One trip to the can is going to kill our momentum?" Nubby asked.

"Dragon, tell Nubby the importance of maintaining

solidarity on the picket line. You let your numbers dip and the *man* immediately smells weakness."

"That may be, Dix, but I think that weakness would be preferable to the smell of Nubby's urine. Plus, I'm just not sure that public urination is going to make us a very sympathetic group," I said.

"Fine. Suit yourselves," Dixie said. "Where are your bandanas?"

"Why do we have to wear bandanas?" Nubby asked.

"To show unity," Dixie said.

"But they're hot pink," Big Nasty said.

"That's not hot pink. It's fuchsia," Dixie said.

"What the hell's fuchsia?" Nubby asked.

"Look, all the other colors are being used," Dixie said. "AIDS took red. Lance Armstrong took yellow. Prince took purple. Fuchsia was the only one left."

"Fuchsia's fine," I said, sensing Dixie's exasperation. "Get your bandanas out and put 'em on, guys."

Big Nasty and Nubby grumbled but followed my lead.

"I've put plenty of bottled water and Luna bars in your backpacks, so you should be all set for snacking," Dixie said.

"Luna bars? Aren't those for chicks?" Nubby asked.

"Yes, Nubby. And if you eat enough of them, you'll start growing breasts. Oh, wait. It looks like you've been gorging yourself on them already," Dixie said, observing Nubby's emerging man-boobs.

"Shut-up, Dixie. Those are called pectorals for your information. Each one represents countless hours in the gym."

"In the gym or on the couch?" Dixie asked.

"Enough, you two," I said.

"Also, there's also a cell phone with the telephone number of the National Lawyers Guild programmed into it in case we get separated."

"Dixie, don't you think that's going a bit overboard?" I asked.

"Come prepared or don't come at all, right? I've also got sun-block for everybody," Dixie said.

"Sun-block? What for? Rochester's ranked number two in the country in total days of annual cloud cover," Big Nasty said.

"Really?" Nubby asked. "Who's number one?"

"Seattle," Big Nasty said.

"God, I hate Seattle. First, the Space Needle, now this," Nubby said. "They're always trying to make us look bad."

"Nubby, if you could momentarily put aside Seattle's vendetta against us, I'd like to remind you that you still need protection against the sun's ultra-violet rays," Dixie said, handing small bottles of Bullfrog to each of us.

"I'll take my chances," Nubby said. "Dudes have climbed Everest with less gear than what I'm toting."

"Shut-up, Nubby," Dixie said. "Okay, Dragon, I think we're ready to go. The picket signs are in my car."

"Dixie, did you call Bono?" Nubby asked.

"No, I didn't call Bono. You have to work up to something like that. He doesn't just appear every time somebody calls," Dixie snapped.

"Hey, how should I know how it all works? I thought he came to all these kinds of rallies," Nubby said.

Marching outside to the Patch's parking lot, Big Nasty dragged his new portable dialysis machine behind him. Mounted on wheels, it looked no different than your average piece of carry-on luggage outfitted with a few tubes and knobs.

"By the way, if this thing gets wet, my doctor says I could get electrocuted," Big Nasty said.

"Aw, cut your whining," Nubby said.

"I'm just saying. I believe in our cause and all, but I'd like to avoid shock therapy if possible."

"Might do you some good," Nubby said.

"Perhaps. You know, I once wrote a poem about electricity called *Ben Franklin's Bitch*. 'Lazy summer, by the ol' swimming hole. Who could predict the downed telephone pole? Two young lovers, skinny-dipping at night. They went up in a flash, like a flambé done right. One of them was poor, and one of them was rich, but both paid their dues to old Ben Franklin's bitch.'"

"Big Nasty, that's horrible," Dixie said. "Please don't use the word 'bitch.'"

"I kind of like that one," Nubby said.

"You would," Dixie said, leading us toward her car to get the picket signs.

March brings at least several major snowstorms to Rochester every year. The month is cold, wet and without a single redeeming quality, other than the fact it's not February, which is even worse. This weather-related reality was just the first of many we'd be facing in our effort to gain publicity for our cause. The plan was one of elegant simplicity. We would picket near the High Falls hoping that the media would take notice of us and pick up our story about saving the site from development. Once in the camera's crosshairs, we would expose the Mayor's plans for Candee Land and announce our intention to go over the falls.

"I don't want to carry this picket sign," Nubby said.

"Why not?" I asked.

"Because I'm not sure I believe in what it says."

I walked closer to Nubby to get a look at the sign he was lugging toward the rally site.

"What are you talking about?" I asked. "It says 'No Hookers or High Rollers in our Hometown.'"

"Exactly," Nubby said. "Are you sure that's a good idea; economically and all?"

"Just carry the sign, okay?"

"I'm only looking out for the city," Nubby said.

At the heart of Brown's Race sits the Pont de Rennes Bridge, a pedestrian walkway named for Rochester's sister city in France, which traverses the Genesee River Gorge and offers a magnificent view of the High Falls. Twenty feet wide and three hundred feet long, it spans majestically above the river. Minutes after arrival, and without fanfare, we began marching back and forth at this dramatic spot armed with nothing but our signage.

"What should we chant?" Big Nasty asked.

"How about something simple like 'Save Our Falls'?" I asked.

"That's lame," Nubby said.

"All right. You come up with something better," I said.

"I always liked 'No Justice No Peace,'" Nubby said.

"But that has nothing to do with our cause," Dixie said.

"How about 'Hell No, We Won't Go,'" Nubby said.

"That has nothing to do with our cause either," Dixie said.

"What if we modify it? We could do something like 'Hell No, the Falls Won't Go,'" Nubby said.

"That's better, but why don't we just stick with 'Save our Falls'?" I asked.

"Wait, I've got it. 'Hell No, the Falls Must *Flow*.'"

"That's just dumb, Nubby," Dixie said. "Big Nasty, you're the poet. Why don't you come up with something?"

"Okay. Let me see. How about this one? 'No Hookers. No Dice. Just Snow and Ice. Leave our Falls Alone.'"

"Oh, that's good," Dixie said.

"The man's a genius," I said.

"I don't think that's so great," Nubby said.

After picketing for two hours, we hadn't attracted one person from the media although a growing number of homeless people found us worthy of stares.

"This isn't going to work," Nubby said. "Dixie, you need to take off your top. That's our only chance."

"Nubby, shut-up," Dixie said. "I'm not taking off my top to get us news coverage."

"Hey, are you committed to the cause or not?" Nubby asked. "I just think we need to try something different. . . . Big Nasty, you got any extra Luna bars? I'm starving."

"Do you know how slow a news town this is? We're going to get coverage if we're patient," Dixie said.

"She's right," I said. "How many waterskiing squirrels can they cover in one year?"

"As many as they want as far as I'm concerned," Big Nasty said. "I love those little guys; so cute with their little paws up on the rope line."

"Did you call the TV stations, Dixie?" I asked.

"Yes. And I also called all the radio stations. I don't know why nobody's here."

With our fuchsia bandanas, goggles and signs proving insufficient to draw the fourth estate, we needed to change tactics.

"So what can we do?" Big Nasty asked.

"I think we have to disturb the peace," Dixie said. With that, she put down her picket sign and returned to her oversized backpack, a purple monstrosity propped up against the bridge's railing. Rummaging through its nether regions, she began to pull various items out.

"I've got a bullhorn. Pots and pans. Kazoos. A trumpet. A tambourine."

"What the hell are we going to do with that stuff?" Nubby asked.

"Make noise, you idiot," Dixie said.

And so we did. For the next half hour, we became the most obnoxious and obscure jam band ever. With Nubby on kazoo and tambourine, yours truly on trumpet, Big Nasty on sauce pan and Dixie on the bullhorn, we let Rochester know we were not to be ignored. Safe to say, we had a unique sound; like five cats in a bag sharing an orgasm. Soon enough, the police arrived.

"Put your goggles on. Right now! Here comes the fuzz," Dixie said, before returning to her bullhorn.

"NO HOOKERS, NO DICE! JUST SNOW AND ICE! LEAVE OUR FALLS ALONE!" Dixie hollered again and again.

As I scrambled to pull my goggles over my eyes and my bandana over my face, I saw a single police officer at the far end of the bridge walking toward us.

"Don't stop playing," Dixie said.

Before I could make it through another verse of *You Light Up My Life*, one of three songs I remembered how to play on the cornet from childhood, the thin blue line was upon us.

"Folks, I need you to put down the instruments," the officer said.

"NO HOOKERS, NO DICE! JUST SNOW AND ICE! LEAVE OUR FALLS ALONE!"

"Ma'am, please cool it with the bullhorn or I'm going to confiscate it."

We stood at attention in front of the officer, lined up like four fuchsia pawns on a chess board.

"Folks, I've received several complaints from local merchants about the noise you're making out here. I'm going to have to ask you to disband and vacate the premises."

"We're not doing anything wrong," I said.

"Yes, you are. You're making too much damn noise," the officer said. "Now, I'm telling you to leave. This is not a request. It's a command."

"Whoa, whoa," Dixie said. "We've got a constitutional right to be here; the right of peaceful public assembly. As long as we're not inciting a riot, we're okay. This is public property."

"Ma'am, you're on city property right now."

"We are?" Dixie asked.

"Yes."

"Are you sure?" Dixie asked.

"Yes, I'm sure. You need to leave."

"Are you *positive* this is city property?" I asked.

"Well, I think so," the officer said, suddenly sounding less certain.

" 'Cause this is a historical district, and I think we have a right to be here," I said.

"Don't make this difficult, people. Just pack up your things and leave," the officer said.

"Don't you want to know why we're here?" Dixie asked.

"To be honest, ma'am, it doesn't matter to me. I deal with wack jobs every day and my job is to remove them from places they're not supposed to be."

"Wait, are you calling us wack jobs?" I asked, pushing my bandana off my forehead and pulling my goggles around my neck.

"I'm not calling you anything. I'm telling you to leave the premises."

"What if we refuse to leave?" Nubby asked.

"Then you'll be forcibly removed," the officer said. "I'm going to need back up here. We've got a disturbance on the Pont de Rennes Bridge in Brown's Race," he radioed.

"Officer, look out at the falls," Dixie said. "Don't you love them?"

The officer turned his gaze toward the High Falls and observed the scenery for a few seconds.

"Sure, I guess. Everyone loves the falls, but I need you guys to take your things and leave."

"How would you feel if I told you this area was going to be turned into a gambling casino and the falls would be part of a waterslide park?" I asked.

"What?" The officer asked, apparently surprised.

"That's what the Mayor and my father are planning to do," Dixie said. "And we're here to protest."

"I haven't heard anything about that plan," the officer said.

"That's because the Mayor is planning it all in secret — just waiting for the right time to pass it through the city council and stick it to the taxpayers," I said

"Is that true?"

The officer looked to the rest of us for confirmation and we each nodded.

"And your father's involved?" The officer asked Dixie.

"He's going to be the builder," Dixie said. "Goliath Industries. Have you heard of it?"

The radio activity initiated by the officer brought a second squad car and, more important, the first reporter to the scene.

"What's going on here, Jake?" the second officer asked upon arrival.

"These folks say the Mayor is going to turn the High Falls area into a gambling casino and waterslide park. Have you heard about that?"

"No."

The first officer stood thinking for a minute as Channel 8's weatherwoman, Breezy Summers, quietly walked up behind him with her cameraman in tow.

"Are you going to use tear gas on us?" Nubby asked.

"No," said the officer.

"What about high-powered hoses? Are you going to blast us?" Nubby asked.

"No. I need to find out for certain if this is city property," he said. "If it is, you'll have to leave. Do you understand?"

Assorted affirmative mumbles spilled from our mouths.

"I'll be back soon," the officer said.

As the officers left, Ms. Summers moved closer, salivating at the prospect of a scoop.

"Are you part of a radical leftist organization?" Breezy asked.

"Aren't you the weatherwoman from Channel 8?" I asked, expecting someone of greater journalistic heft.

"Yes, but don't paint me with that brush. I can do a lot more than weather," Breezy said, understandably defensive about her professional abilities given my tone. "A lot more."

"What's the forecast?" Nubby asked.

"If you don't mind, I'm not here to do the weather. I'm here to find out why you're on this bridge."

"We're protesting the commercial development of the High Falls by the Mayor and Goliath Industries," I said.

"And what's the name of your organization?" Breezy asked.

"Our name? We don't have a name," I said.

"You've got to have a name," she insisted.

"We do?"

"Yes, and an acronym. How else do you expect me to report on this if you don't have an acronym?"

"Look," I said. "We don't have a name or an acronym or anything like that. The High Falls are in danger and the situation is urgent so we're quickly working every angle available for saving this site."

"Got it. Quickly. Working. Every. Angle. For. Saving. Site," Breezy repeated in a staccato fashion as she scribbled on her notepad. "So basically, you're QWEAFS."

"What's a kweef?" I asked.

"Your organization. Your acronym. It's QWEAFS."

"No, we're not kweefs," I said.

"And what's your name?" Breezy asked, ignoring my denial.

"Me? I'm Dragon Horvath. And these are my colleagues: Nubby Jones, Dixie Lee and Big Nasty."

"Do you have a last name, Big Nasty?" Breezy asked.

"Not one I'm disclosing at this time," Big Nasty said.

"And, Mr. Horvath, is Dragon your given name?" Breezy asked.

"Actually it's a nickname my mother gave me, but I *am* a dragon."

"You are?"

"Yes, a reincarnated one."

"Come again," Breezy said.

"I'm a man, but in a prior life, I was a dragon. So, inside, I'm still a dragon. Understand?"

"I think so," Breezy said, a look of bemusement on her face. "And, Dragon, how long do you and your fellow QWEAFS plan to stay out here?" Breezy asked.

"What time is it right now?" Nubby asked, grabbing Big Nasty's wrist to look for a watch. "I want to catch *Speed Week* at ten."

"My friend is just kidding," I said. "We're going to be here as long as it takes to stop the Mayor's project."

"We are?" Big Nasty asked.

"Yes. We will not surrender this bridge until the High Falls are safe," I said, my sense of purpose growing by the moment.

"That's right," Dixie said. "We're going to bivouac out here tonight and every night until the Mayor and my father, Pete Lee, realize that Rochester and its citizens won't put up with their corporate greed."

After interviewing us for another fifteen minutes and learning about our background and future plans, Ms. Summers was ready to record our story for the nightly news.

"Larry, on me in three," Breezy said to the waiting cameraman while we stood in the background. "I'm here on the Pont de Rennes Bridge in downtown Rochester's Brown's Race historic district with Dragon Horvath, a reincarnated dragon and the leader of the QWEAFS, a group that has commandeered this catwalk in protest of what they say is Mayor Candee's secret plan to build Candee Land, a morally-challenged theme park with a reasonably priced all-day fun pass for families. Among the QWEAFS is Dixie Lee, daughter of Pete Lee, who claims that her father's company, Goliath Industries, has been contracted to help build a waterslide park and gambling casino here at the High Falls. The QWEAFS plan to stay here as long as it takes to kill the Mayor's idea, a strategy that might strike viewers as ordinary fare in the protest game. But, trust me; there is nothing ordinary about this story. Dragon," she said, pulling me into the frame. "You have an unusual end game for your protest, don't you?"

"That's right, Breezy. If the Mayor doesn't abandon her plan, we are going to jump into the Genesee River and ride over the High Falls and its 100-foot drop on November 13, the same day Sam Patch jumped in 1829."

"All of you?"

"Yes. All of us," I said, knowing full well that Nubby and Big Nasty had already declined.

"Won't that be dangerous?" Breezy asked.

"No. What's dangerous is doing nothing to save the High Falls."

"You heard it here first, folks. This is Breezy Summers reporting for Channel 8 Action News from Brown's Race in Rochester."

After Breezy left, a few questions and a minor mutiny arose.

"QWEAFS? That's the best name you could come up with?" Nubby asked.

"I didn't come up with anything. What's wrong with QWEAFS anyway?"

"You have to ask? A kweef is a vaginal fart. You know that, right?"

"No, I didn't know that," I said.

"From now on, we're going to be known as the vaginal farts. Nice going," Nubby said.

"I'm sure the name won't catch on. If you guys have a better idea for the name of the group, by all means speak up."

"How about something simple like Four Lovers of Nature?" Dixie asked.

"FLON?" I asked.

"Yes, FLON," Dixie said.

"That's not a name. It's a Mexican dessert," Big Nasty said.

"That's flan, you idiot," Dixie said.

"David, I don't care about our name but I've got to make something clear. I never said I would ride over the falls with you," Big Nasty said.

"Either did I," Nubby said.

"I know, but I wanted us to look united. Will you at least think about it?" I asked.

"I guess," Big Nasty said.

"I'm going home," Nubby said.

"We have to stay out here," Dixie said. "We'll lose all credibility if we don't."

"We have no tents, no sleeping bags, no portable heaters. We don't even have enough Luna bars," Nubby said.

"We can get that stuff," Dixie said. "We'll set up a shanty town and cover it in shifts."

"Sort of a camp, right?" I said.

"Yes, exactly. As long as one of us is here at all times, the protest will continue. And we can recruit others to our cause," Dixie said.

"So I wouldn't have to be here all the time?" Nubby asked, sounding a bit more enthusiastic.

"No. Not all the time," Dixie said. "Just for your shifts."

"It still sounds like a dog," Nubby said.

"You'll look like a hero to Anna," Dixie said.

"I will?"

"Of course. Activism is a major turn-on."

"Do you think we could get Bono to come now?" Nubby asked.

"No, Nubby. I don't think we can get Bono, all right?"

"What about the Edge or Larry Mullen?"

"No. None of the band members of U2 will be showing up. Are you with us or not?"

"I guess," Nubby moaned. "I still think we can get the Edge."

The next morning, the police returned and admitted that we weren't trespassing on city property. From that moment forward, our temporary residency on the Pont de Rennes Bridge officially began.

Fifteen

"I want to thank the entire press corps for gathering here today," Mayor Candee said, nervously glancing down into the orchestra pit from the stage of the Eastman Theatre.

Having aired the night before, Breezy Summers' report was fresh chum in the media shark tank and the assembled reporters wanted answers about the Mayor's alleged proposal for the High Falls.

"Madame Mayor, is it true there are blueprints for an adult theme park called Candee Land? Yes or no?" Chaz Walker, a veteran reporter known for his bowties and bullshit detector, asked.

"Will there be free parking?" Another journalist blurted.

From behind a cherry-wood podium, Mayor Candee ran her fingers through her thinning white hair and leered at the press, her apprehension giving way to disdain. A few feet to her side, in a folding chair, sat Pete Lee, less than happy to be part of Mayor Candee's planned counter-offensive.

"Is this project going to be funded by public tax dollars or the private sector?"

"Hold your gad-blasted horses, people, please," Mayor Candee said. "We're going to answer all of your questions, but first I've got some exciting news to share. As you all know, I issued a public challenge to Hollywood last month to move next year's Academy Awards ceremony to our fair city. As I said then, and as I wrote in my letter to the powers that be, I want to hold the event in this magnificent theatre built by the man who brought film and cameras to the world: George Eastman."

"What's the exciting news?" Breezy Summers asked.

"I'm getting there, Breezy. The exciting news is that we're one step closer to making our Oscar dream a reality. I received a letter this week from the Academy of Motion Picture Arts and Sciences, good ol' AMPAS, that I have right here," Mayor Candee said, pulling it from the breast pocket of her suit and unfolding it.

"Whatzit say?" A reporter in the orchestra pit called out.

"It says *'Dear Mayor Candee: Your written request to have Rochester host next year's Academy Awards ceremony has been received. Although your bullying tone and overt threats of bodily harm were not appreciated, we are keenly aware of your city's historic role in the invention and development of film and cameras, as well as its sterling civil rights heritage. Because of this admirable tradition, a sub-committee has been appointed to determine an appropriate way to honor the contributions of Rochester come Oscar time. Such recognition, however, will take place at the Kodak Theatre in Los Angeles and not in Rochester. Please note that I am hereby returning the envelope of cash, the Cockeye's gift certificate and the "I'd Rather Be in Rochester" bumper sticker that you sent with your correspondence as I am not permitted to accept gifts. Sincerely yours, Marc Engel, President of the Academy of Motion Picture Arts and Sciences.'*"

Upon completion of the letter, Mayor Candee paused before speaking, apparently proud of its contents.

"Do you know what this letter tells me? . . . They're running scared. We've got these Hollywood types by the short and curlies, and it's only a matter of time before that tribute to Rochester turns into a trip to our hometown. We've got the momentum."

"Mayor Candee, with all due respect, it doesn't sound like the Academy has any intention whatsoever of coming to Rochester. How do you respond to that?" A reporter asked.

"I respond to that the way I respond to all stupid questions . . . by telling you to go straight to hell. If you're going to bring that kind of attitude to these affairs, I suggest you stay away."

"But, Madame Mayor, I'm just doing my job," the reporter said.

"And I'm just doing mine. You folks leave the Academy to me. I'll get them turned around on this hosting business like a three-headed ostrich at an orgy. You mark my words."

"What about the QWEAFS?" Breezy Summers asked.

"The QWEAFS are a cancer on this city, and I'm afraid it's malignant," Mayor Candee said.

"Do you believe the High Falls should be saved from commercial development?" Chaz Walker asked.

"What I believe is that the QWEAFS are the single biggest threat to our chances of bringing the Academy Awards ceremony here next year, and its members are all traitors; to this city and to the United States of America. You've got a guy with an eye patch who thinks he's Jesus."

"Actually, he thinks he's a dragon," Breezy said.

"Whatever . . . . Another guy with a missing thumb — a sure sign his mama was hittin' the bottle hard right up 'til birth. A third guy with a dirty bomb that he drags around behind him . . ."

"That's a portable dialysis machine," Breezy said.

"Don't be so certain."

"Isn't Pete Lee's daughter involved?" asked John Lowell, WPXY's drive-time youth demo deejay and hipster, tilting his head toward Mr. Lee, who still sat on stage.

"Regrettably, I must report that Mr. Lee's daughter, a two-faced, rabble-rouser according to everyone I've spoken to, . . . no offense, Pete . . . is one of the QWEAFS. I must also report that the QWEAFS' leader, Dragon Horvath, is a criminal."

"For protesting?"

"No, for beating up Santa Claus. Surely you're aware that he's got an upcoming assault trial on the docket. A few months ago at Midtown Plaza, he pounded St. Nick and half his elves to a pulp just for looking at him the wrong way."

"Aren't you worried your remarks might taint potential jurors? Isn't he innocent until proven guilty?" John Lowell asked.

"No. I changed the local legal standard by executive order last month. From here on out, crooks like Horvath are guilty until proven innocent. We've got a responsibility to lock up delusional wombats like this Dragon fellow. The negative attention he's bringing to Rochester with this High Falls nonsense could scare off the Academy."

"Madame Mayor, you still haven't given us any answers about the High Falls and Brown's Race. Do you plan to develop a theme park there or not?" Breezy asked.

"Develop has become such an ugly word, hasn't it? I prefer the term *enhance*. Don't you?"

"Very well. Do you plan to *enhance* the area?" Breezy asked. "Mr. Horvath says you want to build a gambling casino and waterslide park with Mr. Lee's help."

"And you believe him? Horvath's a one-eyed, lying sack of monkey dung. I'm not in the habit of defaming people, but when I think of Dragon Horvath, two words come to mind: necrophiliac and pedophile."

"Are you saying Mr. Horvath likes to sleep with dead children?" Breezy asked.

"Hey, don't put words in my mouth. I never said that."

"But you just said . . ."

"What I'm saying is that Horvath's a sociopath and a madman and, between us, a little too fond of young boys if you know what I mean."

"Are you saying he's a child molester?" Another reporter asked.

"I never said that. Please, people, don't put words in my mouth. Just picture an unemployed cabbage cutter who loves to hit the sauce, assault people and fondle children. You can't believe anything he says."

"But, Madame Mayor, Dragon Horvath isn't the only one speaking out. Mr. Lee's daughter says that you plan to make prostitution part of this Candee Land. Is that true?" Breezy asked.

"Did I mention that Horvath's a bastard? He doesn't even know who his father is."

"Madame Mayor, please answer the question. Do you plan to make prostitution part of the enhancement of the High Falls?"

"Absolutely not. Prostitution? The very idea is repugnant to me."

"But you introduced a bill in the city council last year to legalize it," Chaz Walker said.

"I don't remember that. Keep in mind that I oversee hundreds of pieces of legislation."

"But you were the bill's principal sponsor."

"Doesn't ring a bell."

"You called it the Prostitute's Bill of Rights, remember? You held a press conference to announce it. We were all there," said Chaz Walker, looking around the orchestra pit as the other reporters nodded. "You even brought three hookers."

"Oh, *that* bill? That wasn't a prostitution bill. The title was entirely misleading. You thought that was a prostitution bill? Oh, that's ripe. That's funny. No, no, not at all. That was an appropriations bill and had it passed, hundreds of unwed mothers and their children would be better off today. See, that bill was part of my faith-based initiative to bring lonely older men together with vulnerable younger women. . . . My God, you try to do something for the people and it just gets kicked back in your face."

"What about gambling, Madame Mayor? Last spring, you introduced a bill to lift the city's ban on craps, blackjack, slot machines and sports betting. Are those the types of activities you want to bring to Brown's Race with this Candee Land?"

"I have no recollection of that bill."

"How is that possible?" Chaz Walker asked. "You proposed city-wide regulation and taxation of all gaming."

The Mayor shook her head defiantly.

"You wanted to change the name of the city from Rochester to Rouletteville," Mr. Walker continued.

"Nope. Wasn't me. Although you gotta admit Rouletteville has more pizzazz."

"But you and your grandson dressed up like a pair of fuzzy dice for a television ad campaign to gin up support for the bill. How can you deny that?"

The Mayor grimaced causing the veins in her neck to become visible.

"I don't recall any dice, Walker. You must be boozin' again."

"But you released copies of the ad on DVD for the media."

"Who told you that lie?" Mayor Candee asked, pointing an angry finger in her accuser's direction.

"Nobody. I've got a copy of it right here," Mr. Walker said, holding up the casing.

"That must be some kind of counterfeit bootleg deal," Mayor Candee said.

"So you deny ever trying to bring gambling to Rochester?"

"Yes, I deny it."

"And you deny ever hiring consultants from Las Vegas to assess Rochester's gaming potential?"

"Another pure fabrication."

"Then I'm sure you'll deny proposing an annual summer Craptacular with a craps table on every street corner. After all, that would take some vision on your part and we know you lack that."

The Mayor, as vulnerable to ego-based badgering as Jack Nicholson's Colonel Jessup in *A Few Good Men*, couldn't take anymore.

"Now *that* I won't deny!"

"That you lack vision?"

"No, that I came up with the idea for a summer Craptacular. You don't like it? Well, tough. I'm sick and tired of those stupid horses and cows on parade. I mean, how many puns can you come up with that use the word 'udder.' How many heifers can you auction off? We needed a fresh revenue stream and craps could've provided it."

"So you *do* want to bring gambling to Brown's Race and the High Falls."

"No, I'm not saying that."

Mayor Candee, dazed from the exchange, pulled a handkerchief from her front pocket and wiped away the moisture clinging to her forehead.

"Mayor Candee, the people of Rochester want answers."

"I, uh . . . this seems as opportune a time as any to bring Pete Lee to the microphone. Pete is the uh . . . CEO of Goliath Industries, one of our model corporate citizens, and uh . . . he'll be able to answer all of your questions. Pete, come up here."

As Mayor Candee retreated to her own folding chair, Pete Lee raised his compact frame from his uncomfortable perch and walked toward the podium. After putting on a pair of bifocals and shuffling his notes, he was ready to speak.

"A lot of false rumors have been swirling around the city about Brown's Race and the High Falls, and the Mayor has asked me to come set the record straight. As for Candee Land, no such plans or blueprints exist. What does exist, however . . . ."

"Are you saying your own daughter is a liar, Mr. Lee?"

"May I finish? What does exist, however, is a burning desire on the part of Mayor Candee to leave a legacy of environmental protection at our beloved Brown's Race, including the High Falls. As you know, she's a tireless proponent of Rochester's Lilac Festival, and the architect of Rochester's revolutionary bikes-for-guns program. She won't tell you this because she's too modest, but countless cities around this country are adopting the same plan."

"Since when was handing out guns in exchange for bikes good for the environment?" A reporter asked.

"Give it a chance to work," Mayor Candee shouted from her folding chair. "Bike use is already up three percent."

"But violent crime is up 109 percent."

"No more questions until I'm done," Pete Lee said. "Now, because of her great devotion to mother nature, her belief in the sanctity of the American family, her profound respect for the elderly, particularly ones with bladder control problems, and her undying commitment to animals, the Mayor has asked me to put together some preliminary drawings of what will one day be the most comprehensively eco-friendly biosphere, family fun center, senior living community and stray dog shelter in the world. When complete, Compost Country will preserve the High Falls, enhance Brown's Race and be something that past, present and future generations of Rochesterians can be proud of for years to come. Questions? . . . Yes, you, in the blue shirt."

"Where are the drawings?"

"They're not ready yet. We'll be making them available in three months. Next question. Yes, you in the red."

"Mr. Lee, don't you think the name of the facility is ridiculous? I mean, 'Compost Country?' C'mon."

"Was there a question in there? It sounded like an editorial."

"Yes, there's a question. Why'd you guys pick that name?"

"Rest assured that we considered many names including Puppyville and Rainbow Village, but ultimately settled on one we felt captured the Mayor's relentless drive to go green."

"So it's not going to be called Candee Land?"

"Of course not. This project isn't about the Mayor. It's about the flowers and small endangered insects . . . things like that. We want to reduce Rochester's carbon footprint. The Mayor was very moved by *An Inconvenient Truth*."

"How big will the biosphere be?"

"Enormous. The biggest in the world. In fact, a gargantuan, biospheric dome will cover most of Brown's Race including the High Falls so that local families, tourists and seniors can enjoy the site throughout the winter. We'll grow flora and fauna, and provide a home for all of God's creatures. For our city's two months of sunlight, a retractable roof will be employed."

"What about gambling, prostitution and waterslides? Will they be part of Compost Country?" Chaz Walker asked, his loss of patience evident.

"Of course not. Every activity will be in harmony with nature and the theme park will be divided into special environmental learning areas. We'll have Recycling Junction, where families can exchange their used aluminum cans and newspapers for worthless, replica arcade tokens; Fertilizer Forest, where a kid can fulfill a lifelong dream by throwing a piece of rotten fruit on a fly-covered heap of garbage in the name of man; and, perhaps most exciting of all, Al Gore Alley, where the former Vice President will conduct seminars on global warming and cars that run on potato skins.

"And you think people will enjoy these activities? Mr. Lee, none of this sounds enjoyable at all. Is that intentional?" Breezy Summers asked.

"In life, you take the bitter with the sweet, right? The point here is that Mayor Candee is going to revive downtown Rochester in a way that's never been imagined. It will be a nature conservatory and a tourist destination; a family entertainment bonanza and a haven for seniors; an educational experience and a pet adoption site; a source of revenue and a greater source of pride for our city and its people."

"That all sounds very nice, but how's the city going to pay for it? It'll cost millions."

"True, and that's the rub. We're going to need funding from the State of New York, but they won't throw good money after bad. They've sunk too many taxpayer dollars into dead end projects, like our shuttered History of the Mail Chute Museum, and they're wary of doing it again. Unless we can demonstrate that a downtown entertainment district is viable by successfully hosting and making profitable an event like the Academy Awards, there's no way Albany will cut us a check for Compost Country. That's why Dragon Horvath is such a dangerous man. The negative publicity that he and all the other QWEAFS are generating is going to cost us the Oscars and what may very well be our last chance at economic survival. So, on behalf of the Mayor, I'm asking for the assistance of all loyal citizens of Rochester. Right now, this Horvath character is out on the Pont de Rennes

Bridge, strutting around like the cock of the walk while this city struggles for its financial life. Let the word go forth that anyone who can knock that cock off his feet will be handsomely rewarded."

"Are you and the Mayor putting a bounty on Mr. Horvath's head?"

"A bounty? Gracious, no. How uncivilized. Although Mr. Horvath is clearly public enemy number one, we wish him no harm whatsoever. We're angry, no doubt, but we'd never do something as unprincipled as that. If, however, Mr. Horvath were to fall prey to a high-powered rifle in an unforeseen hunting accident or an Uzi during random black-on-black gang violence, for instance, we would shed no tears. After all, every war has its casualties and we're fighting for the future of our home town."

"Didn't the Mayor sign into law a ban on assault weapons such as the Uzi?"

"Yes, but she let it lapse, so stock up while you can. I'm kidding, of course . . . but not really."

"What about your daughter? Aren't you worried about her safety?"

"Look, you're either with us or the terrorists or AARP."

"Are you calling the QWEAFS terrorists?"

"I'm calling Dragon Horvath a terrorist."

"Do you consider your daughter a terrorist?"

Pete Lee waved off the final inquiry.

"I'm afraid this concludes today's press conference. Thank you for coming."

Sixteen

Mayor Candee's press conference was the first step in her deliberate plan to turn public opinion against our cause. The next day, she began running a negative attack ad that described me as a "mentally-deranged Santa killer" and showed a man in a dragon costume roughing up an overweight actor in a fur-trimmed red suit. When word of the campaign reached me on the Pont de Rennes Bridge, I immediately called Denton Fink, who reluctantly put me through to the Mayor.

"Stop running that ad," I said.

"Who's this?" Mayor Candee asked.

"You know damn well who it is. I demand you stop running that ad."

"Is this Dragon? You crazy bastard. Disband your gang of eco-thugs and I'll stop running the ad."

"Stop running it, now. It's reprehensible."

"Get real. I've seen tougher stuff at church socials. What's wrong with a little hyperbole?"

"Santa killer? You call that a little hyperbole?"

"You should have seen the ad I wanted to run. That guru guy you tried to murder is still in the hospital, isn't he?"

"No. He's got a broken collarbone. That's all. And I didn't try to murder him"

"I hear he's in a coma."

"No, he's not. That ad has got to be the most depraved thing you've ever done."

"Horvath, you obviously weren't around during my Studio 54 years but, believe me, this doesn't compare."

"This is character assassination."

"You're overreacting. Come off the bridge and the ad will stop running. It's as simple as that. I'll even fix your trial."

"Go to hell."

"That's the plan. See you at the buffet."

Over the next few weeks, tensions mounted further as a small part of the city's population rallied behind us while the misled masses drank Mayor Candee's Kool-Aid. Our camp, which had grown to include many of Dixie's college classmates, Nubby's fellow unemployed Odoriffic salesmen, Big Nasty's beat poetry brethren and several nephrology nurses, was a relentless flurry with an ongoing police presence, live reggae music, the press and a motley assortment of people I didn't recognize who evidently just loved a good protest, whatever the cause. Put Mardi Gras, Haight Asbury and Hands Across America into a blender and you get the mix. Every night, the latest happenings led the local news, a sure sign that we'd simultaneously captured imaginations and incurred wraths, if nothing else. Sleeping out in tents, erected on the concrete bridge, was less than pleasurable, but we were determined to maintain a constant presence and to continue to be heard. The only time I left was for meetings with Bug Boone at his office a few blocks away to try and figure out how to stay out of jail.

"I'm glad I was only charged with assault. Your record for murder trials, Bug, is horrendous," I said.

Out of 26 capital murder and attempted murder trials, Bug had saved only one client from death row.

"What do you expect? Most of my clients were killers," Bug said.

"Isn't the whole idea to create reasonable doubt so even guilty people get off?"

"Eh," he shrugged. "Between us, when I know someone's guilty, I usually don't try as hard. Evidence and witnesses have a nasty habit of disappearing."

"You bury evidence? Isn't that against the legal ethics rules?"

"Not really. Those rules are more like recommendations than actual rules. Nobody pays much attention to them. It's kind of like going 80 in a 55 miles-per-hour speed zone. Is that unethical? Opinions differ. Don't worry. I do better with assault cases anyway. The victim's a lot less sympathetic. So . . . wanna hear some shtick?"

"Bug, I'm here to talk about my case."

"Do you know that the drinking age for Aztecs was 52?"

"No, I was not aware of that," I said.

"Unfortunately, the lifespan of your average Aztec was only 32. Talk about a bitch of a law."

"Bug, I'm really not up for any shtick right now."

"A report was released this week that shows the spouses of sex addicts have intercourse 500 times per year on average. Pretty good, eh?"

"Sure. Can we talk about my case?"

"The problem is the sex addicts themselves average 1000 times per year."

"Bug, no more shtick!"

"Sorry. I'm doing a set tonight at Goofies."

"I just want to talk about my case. I'm sure you understand."

"Of course."

Bug took a seat behind his desk.

"I've got some bad news."

"What is it?" I asked.

"The prosecution is trying to get that kid to testify against you."

"What kid?"

"The one you brought to my office."

"They are?"

"Yes. She was there the day of the incident and I presume she saw the whole thing. It's an obvious strategy."

"So what does this mean?" I asked.

"It means you're screwed."

"What if Willa refuses to testify?"

"That would be helpful but don't count on it. I hear they're leaning on her pretty good. Now there's an outside chance that we could strike a deal and guarantee you no more than six months in prison," Bug said.

"I can't go to prison."

"You attacked Santa, one of the most beloved figures in history."

"I told you he's not Santa. He's a stupid yoga instructor."

"Fine, but society already considers you dangerous and now you've threatened to kill yourself with this nutso High Falls stunt."

"I didn't threaten to kill myself."

"Of course you didn't. And I didn't go to sleep last night clutching a copy of *Hustler* and a box of Kleenex. We all tell ourselves little lies to get by. The important thing is to know when to hold 'em and know when to fold 'em."

"Are you quoting Kenny Rogers' lyrics to me? Is that what my defense is resting on?"

"You can learn a lot about legal strategy from the Gambler."

"Oh, God."

"I'm serious. Have you ever *really* listened to the final chorus from *Coward of the County*?"

"No. And I don't plan to."

"If you insist on going to trial, my advice is that we play this falls thing for all it's worth."

"What do you mean?"

"I'm talking about an insanity plea."

"No way."

"We can't lose. Hear me out. An average, ordinary schmo — that's you — starts attacking beloved figures of authority and religious faith before adopting the pagan name Dragon and threatening to throw himself off a cliff. If that doesn't say insanity, I don't know what does."

"But, I'm not insane."

"Of course you're not. And I'm not wetting my bed anymore. Those secrets can stay between us."

"Bug, I promise you that I'm not insane."

"I don't want to hear that. As far as I'm concerned, you're crazier than the guy who greenlighted Sting's lute album."

"Just prepare a normal defense. I'm not going to plead insanity and I'm not going to cut a deal."

"You've got to give me *something* to work with. Were you ever abused by your parents?"

"No."

"Molested by a priest?"

"No."

"Molested by a teacher?"

"No."

"A guidance counselor?"

"No."

"An Army recruiter?"

"No. Nobody ever molested me."

"Dammit. How about Battered Husband Syndrome?"

"I've never been married."

"No problem. What about a buddy? Has a friend's wife ever beaten you up?"

"No."

"You're making this very hard. The jury needs to see you as sympathetic somehow."

"Guru Ganges stole my girlfriend. Isn't that sympathetic enough?"

"Unfortunately, that's just a mitigating factor. It's not enough for you to walk. Are you sure nobody ever molested you?" Bug asked.

"Yes, I'm sure."

"'Cause I could arrange it."

"Bug, stop it. Let's just stick with the truth. A jury will see things my way."

"Of course, they will. Right. And I hate nymphomaniacs who own liquor stores."

Bug walked over to the window of his modest, unadorned office and looked out at the Genesee River's rushing current. With his back to me, he placed his hands on his hips and exhaled audibly.

"I didn't want it to come to this, but you're giving me no other choice."

"What are you talking about?" I asked.

"What I'm about to suggest is highly illegal so if you ever mention it to anyone, I'll deny everything and possibly kill you."

"You're making me uncomfortable, Bug."

"I got a call from the Mayor about your case."

"What?"

"She knows the trial is scheduled to start next Monday and she says the judge is in her pocket. If you agree to call off your protest, she'll see to it that the charges are dismissed."

I sat frozen in my seat, paralyzed by the power of corruption and revolted by my willingness to hear Bug out.

"What's in it for you?" I asked.

"Let's just say my days as a humble p.d. will be over."

"Christ, Bug. Are you crazy? You could lose your license to practice law."

"You make that sound like a bad thing. I don't think you understand. This'll give me the money to do what I've always wanted to do; go to L.A. and try to make it in the business. That's always been my dream, you know that. Mayor Candee says she'll pay off all of my law school debt and give me $100,000. We both win. You get your freedom and I get my chance at stardom."

"Bug, do you really trust Mayor Candee?"

"I don't have a choice. This is my only opportunity and I want to take it. I'm asking you. I'm begging you. Take the deal. You can't lose."

"We can still win this trial fair and square."

"You're high. Believe me, we've got no chance."

"I don't want Mayor Candee to fix things."

"Why not?"

"Because I'd rather face the consequences than let that idiot think I owe her anything."

"David, I really want this. I know that if I can just get out there, I can make it, but I need money. The Comedy Store on Sunset Boulevard; that's my destination. The agents will be all over me — I'm a star, I swear. People are going to see that. I've got a routine about urinal cakes that kills. Whaddya say? One phone call to the Mayor and we're both home free."

"I'm sorry, Bug, but the answer is no."

"This is no time to let your personal integrity get in the way of your best interests."

"Forget it. I'll see you at the courthouse on Monday."

seventeen

The Genesee is the only river in North America that flows from south to north, and I like to believe this is not an aberration, but rather manifest destiny calling the people who live along her banks to embrace New York State's motto, *Excelsior*, meaning 'ever upward.' This may be wishful thinking given that most local residents think Excelsior is a high-powered laxative requiring a prescription, but I refuse to abandon the idea.

Geologists say the sediment that comprises the Genesee's river bed dates back millions of years and that the High Falls was formed thanks to certain rocks resistant to decay. With my uncertain fate fast approaching, hazy on the horizon above the churning waterway, I needed to be like those rocks and fight valiantly against erosion — of my confidence and my nerve as I headed to court.

Having spent the night at Beatie's, I emerged from the house to find a strangely peaceful and quiet Mt. Hope Avenue. I paused to look at the cemetery across the street in a desperate attempt to garner strength from the daring souls permanently residing there. Surely they'd seen worse days and triumphed nonetheless.

I drove toward the courthouse and quickly discovered that the Mayor had escalated her public relations war against me. Within minutes, I passed four enormous billboards; each with a computer generated picture of me dressed up like a terrorist in a white turban and robe, which read as follows:

> WANTED DEAD OR ALIVE:
> DRAGON HORVATH
> FOR CRIMES AGAINST
> HUMANITY, LOCAL TOURISM,
> DEFENSELESS PETS AND SANTA CLAUS

So much for a fair trial, I thought.

Reaching Brown's Race where the courthouse sat, I saw a dozen or so vans with satellite dishes on top; all parked in a long row. I knew I'd be lucky to make it through the gauntlet of assembled reporters to the small, press-free, safe haven of our camp cordoned off in the visible distance; the place I'd agreed to meet Nubby and Dixie before the trial.

"Hey, it's Dragon Horvath," a reporter shouted.

I was surrounded.

"Mr. Horvath, a few questions please. Are you trying to stop Rochester from getting the Oscars?"

"No."

I pushed my way into the swarm; lousy with journalists, cameramen and protesters.

"Dragon, Wolf Blitzer, CNN. Do you have ties to any terrorist organization?"

"No!"

"Mr. Horvath, what do you have against Santa Claus?"

"Nothing."

"Are you going to commit suicide at the High Falls?"

"No comment."

"Who makes the best calzone in Rochester?"

Arriving at the established check point on the Pont de Rennes Bridge, two of Dixie's classmates recognized me and let me in. Thirty feet away, I found Nubby chewing on a Luna bar and counting a large, stack of cash.

"Nubby, what the hell's going on?" I asked.

"What's going on is T-shirt sales. I'm making a killing. I can't keep 'Have a Penis Day' in stock."

"Where are Dixie and Big Nasty?"

"They're around. They may be at the food court."

"Food court? Since when did we have a food court?"

"You haven't been? Oh, it's great. Bill Gray's, Zebb's, Abbott's, Country Sweet. They've all got set-ups there."

Just then I recognized a familiar face further down the bridge.

"Is that Bono?" I asked.

"Not just Bono. That's U2, the whole band. They're on break. Can you believe it? When they heard about our cause, they showed up to demonstrate solidarity. They're even taking requests. Hey guys, play *Pride in the Name of Love* again," Nubby yelled.

"Yuh got it, Nub," Bono called back.

"You can't ask him to play that," I said.

"Why not?"

"Because he wrote it in memory of Martin Luther King, Jr.—Not for our protest rally."

"So now it'll have two meanings. Songs have to evolve or they die."

"You're warped. You know that, right?"

"Just relax."

"How can I? You realize my trial is today, don't you?"

"It is?"

"Yes. When did all these national media people show up?"

"This morning. Turns out Mayor Candee's harassment of Hollywood hasn't gone unnoticed. All of her charges of industry discrimination got the press sniffing around and when they did, they discovered you."

"Me?"

"Yeah, of course. Your whole feud with the Mayor."

"*Our* feud. I'm not the only one in this. We're a team, remember?"

"Of course, but you're the head of the QWEAFS."

"This is unbelievable," I said, looking around at the carnival we'd created.

"This story has it all. It's like that compound in Waco. Start with a crazy, charismatic leader . . ."

"I am *not* crazy."

"All right, fine, but the story's still got Academy Award intrigue, environmental activists, gambling, prostitution, charges of racism and sexism, violence, suicide."

"Suicide? What suicide?" I asked.

"Just your ride over the falls and all," Nubby said.

"I'm not committing suicide."

"Of course not, but the press doesn't know that. All they know is that death sells newspapers and they want their piece of the action."

"That's sick."

"What's sick is the number of U2 concert jerseys I'm going to sell when the public realizes they're down here. And wait'll the other groups show up."

"What other groups?"

"Protests attract musicians. For God's sake, Peter, Paul and Mary were here a half hour ago."

"I thought Mary died."

"They must have replaced her with a new Mary."

"Good grief."

"What a bunch of peaceniks. I sent them over to Nick Tahou's to pick me up a garbage plate, but they'll be back. Look, you wanted to create a stir, and you've done it."

"Are you coming with me to court?"

"Can't right now, buddy; too many T-shirts to sell. I'll be over in a bit. Good luck."

And so it was amidst this chaos, with U2 playing in the background, that I began making my way to the Edward Menendez Courthouse by myself.

"Dragon, do you have impulse control issues?" A reporter asked. "Have you ever killed anyone?"

"No comment," I said.

"So that's a yes?"

"No."

"Mr. Horvath, what kinds of prescription medication are you on?"

"Folks, please give me some room."

Bug Boone met me on the white marble steps of the courthouse and whisked me inside to an anteroom where he assessed my attire.

"Okay, good, that off-the-rack suit is perfect. You look plain and humble. Just what we need."

"I thought you said no flashy clothes or jewelry, Bug."

"I did."

"But your suit is salmon-colored, and you're wearing two diamond-encrusted pinky rings."

"I meant no flashy clothes for you, not me."

"Do you really think your suit will play well with the jurors?" I asked.

"Hey, there could be a talent scout in the courthouse — stranger things have happened. You don't expect me to give up my sense of style just for you, do you?"

"It'd be nice."

"Just calm down and put this on," Bug said, handing me a gold ring.

"What's this for?"

"It's a wedding band. Now, put it on."

"But I'm not married."

"The jurors don't know that. They want to see you as an upstanding member of society. Married men don't haul off and hit Santa unless they're unreasonably provoked."

"But I'd be telling a lie."

"No, you wouldn't. You'd only be conveying an impression. There is a *huge* difference. You're not telling anyone you're married. You're just wearing a ring. Let them draw whatever inferences they want."

"I'm not wearing it."

"Are you going to give me anything to work with here?"

"Just stick to the facts."

"Sure. Like those ever helped one of my clients. Are you sure you were never molested?"

"Yes, I'm sure."

Forty-five minutes later, every seat in the courtroom was filled as we made our way toward the table assigned to defense counsel. To my slight surprise, Big Nasty, Nubby and Dixie were seated in the front row, having left the camp in the hands of proxy leadership. Behind them sat Beatie, unmistakable in her bright yellow smock and turquoise costume jewelry, and Biff, attired in his olive green bathrobe. Notably absent were Kit and Willa, who had declined the government's request to testify against me.

Across the aisle from my friends and family, I spied Mayor Candee, Denton Fink, Pete Lee and Miranda, who avoided eye contact with me and sat with her crossed arms pressed tightly against a cherry red blouse. Soon, Judge Branch Kerfoot, devoid of emotion, brought the court to order and instructed legendary local prosecutor, Woody Curtin, a tall, bald man with a booming voice, to make his opening statement.

"May it please the court, your honor? Ladies and gentlemen of the jury, this past December, the city of Rochester and every one of its children was victimized by this man, David Horvath," Curtin said, pointing a long, accusatory finger toward me.

"Objection, your honor," Bug said, springing to his feet. "Counsel is badgering the witness."

"Sit down, Mr. Boone," Judge Kerfoot said. "You can't object during an opening statement."

"Sorry, your honor. My fault. I'm a little jittery, today. Gonna need a mulligan."

Judge Kerfoot looked at Bug like a stain on his favorite shirt.

"Mr. Boone, let me remind you that this is not a golf course. There are no *mulligans*. It is a court of law and you will act accordingly. Please continue, Mr. Curtin," Judge Kerfoot said.

"As I was saying, this man, this *monster* sitting before you today, destroyed the dreams of hundreds of our community's children when, for no reason at all, he brutally attacked Midtown Plaza's beloved Santa Claus. This cretin, who calls himself *Dragon*, single-handedly snuffed out the sugarplum faerie of innocence that we call childhood by sending St. Nick to the intensive care unit at St. Mary's Hospital for two months and rendering him unable to deliver presents or go to the bathroom without assistance from at least three elves. We must take this piece of scum off our streets so that they are safe again for our families, our homeless and our gangs."

Woody Curtin had sent hundreds of men to prison and his opening statement gave me reason to believe I'd be joining them soon. For the first two hours, the trial proceeded uneventfully as Curtin called a half a dozen witnesses, including two security guards and the manager of the mall's Hot Sam Pretzel kiosk; all of whom told the jury that my attack was unprovoked. My dragon dream of riding over the High Falls to correct the course of my hometown and my own life was already in serious jeopardy when the proceedings, which were farcical to begin with, began resembling an Anna Nicole Smith paternity hearing.

"For my next witness, your honor, I'd like to call to the stand Guru Ganesh Ganges."

The doors at the back of the courtroom opened and, just as Bug predicted, in came Guru Ganges, wearing full Santa regalia and riding a sleigh towed by a team of dwarves, all of them dressed like elves — the same ones who'd danced around me shouting epithets the day of the incident.

"That bastard, Curtin," Bug muttered under his breath. "I knew he'd bring Santa in on a sleigh."

Guru Ganges was sworn in, temporarily taking off his Santa hat while the oath was administered, and Curtin went to work.

"Mr. Ganges, will you please tell the jury what happened to you on the day in question?"

"Of course. It vas a beautiful vinter day. Children vere laughing, happily vaiting in line to see Son-ta. The elves vere joyful, so happy that the last toy had been made and wrapped."

"Objection, your honor. Speculation," Bug said. "Does he really expect us to believe he knew how the elves were feeling that day?"

"I'll allow it."

"Dammit," Bug said.

"Go on, Mr. Ganges," Curtin said.

"So the elves vere singing when I saw a highly disturbed man in line."

"Objection, you honor. Witness is expressing his own, non-expert, personal opinion about defendant's mental state."

"I'll allow it."

"Dammit," Bug said.

"Mr. Ganges, is that *highly* disturbed man in this courtroom, today?" Curtin asked.

"Yes."

"Can you point him out for the members of the jury?"

"Yes. He's right over there," Ganges said, pointing toward me.

Woody Curtin proceeded to take his primary witness through a rose-colored creation of revisionist history, the likes of which I'd never seen. Exhibit A, the digital recording that showed me attacking Guru Ganges after what appeared to be a routine exchange of words, admittedly didn't help my case. Once Bug Boone got to cross-examine my accuser, however, he sought to turn the topic of digital video to our advantage.

"So, Mr. Ganges, if that is your real name, I see you're wearing your Santa suit, today."

"Vell, yes. I'm vearing it. So vut?"

"You're like a murderer in a pastel sweater, aren't you?"

"Vut does that mean?"

"Are you the third Menendez brother?"

"Vut?"

"Did you eat your parents?"

"Objection, your honor. Irrelevant," Curtin said.

"Question withdrawn. I just noticed they weren't here and wondered why. That's all."

"They live in India," Guru Ganges said.

"Sure they do. And I live with my mother by choice. Tell me, did you have that Santa suit dry-cleaned for today's court appearance?"

Bug hadn't learned to avoid questions he didn't know the answers to.

"Yes, I had to get the bloodstains out of it from your client's attack."

"I see. Very convenient for you, wasn't it?"

"No. It cost me $37.00 and took two veeks."

"Okay. Moving on. Isn't it true that you were sleeping with Mr. Horvath's girlfriend, Ms. Miranda Jennings, at the time of the Midtown Plaza incident?"

"No, that is a lie."

"Oh, is it? And what would you say if I told you I had a DVD of the two of you in flagrante delicto?"

"Flagrante delicto? Vut is flagrante delicto?"

"It means having sex, doing the nasty, knockin' boots, bumping uglies, making the two-backed monster."

"Vut? That is a lie. Vee never bumped uglies."

"May it please the court, your honor? I'd like to bring in a big-screen TV. Bailiff, would you assist me please?"

From a small room to the side of the judge's bench, Bug and the head bailiff rolled out a TV with what must have been a 70-inch screen.

"Bailiff, please set the volume as high as it can go while I insert the DVD because there is some heavy breathing and moaning that the jurors won't want to miss."

Guru Ganges shifted uncomfortably in the witness box.

"Can everyone in the jury see from where you're seated?" Bug asked.

The jurors nodded in anticipation.

"All right. Here we go," Bug said, turning on the DVD player. "Too bad we don't have popcorn and Twizzlers," he chuckled.

Finally, Guru Ganges broke.

"Stop it. Stop it right now!"

Bug stopped the machine.

"So, you admit it? You were sleeping with Miranda Jennings?"

"Yes, I admit it," he said, flustered from his near unveiling. "I admit it."

"Did everyone in the jury hear that?" Bug asked.

The jurors nodded.

"Well, good. I'm glad 'cause I had nothing on this disc but footage from my 15-year high school reunion, and God knows that was a train wreck."

"You bustard," Ganges shouted. "You vill burn in hell, Boone."

Unfortunately, for me, this embarrassing admission was the high point of the morning's testimony. Like a fighter stung by a left uppercut, Woody Curtin immediately set about rehabilitating his client's reputation with the story of Guru Ganges' impoverished childhood in an Indian leper colony selling ice to support his parents and 17 siblings. This was followed by the tale of his voyage to America in a boat made of nothing but rice and curry that he built with his own two hands and the frequent shark attacks that nearly took his life. By the time the twelfth elf testified that I had *maliciously* attacked Guru Ganges, most jurors were weeping in sympathy for him and Judge Kerfoot had to call a recess until the afternoon to let them gather their emotions.

Bug and I grabbed sandwiches from a courthouse vendor and retreated to his office two blocks away to strategize for the afternoon session.

"What do you think?" I asked.

"I'm not going to lie to you. It didn't go as well as I had hoped," Bug said. "I think we should try to cut a deal while there's still time."

"No way. We're not cutting any deal."

"You're facing possible jail time. Do you get that?"

"I don't care."

"Okay, fine. Be that way. But if you're going to completely ignore my advice, you better be prepared for what's coming this afternoon. Miranda Jennings is the next witness and things could get ugly."

"Why? Don't we already know what she's going to say?"

"About the attack, yes. But about the rest, I'm not sure."

"What else is there?"

"Oh, didn't I tell you? The judge has decided to allow past sexual history into the trial."

"Past sexual history?"

"Yes."

"My past sexual history?"

"Yes."

"What does that have to do with anything? This isn't a rape case. What the hell's going on?"

"Hey, don't overreact. This morning's testimony opened the door to this stuff."

"You mean *you* opened the door to this stuff."

"You wanted me to establish that Ganges was sleeping with your girlfriend, right? I'm sure the judge will only allow testimony he thinks is relevant to the trial — basically anything that might bear on why Miranda left you."

"Our break-up was mutual."

"Of course it was. And I only wear women's panties to improve my circulation. Listen, I need to warn you that Miranda may be answering some very unpleasant questions about your sex life with her. You aren't into a lot of kinky stuff, are you?"

"No."

"You never put this Miranda into bondage or sold her as a sex slave to anyone?"

"A sex slave? No, of course not."

"And you guys were never into the whole group thing, right?"

"No, absolutely not."

"I don't blame you one bit. It can really get sticky. Ever attend the sex toy expo at the Dome Arena?"

"No!"

"Good. It's not much to see, believe me. Selection is poor at best."

"Why are you asking me these things?"

"I want to make sure I know what I'm dealing with here. If it turns out you're some kind of depraved sicko, we could have a problem."

"I am not a depraved sicko. I have a normal sex life and normal sexual appetites."

"I'm sure you do, Long Duk Dong. Now, just try and relax."

"I can't believe you couldn't get my past sexual history excluded."

"I told you I was a better comedian than a lawyer."

"You're going to put me on the witness stand so I can set the record straight, right?"

"Not if I can help it. I think that would be a disaster."

"Why?"

"Because Curtin would destroy you on cross."

"Just give me a chance."

"I'm not putting you on. I've made up my mind."

Back inside the courtroom, Woody Curtin stalked the jury like an opera singer at a make-your-own sundae bar. He put Miranda on the stand and began his ruthless line of questioning.

"Ms. Jennings, what kind of lover was Mr. Horvath?"

"Objection," Bug said, rising to his feet. "Too personal."

"Too personal?" Judge Kerfoot asked. "That's not an allowable objection."

"Too embarrassing?" Bug asked.

"That's not one either."

"All right. How about good, old irrelevant?"

"Overruled."

"Dammit," Bug said.

"As I was saying, Ms. Jennings," Curtin continued. "What kind of lover was Mr. Horvath?"

"Terrible. His idea of foreplay was watching *Sportscenter* together."

"So you were unsatisfied in the bedroom?"

"Very unsatisfied."

"I see. And that's when Guru Ganges came along, correct?"

"That's right."

"And this is a man who can put both feet behind his head. Is that right?"

"Yes."

Guru Ganges, still dressed in his Santa suit, beamed from the gallery.

"Which opens up a whole new sexual galaxy I presume?"

"Oh, definitely. We once made love in a two-foot by two-foot box."

"Remarkable."

"He can bring me to climax through mind control without ever touching me."

"Truly incredible. So, Mr. Horvath and his sub-par sexual abilities drove you into the arms of another man?"

"Yes."

"And this led to the incident at Midtown Plaza?"

"Yes, I believe so."

"Can you tell us about it?"

"I'll try."

"I'm sure it's very painful so, please, take your time."

Curtin brought a box of tissues from counsel's table to the witness stand and placed it next to Miranda.

"The day started out with such hope. Guru Ganges loves

Christmas as much as I do, and we couldn't wait to see the children with their innocent smiles."

"And the elves?"

"The elves were like shooting stars. I was throwing them bread crumbs. It was wonderful."

"Sounds like a magical Christmas scene."

"It was."

"Tell me. Did there come a time when this scene was spoiled?"

"Yes. When he arrived," Miranda said, looking directly at me.

"Your honor, let the record reflect that the witness identified Mr. Horvath."

"So noted."

"Miranda, did Mr. Horvath appear to be under the influence of narcotics that day?"

"I would have to say yes."

"Objection your honor. Speculative," Bug said.

"I'll allow it."

"Son-of-a-bitch," Bug said.

"And he was with a young child, am I right?" Curtin asked.

"Yes, he was with a darling little girl," Miranda said.

"So, entrusted with a young child and gorked out of his mind on a dangerous cocktail of narcotics and, presumably, grain alcohol, this *Dragon*, as he fancies himself, attacked Santa Claus, in a fit of jealousy and rage?"

"Yes, that's exactly what happened. It was horrible. My Ganesh was listening to what the children wanted, passing out presents and spreading good cheer, and then all of sudden fists and presents and elves were flying through the air. There was blood and screaming, and I even broke a nail."

"Would you say Mr. Horvath had murder in his eyes?"

"Oh, definitely. I thought he was going to kill us all."

"The whole thing sounds just awful. I know this may be

hard to answer, but tell me how this tragedy has impacted you."

"I've had to seek counseling. I haven't been able to work. I don't even enjoy shopping as much anymore."

"That's terrible. Mr. Horvath cut a remorseless path of destruction, didn't he?"

"Yes, he did."

A woman can single-handedly seal your doom in so many ways. Usually, it's right after you fall in love with her but, in this case, it was in a courtroom, out in the open for the world to see. Although Bug did his best to discredit Miranda on cross-examination, the damage had been done. He poked a few holes in her story, but he'd been right about one thing all along. Santa Claus, even when played by a yoga-teaching, girlfriend-robbing, Hinduism-practicing Indian, is a sympathetic figure and tough opponent in court. The jury recessed for the night and would begin deliberations in the morning. Bug was more candid than I wanted about my odds, suggesting that I update my will and start packing a prison bag full of *Playboys*, Skittles and smokes.

eighteen

At Frederick Douglass's funeral in 1895, the eulogy was delivered by Susan B. Anthony, an apt person to speak given that Rochester's reputation as a receptive home for suffrage advocates, such as Anthony, was one of the factors that originally brought Douglass to the city to start *The North Star*, his abolitionist newspaper, and to live. His belief that we were all brethren might have been tested, however, if he'd lived to see Mayor Candee's attempt to exploit the civil rights struggle for commercial purposes.

The Mayor's plan to use gender and race to bait Hollywood into moving the Oscars while simultaneously destroying me ruled her every move now, including her decision to appear on *The O'Reilly Factor* following day one of my trial. Having bribed Judge Kerfoot in advance, Mayor Candee worried little about the jury's deliberations scheduled for the next day.

Home with Beatie and Biff eating eight-calorie lime Jell-O with Reddi-wip, I watched helplessly from the couch.

"In *The Factor* follow-up segment tonight, a story we've been following about Hollywood and, you guessed it, the pinheads that run that asylum. Live via satellite is the respected

Mayor of Rochester, New York, Cornelia Candee. Madame Mayor, good to see you," O'Reilly said.

"Likewise, Bill."

"Let me see if I can get this straight. You're trying to get these jokers out in Hollywood, the same ones who won't come on *The Factor* and take the heat, to move the Academy Awards to Rochester because it's the home of Kodak. They claim that a ceremony honoring Rochester at the event in Los Angeles is sufficient. What say you?"

"Bill, pardon my Portuguese, but you've just grazed the tip of tittie. Rochester *is* the indisputable home of film, but we also played a historic role in the civil rights movements for both women and blacks, two groups that Hollywood has notoriously mistreated."

"These actresses get a little older and they're done. Just done. Am I right?"

"That's right. Susan B. Anthony, one of the original actresses on *Charlie's Angels*, isn't even working these days."

"It's outrageous. And from what I can see, their record with minorities is even worse."

"Tell me about it. Bill, the truth is that there are only three or four black actors who get offered anything but parts playing jive turkeys, shoeshine boys and crack dealers. The late, great Frederick Douglass, a terrific actor *and* the inventor of peanut butter, would be lucky to get an audition today."

"They're hypocrites. Complete hypocrites. And they won't come on *The Factor* and take the heat. First they steal money from the nine eleven funds, and now this. I really think George Clooney's behind it all. I'm convinced. He runs the place from his villa in Italy."

"I have no doubt. I've contacted the Academy and told them that it's time to do the right thing by recognizing the industry's roots and its shameful civil rights record and coming home to Rochester."

"Well, I hope they come around, but don't count on it. We'll keep the pressure on them here at *The Factor*."

"I appreciate that, Bill."

"I understand that Hollywood isn't your only obstacle, however. You're also dealing with some wacko activist, right?"

"That's right, Bill — a real environmental nut-job who goes by the name Dragon Horvath. He and his eco-terrorist lickspittles are trying to block our ability to bring Oscar to town by threatening to throw themselves over the city's High Falls."

"What a bunch of derelicts. Have you contacted the National Guard?"

"I've tried, but they're all tied up in the Middle East."

"That's where we ought to send these environmentalists. They'll stop bitching about gas mileage and fur coats pretty damn quick; that I can assure you."

"You said it. They're holding our fair city hostage and creating a lot of ill will but, fortunately, I don't think they'll be a problem for long."

"Why's that?"

"Well, this Dragon Horvath I mentioned is on trial for criminal assault and I have every expectation that the jury will find him guilty and put him away for life or give him the chair."

"My God. What did he do?"

"He tried to kill Santa Claus, Bill, and I think a message needs to be sent that our society is not going to tolerate the ongoing desecration and secularization of our institutions and symbols."

"You are so right, Madame Mayor."

"I'm sick of it, Bill."

"I am right there with you. If this Horvath guy tried to kill Santa Claus, he ought to burn at the stake."

"We'll do our best to light the fire, Bill. You've got to cut off the head to kill the snake, right? Once we get rid of Horvath, his organization will crumble."

"We can't let the terrorists win. Listen, you're a stand-up gal to come on *The Factor* tonight. I'm going to give you the last word."

"Thanks, Bill. I want America to know that a challenge has been issued to the Hollywood community to atone for its sins by bringing Oscar to Rochester, New York. The people of this city deserve it and, as their Mayor, I'm determined to make it a reality. If our citizens and the rest of the country stand side by side with me against Hollywood bigotry and Dragon Horvath, I know we'll be celebrating a great victory very, very soon."

I turned off the TV.

"What the hell are you doing?" Biff asked. "That was just starting to get good."

"Biff, we're you listening to the same interview I was? Everything Mayor Candee said was a lie."

"I think she had some good points."

"Mayor Candee's a jackass," Beatie said.

"I'm going to bed," I said, rising from my chair; my spirit severely bent if not broken.

"Since you're up, could you get me a little more Reddi-wip?"

"Shut-up, Biff," I said.

The next morning, the three of us drove to the courthouse to await the jury's verdict with Bug Boone. A mob, twice as large as the day before, lined the walkway from the parking lot to the courthouse and chanted in a threatening manner as we stepped out of Biff's Crown Vic.

"BURN! BURN! BURN! BURN! BURN! BURN!"

Either the crowd thought it was witnessing the Salem witch trials part deux or it had taken the Mayor's televised, incendiary remarks to heart and now saw me as a threat to the Oscars, Compost Country *and* the continuing existence of Christmas as a national holiday.

"BURN! BURN! BURN! BURN! BURN! BURN!"

Though they were mostly drowned out by the angry rabble calling for my death Joan of Arc-style, a small but vocal group, attired mostly in "Have a Penis Day" T-Shirts, attempted to compete with its own chant of "Free Dragon! Free Dragon! Free Dragon!"

"BURN! BURN! BURN! BURN! BURN! BURN!"

Bug Boone, wearing his salmon-colored suit for a second day in a row, met us on the front steps of the courthouse and helped usher us past a thick line of police protection and into the building.

"Looks like Candee's got the Christian conservatives all stirred up," Bug said.

"Yeah, I noticed," I said. "I almost got killed out there."

"Maybe we should ask them to pray for Judge Kerfoot to be lenient."

"Are you kidding? They don't seem to be in a praying mood. They want to light me on fire for chrissakes."

"Might knock some sense into you," Biff said, tightening the belt on his robe.

"Thanks a lot, Biff. Why don't you take Beatie to the courtroom and get settled, okay? I need to meet with Bug for a bit."

Biff and Beatie headed down the center hallway of the courthouse while Bug took me to counsel's chambers where we found a quiet alcove to sit and talk.

"Look, with regard to the jury verdict, I think you need to be prepared for the worst."

"I do?"

"Yes. I don't think I was able to convince anyone that you're innocent."

"What kind of attitude is that?" I asked.

"It's one that ensures you're never disappointed. Look, we both know that Judge Kerfoot is on the Mayor's payroll. The fix was in from the start."

"Can't we report them to someone?"

"Like who?"

"I don't know. How about the New York Bar Association?"

Bug laughed.

"Oh, right. That would be a great idea except for one small fact: the New York Bar Association is nothing more than a front organization for the Russian mafia."

"What? Where do you get this stuff?"

"I think the real problem was that Kerfoot didn't like you."

"I didn't know I was in a popularity contest. What did I do?"

"You came across a little cocky."

"Cocky? I'm not cocky."

"Of course not. And I'm not a huge disappointment to my parents."

"How the hell could I come across as anything? I never testified."

"Maybe he thought you were standoffish."

"I wasn't standoffish. You never put me on the stand. That's the problem."

"Hey, Monday morning quarterbacking isn't going to help us now. If the jury comes back with a guilty verdict, I'm just going to have to throw a Hail Mary."

"What Hail Mary?"

"I'm going to request community service and see if the Judge Kerfoot will bite. We might get lucky."

"How much community service?"

"About four thousand hours."

"Isn't that a little extreme? I don't think Mother Teresa did four thousand hours of community service."

"She probably had a better lawyer. Would you rather go to jail?"

"No."

"It won't be so bad. You'll spend lots of time teaching people to read, serving meals, picking lice off the heads of alcoholic bums — that sort of thing. Trust me, the hours will fly by."

"I bet."

Bug's cell phone rang to the tune of *Jailhouse Rock*.

"Boone, here. Yeah, okay. We'll be right down."

Bug hung up and looked my way.

"Verdict's in. It's showtime."

Back inside the courtroom, the air buzzed with the anticipation of my impending fate as Bug and I made our way to counsel's table. The usual suspects — Nubby, Big Nasty, Dixie, Beatie and Biff — sat behind me.

On the prosecution side, I saw all my enemies: Mayor Candee, Denton Fink, Pete Lee, Guru Ganges and Miranda, each of them gleefully awaiting my demise. The rest of the crowd was a blur to me, their faces melding into an impressionistic painting. Soon the jury filed in and court was called to order.

"Mr. Foreman, have you reached a verdict?" Judge Kerfoot asked.

"Yes, we have your honor."

As soon as the guilty verdict was read and Judge Kerfoot quieted the crowd, he wasted no time in handing down my sentence.

"In all my years on the bench, I've seen some bizarre cases, but this one ranks right up there on the freak-o-meter. I've tried my best to be an impartial vein in the leg of Lady

Justice and I believe I've succeeded. Mr. Horvath, do you have anything to say before I render my decision?"

Bug rose to his feet.

"Your honor, in the spirit of Mother Theresa and Naomi Campbell, I'd like to request a sentence that's limited to community service."

"Will you please sit down, Mr. Boone? I was speaking to Mr. Horvath."

I stood and moved front and center before the judge.

"Yes, your honor. I'd like to say a few words. Much of what's been said about me during this trial has been false. Some of it, however, has been true. When you get right down to it, I felt an injustice had been done to me and I decided to take the law into my own hands."

"And you still think that was the right thing to do?" Judge Kerfoot asked.

I had seen enough movies to know that taking the law into your own hands was never viewed favorably in a court of law. With no cards to play, I looked back at Bug, still seated at our table, to see if he had a pair of dice to roll. To my surprise, Bug started scribbling madly on a legal pad, then tore off the top page and handed it to me. Here goes nothing, I thought after reading Bug's scratch.

"Your honor, are you familiar with the final chorus from *Coward of the County* by Kenny Rogers?"

"Are you kidding?"

"No, sir, see I've got the lyrics here and, if the court will indulge me for a moment, I'd like to read them to you because I believe they go a long way toward explaining what happened in this case. The chorus goes like this: 'I promised you, dad, not to do the things you'd done. I walked away from trouble when I could. Now, please don't think I'm weak; I didn't turn the other cheek. And papa, I should hope you'd understand.

Sometimes you gotta fight when you're a man.' See, as you probably know, the guy singing the song had to finally beat up the Gatlin brothers who had slept with his girlfriend."

"Are you telling me you're using the chorus from a Kenny Rogers song as a justification for nearly bludgeoning to death a man in a Santa suit?"

"Well, yes. I guess I am."

Judge Kerfoot paused and thought about it for a moment.

"Well, this makes things much harder, because I absolutely adore Kenny Rogers. The second verse of *She Believes in Me* brings me to tears every time."

"Me, too. It's a classic," Bug said, rising to his feet. "Just a great, great song. 'While she layyyss sleeping, I stay out late at night and play my soonnngs.'"

"Shut-up and sit down, Mr. Boone."

"Got it," Bug said, doing as told.

"Your honor," Woody Curtin interjected. "I find this highly unusual and inappropriate. The defendant is clearly pandering to the court."

"Shut-up, Curtin! You'll get your turn," Judge Kerfoot boomed. "Mr. Horvath, when I went to Starbucks this morning, they screwed up my order and it nearly wrecked my whole day. I was so pissed, I was thinking of completely abusing my judicial discretion today and putting you away for 30 years, but I've changed my mind."

"You have?"

"Yes. I'm only going to put you away for two."

"What? Two years?"

"Yes."

"But the song, your honor. What about the *Coward of the County*?"

"Good but not his best. If you'd quoted *Lucille*, you might have gone free. I really love that one."

"Wait, I can sing it for you now if you'd like. 'In a bar in Toleedo . . .'"

"It's too late, Mr. Horvath. Please stop."

"But what about the High Falls, your honor? I've got to go over the falls."

"I've been following your exploits, Mr. Horvath, and I've given this a lot of thought."

The Mayor stared hard at Judge Kerfoot, who'd evidently grown resentful of the Mayor's overbearing expectation of unquestioning loyalty.

"I've decided your incarceration will begin the day *after* you go over the falls. Until then, you are a free man."

"Thank you, your honor. Thank you very much."

Though she was visibly beyond furious, the Mayor was smart enough to avoid throwing a tantrum with the press in such close proximity. As soon as the crowd dispersed and an hour had passed, however, my cell phone went off. It was Candee.

"You got lucky, Horvath, but I want you to know I'm glad you did. I look forward to seeing you smash your skull on the rocks. I really do. One way or another you're going to die and when you do, I'll have the High Falls all to myself for Candee Land or anything else I want. Your protest will mean nothing."

"Go to hell," I said.

"You first. And save me a seat when you get there, asshole."

The victory party was held back at camp. Around a large bonfire built by Big Nasty, I danced with Dixie and Nubby nuzzled with Anna while U2, accompanied by Peter, Paul and the new Mary, played a three-hour set lasting late into the night, including the only rendition of *Leaving on a Jet Plane* that ever pinned my ears back. Standing on the Pont de Rennes Bridge with a beer in my hand, I gazed out at the High Falls — the white peaks of water crashing down into the dark abyss — and realized that nothing could stop me from going over them now.

Nineteen

Although Kit Nash offered to buy the principal of Park Road Elementary School a Jaguar and a vacation home in the Cayman Islands, Willa Nash was not designated a gifted child. In fact, upon conclusion of the school year in June, Kit was informed that his daughter would need to repeat the fifth grade and spend the summer taking a remedial math class and seeing a psychologist. Of course, I was fired as her mentor and barred from all contact with Willa immediately, so it was a great surprise to see her skateboarding toward me on the Pont de Rennes Bridge with Plank in tow.

"Willa, what are you doing here?"

"Is it true you got fired from Royal Flush?"

"Yes."

"That place sucks."

"They said they didn't want a convicted felon on their pro staff. I can't say I blame them."

"I do."

"Tell me what you're doing here."

"I came to join the cause," Willa said.

"What?"

"I saw you on TV. I want to raise some hell; stick it to the man. Isn't that what you're doing?"

"Do your parents know you're here?"

"No, and I don't care. They lied to me. They said they were just separating for awhile but now they're getting a divorce."

"I'm sorry, Willa. I really am," I said, offering up a hug.

"Dude, this isn't a Hallmark moment," Willa said, recoiling. "I just came down to hang out."

"Hang out? That's great, but your father has made it very clear he doesn't want you spending time with me."

"He doesn't want me doing a lot of things."

"How did you get down here?"

"I took the bus."

"That's impossible."

"Why? You don't think I could get on a bus by myself?"

"No, I just thought the Mayor discontinued all public transportation."

"Well, there's still a bus that runs downtown from Thornell Farm Park and I got on it."

"I'm calling your father."

"You can't. He's in Europe on some dumb trip."

"What about your mother?"

"She's away, too."

"So who's watching you?"

"Ona. She's one of the nannies."

"I thought she was getting deported."

"She was, but my dad paid off the I.N.S."

"What about summer school?"

"It's Saturday."

"Oh."

Willa stared down at her sneakers.

"My parents are going to send me away."

"Send you away where?"

"Some prep school. They said it means I'm special but I know it just means I'm stupid."

"You're not stupid."

"Yes, I am."

"No, you're not."

"Whatever. I don't get good grades."

"So what? I never got good grades and look at me. I turned out all right."

"Aren't you unemployed?" Willa asked.

"Technically, yes, but . . ."

"And broke?"

"Well, yes, but I'm a work in progress."

"Maybe that's what I am, too."

"Of course you are. We all are."

"My father says if I don't go to an Ivy League college I won't be successful, but he doesn't get it. I don't care about school. I only care about skateboarding. I need you to talk to him; tell him you'll take me for the rest of the summer."

"Willa, this isn't summer camp," I said.

"Looks like camp to me," Willa said, as a Frisbee zoomed past her head.

"You know as well as I do your parents don't want you around me. Plus, what would you do down here?" I asked.

"Skate. All this concrete is a boarder's paradise."

"You'll get bored."

"No, I won't. And, anyway, you owe me."

"I owe you?" I asked.

"Yes. They wanted me to testify against you at your trial but I refused. . . ."

Willa had me there.

". . . Why didn't you plead insanity? I thought that was the plan. You really blew it. You could've gotten off completely," Willa said.

"Who told you I was going to plead insanity?" I asked.

"Bug Boone. He said you got groped by a guidance counselor or something and it drove you nuts."

"I didn't get groped by a guidance counselor."

"But you *are* going over the falls, right?"

"Yes."

"So you're insane."

"No, I'm not."

"Whatever. I don't really care. Either way, I think it's cool."

"You do?"

"Yeah, it's like an X Games event. Going over the falls? That's rad. If you die, can I have your car?"

"No, you can't have my car. I'm not going to die."

"You might. Look at that beast," Willa said, motioning toward the High Falls. "It's pretty ferocious. Aren't you worried?"

"Why would you want my car? You hate my car."

"I changed my mind. Sue me. What are you going over the falls for anyway? You're not trying to kill yourself, are you?"

"No, of course not. Why would you say that?"

"It just seems like a desperate cry for help, or maybe a mental illness."

"Let me assure you that it's nothing of the sort."

"Then what's it about?"

"It's about trying to save the High Falls from development."

"Is that all?"

"Well, no, that's not all. It's also about trying to do something that will inspire the people of Rochester."

"By killing yourself?"

"I told you I'm not going to kill myself. I'm trying to change my life and change the city."

"What for?"

"Let me try to equate this to tennis."

"Don't bother. I told you I hate tennis."

"Right. Look, I suppose what I'm trying to say is that going over the falls is intended to be an act of aspiration."

"What's aspiration?"

"It means hope."

"So by doing this, you're trying to give others hope?"

"Yes. It's a bit complicated but basically that's the reason. Do you get it?"

"I'm not sure."

"Okay. Let me try to explain this another way. Let's see . . . . Did you see the movie *Forrest Gump*?"

"Only about 800 times."

"Good. Remember the line, 'Life is like a box of chocolates. You never know what you're gonna get.'"

"Yeah. What about it?"

"It's wrong. Completely wrong. Life is not like a box of chocolates."

"Why not?"

"Because in life you know *exactly* what you're going to get. And a lot of it's not very good. For every time you're happy, there will be at least two times when you're sad. For every moment of exhilaration, there will be several moments of despair. For every win, there will be many losses."

"Dude, you're bumming me out."

"I'm just trying to tell you the truth. See the secret is that once you accept the nature of life, you become more resilient to the bad things everybody faces and you realize you can get through them and keep going."

"Like my parents' divorce?"

"Yes. And, without fail, when you get through a bad thing, something good eventually comes around."

"So what does that have to do with going over the falls?"

"Well, a lot of bad things have happened in Rochester lately, and I'm trying to remind the people here that good things can happen, too. Do you understand?"

"I guess so."

I couldn't expect Willa to fully understand my motivation. How could a 10-year old little girl ever grasp all the reasons why a grown man would choose to dive off a 100-foot waterfall? She was only beginning to learn about life's disappointments and had miles to go before she'd come face to face with her own cynicism. Despite her parents' impending split, she hadn't truly trafficked in life's lesser moments; the rejection, humiliation, loneliness and fear that we all experience. And she certainly hadn't tangled with the cruel effect of time on one's body or the psychic toll that aging exacts. I envied her ignorance. Had I done her and my other tennis students a disservice by introducing these themes into their lives with my lessons? I wasn't sure. On balance, I wish that someone had told me what was coming when I got older. I might have been better prepared.

"We have to call your house right now and let your nanny know where you are. What's your number?"

"Ona won't care. She lets me do whatever I want."

"What's your number?"

"I want to go over the falls with you."

"What?"

"You know that extreme sports are my thing."

"The answer is no."

"How am I ever going to make it to the X Games if I don't start ripping now. No kids's ever done something like this. If I make it, I'll be a ledge."

"Forget it, *ledge*."

"This is my chance to show my parents what I can do. Pleeease."

Between her parents' divorce, her father's unrealistic expectations, and her mother's inattention, I couldn't help but empathize with Willa. At some level, I identified with her and the frustration she felt trying to relate to adults; something that never seemed to get easier. Although she was only ten, she was already feeling the desire to do something memorable and make her own mark; to matter.

"If your nanny, Ona, says it's okay, you can stay down here for the weekend. That's the best I can do."

"I don't want to go to prep school," Willa said.

"I know."

"Will you talk to my parents?"

"We'll see. Okay?"

Willa was disappointed by my response, but her spirits improved after Ona confirmed that the Nash's were away and agreed to my weekend sleepover proposal. The only condition was that I deliver my protégé to her remedial math class first thing Monday morning. As I watched Willa skateboard along the Pont de Rennes Bridge, past the reggae band and food court, she looked happy, as if a large boulder pinning her down had been lifted, if only temporarily, and I longed to feel the same way.

twenty

"You can't go over the falls."

"What are you talking about?" I asked.

"You heard me. You can't go over the falls," Nubby said, pulling me aside.

I shouldn't have been surprised by Nubby's declaration. He was, after all, the biggest buzzkill walking the planet. Still, things were different now. The publicity surrounding my trial had given our cause national exposure, attracted celebrities and turned my best friend into a local media darling. From the cozy confines of his hackysack circle on the Pont de Rennes Bridge, Nubby reveled in his role as zinger-in-chief, repeatedly ridiculing Mayor Candee in the press for her transparent attempt to cover up her plans for Candee Land with Compost Country. And as the summer passed, I'd never seen Nubby happier, a condition I attributed primarily to his relationship with Anna. For the first time ever, he appeared comfortable with himself, and the volume of the blues that had dominated his entire life seemed to be lower. So it was difficult to accept that, beneath my buddy's outer layer of contentment, Blind Lemon Jefferson, Robert Johnson and the rest were still playing loudly.

"Why not?" I asked.

"You just can't," Nubby said. "It's too dangerous."

"I'll be fine."

"I don't want you to do it," Nubby said, sounding perturbed rather than concerned.

"What's going on with you?" I asked. "You don't seem right."

"Nothing's going on."

"Look at you. You're all agitated. You're dressed like an L.L. Bean clearance sale. And you're trying to talk me out of something that you know means everything to me. What's this all about?"

Despite Nubby's denial, he couldn't conceal the troubled look on his face. Glancing over the guardrail at the water below every few seconds, he appeared anxious, as if he feared for his own safety.

"Does this have to do with your mother?" I asked.

Nubby and I had talked frequently about the absence of our parents in our lives. "At least you had your mom for nineteen years," he said to me every time the topic came up. He'd made several attempts to find his own mother over the years, but had no luck. For all he knew, she could be dead. He confided to me once that he felt a perverse pride having survived on his own, but I knew he'd trade that sentiment in an instant for a reunion with her. As for his father, he'd been trying to convince himself that he didn't care about him forever; a struggle I knew too well.

"No. It's not about her. It's about Anna."

"But things with Anna are good, aren't they?"

"Yeah, sure, but I did something stupid," Nubby said.

"Is she pregnant?"

"No. It's worse. She's in love with me."

"That's your *problem*? An attractive, intelligent woman with all of her own teeth and a driver's license is in love with you?"

"It's all a façade. She's in love with a lie."

"What are you talking about?"

"After our first few dates, I felt more and more pressure to impress her. I needed money, but I didn't have any. I got panicky and borrowed some money. Now, I'm in debt."

"How much are we talking about?"

"Forty-five grand."

"You're kidding me. What did you need that kind of dough for?"

"Everything; cash, clothes, a new apartment."

"You got a new apartment?"

"I rented it."

"For what?"

"So I'd have someplace decent to bring Anna. Soon these tents will be gone and I'll have to show her where I live."

"What about your trailer? You have a home."

"Not for long. I used part of the money I borrowed to stay out of foreclosure, but if I don't get a job soon, I'm going to lose it to the bank. It's just as well. A woman like Anna doesn't want to date a guy who lives in a trailer park," Nubby said. "She's a professor for God's sake."

"Maybe so, but you can't hide your life from her forever."

"Look, are you going to help me or not?"

"What the hell can I do? I don't have that kind of money."

"You can call off your trip over the falls."

"Why would that help you?"

"It just would."

"Why? Who'd you borrow the money from?"

Nubby hung his head and sighed.

"His name is Knuckles Tate."

"Knuckles Tate? You borrowed money from a guy named Knuckles? Are you mental? That's like taking driving lessons from a guy named Crash."

"It gets worse. He works for Mayor Candee."

"Oh, shit."

"He does odd jobs for her."

"You mean hit jobs, right? You are without a single doubt in my mind the world's biggest idiot. Do you know that?"

"I had no idea the guy worked for Candee. I swear."

"So the money you borrowed actually belongs to the Mayor?"

"Yes."

"That's just great, Nubby. Really, really great."

"I told you I didn't know that Knuckles...."

"You knew he was a loan shark. That should've been enough to stop you right there. Where's your common sense?"

"There was no place else to go. He said I could pay it back over time. He played it down; said it was no big deal. Now he says he's going to break my legs if I don't pay it all back by the end of the month," Nubby said.

"I can't believe you did this."

"Look, I didn't know what to do. Robert Johnson sold his soul to the Devil in order to play guitar the way he did. I suppose I did the same thing to keep Anna."

"Well, it was *stupid*."

"I'm ashamed to ask you to stop, but there's only one way out. The Mayor will forgive my debt if I talk you out of going over the falls. She says she'll even pay off the note on my trailer."

"There's no way I'm calling it off. Not a chance in hell."

"Why not?"

"How can you ask me that? Don't you see what she's doing? She's blackmailing you."

"And it's working. I'm trapped."

"No you're not. We'll figure something out together," I said. "All we need to do is go on offense," I said.

"Offense?"

For guys like Nubby and me, two people who'd spent their entire lives on defense, this was a foreign concept.

"Yes, *offense*. We need to go on the attack."

"How are we going to do that?"

"It's a two-part plan," I said.

"Aw, Christ. I hate it already."

"Shut-up. First, you've got to agree to go over the falls with me."

"What? I'm not doing that. I've told you 100 times."

Despite repeated requests from me over the past months to commit to the daring act, Nubby refused to do so.

"Do you want to keep Anna?"

"Of course."

"Do you want her to admire you and respect you?"

"Of course."

"Then strap on a pair and ride the High Falls with me. Be my Sancho Panza."

"Sancho who?"

"Sancho Panza. He was the trusty sidekick of Don Quixote."

"Who the hell is Don Quixote?"

"He was a knight on a quest. You know, 'dream the impossible dream, right the unrightable wrong, fight the unbeatable foe.'"

"If the foe's unbeatable, what's the point?" Nubby asked.

"The point is to try. Like you're trying with Anna," I said.

"I'm not trying that hard."

"Oh, no? Since when did you buy Slim-Fast in bulk?"

"All right, maybe I'm trying, but I bet this Sancho guy never had to jump off a 100-foot waterfall."

"Well, no, he didn't. But he traveled very far and endured many hardships with his friend."

"They sound like a couple of suckers."

"They weren't suckers. Come on."

"All right, all right, I'll do it. I'll go over the falls with you."

"That's great! You won't regret it."

"I'm sure I will. . . . What's the second part of the plan?" Nubby asked.

"We've got to call the Mayor out on her loan-sharking. What she's doing is criminal."

"Wait a minute. I'm already having nightmares about Knuckles, and now you're going to provoke him by tattling on his boss."

"Just leave Knuckles to me, okay?"

"Forgive me if that's no comfort whatsoever."

As 1:00 a.m. approached, I went to my tent to sleep. For weeks, my only companion at night had been a dog-eared copy of Cervantes' *Don Quixote*, a book I'd learned was Chester Carlson's favorite. Spending every waking hour trying to invent what he called electrophotography, something that had never been imagined before; he found strength in the story's themes of determination and persistence. The inventor endured crippling arthritis, a broken marriage, unemployment and endless rejection, but when he finally met with success and the first Xerox machine rolled off the assembly line, he had become an expert on the topic of believing in the impossible.

Was it foolish to embrace hackneyed clichés about never giving up? It would be easy to say yes at this juncture in my life. The older I got, the more cynical I'd become. No matter how hard I tried to escape, my mistrust of the world and those in it continued to encircle me. Were Don Quixote and Sancho Panza suckers? Chester Carlson didn't think so and neither did I.

twenty-one

In early August, organizers of the High Falls Film Festival, the city's celebration of female cinema slated for November, began to put up publicity signs around Brown's Race and take out ads in the *Democrat and Chronicle*. With our plunge planned to coincide with the opening night of the event, the intensity of press interest in our story continued to grow as did the pressure on Mayor Candee and Pete Lee to produce the architectural drawings they'd promised for Compost Country.

Simultaneously, nominations for the film festival's Susan B. Anthony "Failure is Impossible" Award were being accepted, stirring debate at camp about which female might be coming to town to receive it.

"I think it's going to be Maya Angelou," Big Nasty said.

"But she's not an actress," Dixie said. "She's a poet. The award is for actresses only."

"Reading poems is a performance art," Big Nasty said.

"They should give it to Beyonce," Nubby said.

"She's more of a singer than an actress," Dixie said.

"Who cares? She's hot," Nubby said.

"She's not as hot as Maya Angelou," Big Nasty said.

"How can you say that?" Nubby asked.

"Because I'm more attracted to brains than bodies."

"You would be," Nubby said.

"What's that supposed to mean?" Big Nasty asked.

"Hey, guys, hold on. I really don't want to hear the two of you debate the relative hotness of Beyonce and Maya Angelou," I said.

"I should clarify. Just because I'm primarily drawn to her intellect, I'm not saying I wouldn't sleep with her," Big Nasty said. I even wrote her a poem. *'Knock, knock, it's the Nasty man. You're the brownie mix and I'm the pan. All greased up and ready to cook, you heat my oven with your every look...'*"

"Stop that now. You're grossing me out," Dixie said. "Are you comparing Maya Angelou to brownie mix?" Dixie asked. "That's incredibly racist."

"It's just a poem, Dixie. Relax," Big Nasty said. "She's a sweet, sexy woman. You know I invited her, right?" Big Nasty asked.

"To what?" I asked.

"To the opening of the film festival; our big moment. I thought she could say a few words before we go over the falls."

"We? Does that mean you're in, Big Nasty? I asked.

"I'm in. I'll pretty much do anything to impress a woman."

"I hear ya," I said, reaching out to give Big Nasty a high five for his decision.

"Well, don't get your hopes up. There's no way Maya Angelou is going to come," Dixie said. "Look, are you guys going to stand around all day and play hackysack or actually do something useful?"

"Hey, we've been out here for over four months. In case you don't know it, recreation is important for morale," Nubby said.

"So is making new signs and distributing supplies," Dixie said.

"Speaking of supplies, do you have any extra Luna bars?"

"Get your own, Nubby," Dixie said. "Sometimes I don't think you realize that we're the only thing standing in the way of the destruction of the High Falls. Are you serious about this or not?"

"Hey, when the time comes, I'll chain myself to a bulldozer. Is that serious enough for you?" Nubby asked.

"You're in a bit a foul mood, Dixie," Big Nasty said. "What gives?"

Dixie's eyes moistened.

"I'm sorry, guys."

She took a moment to gather herself.

"I got word this morning from the New York State Fair. My butter sculpture of Susan B. Anthony wasn't selected for display."

"I'm sorry, Dixie," I said.

"I guess it just wasn't good enough," Dixie said.

"So who won?" Nubby asked.

"Some guy who sculpted a leprechaun sitting on top of a cheese pastry. He called it 'Luck of the Danish.' Can you believe it?" Dixie asked.

"There's no such thing as luck of the Danish," I said.

"I hear they're all inbred," Big Nasty said.

"I suppose his message was there's nothing better than eating an enormous cheese danish," Dixie said. "He was obviously kissing up to the dairy farmers."

"Stupid dairy farmers," Nubby said. "They're always screwing things up for everybody."

"But there's no historical significance to his sculpture. It has nothing to do with the State of New York. Isn't that what the fair is supposed to be celebrating? New York? Not Denmark. The judges should be ashamed of themselves. At least you stayed true to yourself and your home state. You should be proud of that," I said.

"I guess," Dixie said.

"I told you not to do a feminist," Nubby said. "Nobody wants to see that at a state fair."

"Shut-up, Nubby," I said. "Show a little sensitivity for once, all right?"

"All I'm saying is she should've done Muddy Waters or Dale Earnhardt, Jr. That's who people want to see. Either of those guys would've blown that Danish dude right out of the water."

"Will you cool it about Dale Earnhardt, Jr.?" I asked.

"I'm just saying he's an automotive racing god who . . ."

"Just *don't*, okay?"

"Dixie, maybe we could get your sculpture displayed at Brown's Race during the film festival," I said. "It would make perfect sense what with the Susan B. Anthony award and all."

"It doesn't matter," Dixie said, getting teary again. "I've got other problems."

"What's wrong?" I asked.

"I went to see my father last night."

"And?"

"He's not going to back down from developing the High Falls site. He says the project is too important to Goliath Industries, too important to him and too important to the future of my brothers. He doesn't give a shit about me."

"I'm sure he does," I said.

"No, he doesn't. He knows what we're planning to do in November and he's not trying to stop me. He knows that my physical safety may be in jeopardy and yet he said nothing to me. All I ever wanted from him was the kind of approval he gives my brothers."

"That's natural. That's what everyone wants from their parents," I said.

"God knows I do," Nubby said.

"What makes me so mad is that I realize my motive for entering the butter sculpture contest was more about him than about me or about women's rights. I wanted to show him that I could do something he'd be proud of; something that was a big deal. I'm reconsidering my need to blow up his warehouse and headquarters."

"That's not going to solve anything, Dixie," I said.

"Yes, it will. It'll stop this stupid project," Dixie said.

"Dixie, if you need help. I'm still game," Nubby said. "I've got the C-4 explosives in my mini-frige."

"Nubby, shut-up about the mini-frige. Dixie, the Mayor is going to try to build Candee Land with or without Goliath Industries. All your father has right now is a construction contract," I said.

"A construction contract and a missing spine," Dixie said.

In the middle of consoling Dixie, my cell phone rang and the call I'd been dreading arrived. It was Biff. Beatie's health had taken a nosedive and they were on their way to the hospital.

I left the Pont de Rennes Bridge deep in thought about my grandmother. In the years that followed the death of my grandfather, before the arrival of Biff, Beatie would set out two champagne flutes and fill them for significant events like her birthday, July 4th and New Year's Eve, then talk aloud to the one true love of her life and celebrate as if he was alive. Her devotion was touching, but I was happy when she found someone to fill those terrible spaces we all know; the ones that never fully disappear but greatly diminish when we're in a relationship. Though she hid it well beneath a blustery veneer, Beatie had a very sentimental side and her illness had brought it back to the surface. She had been calling me often on the bridge to tell me she missed having me around the house but that she was one hundred percent behind our protest and wanted me to keep going.

Beatie looked pale and pitiable in her hospital bed when I entered her third floor room. She was hooked up to all forms of alien machinery and wiring, but Biff was by her side, rubbing her hands to assure her of his presence. There was no more bickering over Reddi-wip, *Kid Boots* or anything else. Only harmony and a quiet serenity passed between them now, a connection earned with shared intimacies unseen, memories that I was excluded from and the world couldn't touch or know. When Biff went for a cup of coffee, she and I got to talk.

"I've realized something," Beatie said.

"What's that?"

"I don't want to die anymore."

"You don't?"

"No, but I still want to go over the falls with ya."

"Wait — we talked about this before. I'm not so sure that's a good . . ."

"I know yer gonna try and talk me out of it, but I've made up my mind."

"But . . ."

"And I want Woofie to come, too."

"Over the falls?"

"Yes."

"But Woofie's a pot-bellied pig."

"And he's got four good legs. Plus, he's a good swimmah."

"This isn't the Olympic relay we're talking about."

"When I put him in the tub, he does real good."

"We're talking about a 100-foot drop off a waterfall. I don't think pigs are designed for that."

"Nobody is, but that doesn't mattah."

"It's too dangerous — for him and for you."

"I'll be fine."

"There's a reason 102-year old women don't do stunt work — particularly ones battling cancer."

"It'll be exciting."

"But I don't want anything to happen to you."

"What else can happen? I'm not afraid to die. This is my choice. It's what I want."

I shook my head and smiled.

"You realize the animal cruelty groups are going to be all over us."

"Buncha ninnies."

When it came right down to it, Beatie was right. This was her life, and she was free to live it any way she wanted, whether she was dying of cancer or not. My reasons for denying her wish were all about me and, as difficult as it would be to do, it was time to cut my Gordian knot. If something happened to Beatie on the way over the falls, was I worried that that the last link to my mother's prophecies wouldn't be around to witness my fulfillment of them or was it something more?

Growing up without a father isn't something I recommend. My mother and grandmother did their best to convince me that I wasn't missing out on anything but questions concerning his whereabouts from teachers at school and from kids at birthday parties, little league games and a never-ending assortment of events, constantly reminded me of his absence. Father's Day was particularly hard and invariably filled my mind with imaginings of who he might be and the possibility of a reunion one day. Nevertheless, with two strong, loving women hovering over me and lavishing me with encouragement and understanding, I made it to eighteen without feeling any strong compulsion to find him. That all changed, however, when my mother died the next year and I felt a sudden, urgent need to locate my dad.

Using a local investigator and in due course, the Internet, I tried repeatedly to identify the man my mother had romanticized and whose departure she defended for reasons she believed were in my best interests. Beatie gave me his name and a few odd facts, but time after time my search proved fruitless and eventually I gave up on the idea of ever meeting him and hearing him say the things a son longs to hear from his father. I wrote him off; frustrated and angry that he had no interest in me. 'The hell with him,' I said to myself whenever he crept into my head; trying repeatedly to persuade myself that I didn't care until I actually thought I believed it. Unfortunately, the mind can't always accomplish what the heart wants it to when it comes to your parents.

What I was discovering now, in a painful way, was that I'd never completely let go and that a small piece of me had clung to the hope that one day my father would arrive and give me the kind of validation I sought. Had I married and started a family things might have been different, but as my life evolved and I remained alone, Beatie became disproportionately important to me as my only parent; the only person who could give me the approval every child craves. The prospect of losing her now was forcing me to face the truth that once she was gone I would no longer have a parent to turn to as a source of love or anything else and it terrified me.

twenty-two

Kodak announced more layoffs in October. Two thousand people would lose their jobs and, like a punch to the stomach, the experience would leave them breathless and temporarily paralyzed. Some of the newly unemployed would no doubt find their way to the Patch, just a short walk from Kodak Park, where a pink slip constituted ample permission to rail against the world and its inequities while drinking Genesee Cream Ale and plotting revenge; the kind that's obsessed about but rarely taken.

Months before, I'd unfavorably compared these sorts of people to those depicted in the old black and white photographs on the wall of the bar; early Rochesterians full of hope and discipline. But I wondered now if I'd been too quick to judge. Perhaps it wasn't the quality of the people that had changed, but rather the quality of the opportunities presented to them by the city. I didn't want to believe that either had been diminished. This was my home; one that I still loved, and my hopes for it and the individuals who resided here remained as endless as any summer ever spent in the Finger Lakes.

Unfortunately, conditions in the city and at camp were deteriorating as fall arrived. The weather was turning colder and life on the bridge was getting harder. I had come to detest sleeping on cement, the taste of Luna bars and the sound of steel drums, which had been playing non-stop for nearly five months by my estimate. Hot showers and hot meals were non-existent, save the occasional garbage plate from Nick Tahou's or plate of wings from Sal's Birdland, another favorite dive. Peter, Paul and the new Mary had played *If I Had a Hammer* 700 times by my count and I was ready to kill all three of them.

"Do you guys know anything by The Who?"

"Uh, no."

"AC/DC?"

"No."

"Black Sabbath?"

"I don't think so. What if we play *Lemon Tree* again?"

"Uh, yeah, I guess so. Let her rip."

As the calendar moved inexorably toward November 13, I only left the bridge to visit Beatie, whose condition continued to worsen but whose spirit was undiminished. "Stay out on that bridge, ya stinka," she said to me every time we spoke. And so I did, along with my fellow QWEAFS, as we refused to yield to Mayor Candee's repeated threats; a feat growing harder by the day. So far, by reminding her of our easy access to the media and high profile, I'd been able to convince her that sicking Knuckles Tate on Nubby was a bad idea, but I feared her mind could change at any time.

"Hey, Dragon, there's a call for you," shouted Edwin, a bartender, from the Patch's front door, two hundred feet from our camp.

"Who is it?" I asked.

"It's the Mayor again."

Although she'd done a good job of shifting public opinion against us by dangling the promise of Oscar and Compost

Country in front of Rochester's citizens while running her 'Santa Killer' ads non-stop even after my trial ended, the Mayor was baffled as to why we hadn't quit protesting and abandoned our plan to go over the falls. Of late, she'd been calling me every few days to convince me that our efforts were futile. Typically, what started out as cajoling quickly gave way to begging then bribing and, ultimately, a hostile slew of profanities each time I refused her offer. Today, however, her call was different.

"Mayor Candee, what do you want? I've told you 10 times now we're not for sale. No amount of money will get us off the bridge or stop us from going over the falls."

"Who said anything about stopping you?"

"You did; every time you've called me."

"Not anymore, Horvath. Let me be clear. I support what you're doing."

"What the hell's going on, Candee?"

The Mayor's new attitude, plus the static on the line, put me on edge.

"I'm making lemonade, and you and your Woodsy Owl terrorist friends are the lemnzzz."

"What did you say? I can barely hear you."

"Yeah, sorry about the reception; I'm in Paris on vacation. The cell service stinks but it's hard to complain when you're nibbling on a tasty piece of brie and guzzling champagne."

"I'll be sure to tell everyone how much you're enjoying the French food," I said, my sarcasm laid bare.

"Who said anything about food? Brie and Champagne are two dancers I just met. Real nice girls; at least I think they're girls. I'll find out soon enough. Anyway, Horvath, about my lemonade; here I was fighting you every step of the way, but getting nowhere. I was puzzling over it all last night during an all-nude game of Twister when it hit me: I need to promote this event not prevent it."

The static continued to make the Mayor's words hard to hear.

"Did you say that you want to *promote* our trip over the High Falls?"

"That's right."

"Wait a minute. Is this one of your practical jokes? Like when you told those orphans they'd been adopted on April Fool's Day?"

"No, this is not a practical joke. I've already commissioned Chuck Mangione to write a song for the occasion called *Hittin' the Rocks*. For my money, nothing evokes tragedy quite like a flugelhorn. He may have scored an Olympic Games, but he's never scored a group suicide."

"Screw you. What we're doing has nothing to do with group suicide," I said.

"Of course not. But, let's face it; the strong possibility of your collective death is what'll put fannies in the seats. Why do you think NASCAR races draw record crowds? It sure as hell isn't the fine cuisine; that I can tell you. The real reason is because people know there's a very good chance that someone, somehow, someway, is going to get killed; either on the racetrack or in the stands. You ever see a redneck get hit by a flying tire in the face? Pure magic. I see this thing the same way."

"I told you this has nothing to do with suicide or death, and you can't exploit it as some death-defying stunt."

"I can and I will. A big event like this is my chance to show the voters that I can create a viable entertainment district in downtown Rochester. Once I do that, it's going to be cake to get state funding for Candee Land and to get the Oscars, not to mention get re-elected. Now, I've put my ad people on the case and they're coming up with some great stuff; all of it tying your public plunge to the High Falls Film Festival since the events coincide. 'Come for the nitwits, stay for the chick flicks,' is my favorite so far. It's going to be a family-friendly evening of entertainment and *your* final curtain."

"I hate to disappoint you, but we're all going to survive."

"Oh, sure, I'm with you. Keep up that front. That's what's going to drive the gambling on this baby. Will they live or will they be smashed to smithereens? Place your bets. Place your bets. I may hire a carnival barker. What do you think?"

"You're despicable."

"I feel like P.T. Barnum. This is going to be one first-class spectacle. The Genesee River will be lined with thousands, all of them anxiously awaiting the sound of bodies hitting boulders."

"Why the hell are you so evil?"

"I don't know. I've never really thought about it. I guess it's because it's so much damn fun."

I hung up on the Mayor and returned to the bridge where, to my surprise, I found Big Nasty bent over in obvious pain and steadying himself with a hand on the railing.

"Big Nasty, what's wrong?" I asked, racing over to him. "Are you all right?"

"Oh, sure. I'm good," he said, his face pale and puffy. "Just a little tired that's all."

"Here, lean on me," I said, draping his arm around my shoulder. "Let's get you inside the bar. Nubby, help us out over here," I called.

"I don't think that's a good idea," Big Nasty said, gasping for air. "Something's not right."

"We need to get you to the hospital," I said. "Hey, Nubby, I need some help over here."

Straining under the burden of Big Nasty's considerable weight, I felt grateful when Nubby and another protester joined me in propping him up.

"Help me get him to my car," I said. "I'm going to take him to St. Mary's. That's the closest."

Although the physical demands of being on the bridge were tough for everybody, they were particularly hard for Big Nasty given his defective kidneys. Nevertheless, despite repeated warnings to take it easy from myself and others, he felt like a brother-in-arms only when protesting alongside the rest of us and thus kept his absences to a bare minimum. As I walked him toward my car, however, he put up no resistance.

"Everything's going to be okay," I said. "Just hang in there."

"I don't know. This could be it."

"Don't say that. You're going to be fine."

"I wrote a poem about my death," Big Nasty said, as we plopped him down in the front passenger seat of my car.

"No poems," I said, rushing around to the other side of the vehicle and sliding behind the wheel. "Save your energy."

"Hello, darkness, my old friend. I've come to be with you again . . ."

"That's Simon and Garfunkel."

"It is?"

"Yes. Look, no poems. Let's just get you to St. Mary's."

I peeled out of Brown's Race and headed for the hospital.

"Wait, I've got it," Big Nasty said. "'Death, my friend, I'm glad you've come.'"

"You're not going to die. Now, knock it off."

"'In your black hands, I'm comfortably numb.'"

"Stop it! We'll be at the hospital in two minutes."

"Tell Maya Angelou that I loved her."

"You can tell her yourself."

"I doubt it. She still hasn't answered my letter."

"Don't worry. She will."

Big Nasty was delirious now, but St. Mary's was mercifully close, located at the east end of Main Street a few miles away.

Speeding past boarded up stores and buildings, the severity of the city's decay registered with me even in the midst of a crisis. At the hospital's emergency entrance, I helped an orderly escort Big Nasty inside and onto a gurney. I was told to wait and then watched as two nurses took him away. A pair of swinging doors closed behind them and he was gone. There was nobody to call. Big Nasty had no family. So I sat in the waiting area and worried; wondering if I'd ever see my friend alive again. Soon, Nubby and Dixie arrived to join me.

"I didn't realize Big Nasty was in such bad shape," Nubby said.

"What are you talking about? He's been walking around with a portable dialysis machine for months," Dixie said.

"Is *that* what that was?" Nubby asked.

"Yes. What did you think it was?"

"I don't know. I thought he was going on a trip. It looked like luggage."

"Nubby, he's been sick for years."

"I know, but I didn't think he was going to die."

"He won't if we do something about it," I said.

"Like what?" Nubby asked.

"We have to get tested to see if any of us is a match," Dixie said.

"She's right," I said.

"A match for what?" Nubby asked.

"For Big Nasty's blood and tissue type," Dixie said.

"What would that prove?" Nubby asked.

"That one of us could be a donor," Dixie said.

"Oh, okay. . . . A donor of what?" Nubby asked.

"A kidney, you moron," Dixie said.

"Whoa. Hold on. There's no way I'm giving away my only kidney," Nubby said.

"You have two of them, and you only need one to function," I said.

"I don't care. I like Big Nasty and all. He's a great guy and I like his poems, but I'm not getting cut up like some Frankenstein for him. Forget that. What if I need the spare? Is he going to give it back?"

"Try to think about someone else for once," Dixie said. "It's very likely that a kidney transplant is the only way he'll survive."

"Take it easy, you guys," I said. "Let's see if any of us is a match before we start bashing each other."

An hour later, a doctor emerged and told us that Big Nasty had suffered a seizure shortly after arrival. His condition was worsening and, just as we suspected, a kidney transplant was needed to save his life. How much time he had left was unknown, but it wasn't long.

twenty-three

The dramatic appearance of the largest urban waterfall in North America is striking to first-time visitors to Rochester. They never expect to see something so beautiful and alive at the center of a city known for its deadly cold winters. This remarkable, cascading image was the first thing that the filmmakers and luminaries arriving for the High Falls Film Festival would notice and fittingly so. To natives, however, the High Falls had taken on a whole new look; one part potential mortuary, one part publicity mecca.

November brings ice cold winds down from Canada making it an unwelcome month in western New York, but this season it was bringing something else; the air of expectation and excitement. Ordinarily, at this time of year, city dwellers instinctively brace themselves for the six-month siege ahead, but the prospect of our trip over the falls and the impending festival had disrupted the rhythm of Rochester's hibernatory clock and its state of low respiration. Never before had the Mayor's office issued so many press credentials as journalists from around the world closed in to cover the various happenings. Having returned from Paris with her new attitude, the Mayor publicly raved about the undeniable synergy between the opening night of the film festival and the accompanying daredevil theatrics. "Come see a film and a fatality," she crowed at every press conference while touting her downtown revitalization efforts and priming the pump for the Oscars, Candee Land and her own re-election.

Out on the bridge, I shared my skepticism about the Mayor's recent epiphany with the media, but my focus was elsewhere. With only two days to go until the big event, nothing felt quite right. Beatie and Big Nasty were still in the hospital, Dixie was distraught about her butter sculpture and Nubby was losing his will.

"I think I'm going to be sick," Nubby said.

"What's wrong?" I asked.

"What's wrong is your stupid plan to have us jump off a cliff. That's what's wrong, David — oh wait, excuse me — *Dragon*."

"What are you talking about? I'm not forcing you to do anything."

"Do you know what I realized last night? I realized that I want to marry Anna. Can you believe that? Me: the biggest commitment-phobe on the planet; the guy who can't commit to the same breakfast cereal for more than a week, wants to get hitched. But, guess what? I'm not going to get the chance."

"Why not?"

"Because I'll be dead, you twit. My skull will be crushed like a walnut shell. My guts will be floating down the Genesee River, completely detached from the rest of my body. My blood will be spilling like an overturned bucket of horse piss. That's why not, you idiot."

"None of that is going to happen."

"And you can guarantee me that?"

"I can't guarantee that but . . ."

"Of course you can't, because you don't know anything you God damn lunatic. I can't believe you got me into this mess.

'Jump with me, Nubby. Strap on a pair, Nubby. Be my Sancho Panza.' That's what you said and, like a moron, I agreed."

"Calm down, Nub."

"And here's the worst part. I still don't know who the hell this Sancho Panza guy is. All I know is because of you, *he's* not going over the falls like some mental defective, but I am."

"You don't have to do anything you don't want to do. I was only trying to help you with Anna and protect you from the Mayor's henchmen, remember? I thought you wanted to be a part of it."

"It's suicide for God's sake."

"No, it's not. You wanted to show Anna that you weren't some unemployed schmuck who lived in a trailer park, didn't you? Isn't that what you said? You were afraid that when she found out the truth about what a putz you really are, she wouldn't want to have anything to do with you. Isn't that what you told me?"

"Yes, but that didn't mean I wanted to go over the falls. You talked me into this."

"I gave you an option; a way to show Anna that you have some balls; a way to show *yourself* that you have some balls."

"Well, maybe I don't. All right? Maybe I don't have balls. Does that make you happy?"

"No, that does *not* make me happy. That doesn't make me happy at all. Jesus, what's wrong with you?"

Nubby took a deep breath and regained his composure.

"I don't know, but whatever it is, it happened a long time ago."

Unable to reach accord with Nubby, I headed over to St. Mary's to check on Big Nasty and to deliver some bad news — none of us were a match for a kidney transplant. Entering his room, I found him awake, but groggy; his gangly frame covering the entire bed.

"Big Nasty, how are you, man?"

"What are you doing here, David?"

"What do you think I'm doing here? I came to see the heart and soul of the QWEAFS."

Big Nasty smiled ruefully at my use of the name foisted upon us.

"How are things down on the bridge?"

"Everybody's thinking about you. Last night, a candlelight vigil was held in your honor at camp and some of your poems were read aloud."

"Really? Which ones?"

"Which ones? Well . . . I'm not sure of all the titles. I know a lot of them involved sex and violence, but the overall message was very uplifting."

"So everybody thinks I'm going to die?"

"No, I didn't say that."

"Yes, you did. Candlelight vigils equal death. Everybody knows that."

"Well, you're going to be the exception. Any word on a donor?"

"No, nothing yet."

"Dixie and I got tested, but we're not a match for you. Nubby got tested, too."

"You didn't need to do that."

"We wanted to. We knew it was a long shot. How do you feel?"

"I'm not in any pain but I'm scared. The doctor says if they don't find a kidney for me in the next few weeks, I'm not going to make it."

"They'll find a match. You've got to stay positive."

"I'm trying, but it's getting harder."

Big Nasty closed his eyes as if deep in thought and then re-opened them, slowly focusing on my face.

"I won't be able to go over the falls with you, David."

"Of course not; I just assumed. You're not worrying about that, are you?"

"Not exactly, but I've got to tell you something else that I don't think you're going to like," he said.

"You do?"

"I've been debating whether or not to tell you."

"What is it?"

"It's just been on my mind. But after everything that's happened, it's kind of hard to say."

"Just tell me."

"Okay . . . see the thing is . . . I don't think you should go over the falls."

"What? Why not?"

"Because there's no such thing as reincarnation."

"How do you know that?"

"I just do."

"How? And what difference does that make anyway?"

"It makes all the difference, David. I've been listening to you for six months. I know what's in your head. You're obsessed with Chester Carlson and Dr. Stevenson and reincarnation and what awaits us on the other side. For the love of Christ, you've been telling the world you're a dragon from a past life."

"So what?"

"So I don't think you realize how dangerous what you're about to do really is. Somewhere in the back of your mind, you think that if something goes horribly wrong at the falls tomorrow night, you'll be reborn into another life."

"What's your point?"

"My point is that *this* is the only life you've got and I don't want to see you throw it away. I'm not a religious scholar and I won't pretend to know anything about God or heaven, but when it comes to reincarnation I can tell you based on my own experience that it doesn't exist."

"How could you possibly know that?"

"Because I've died before."

"Oh, come on. Are you heavily medicated right now?"

"No, I'm perfectly lucid and I'm telling you that I've died before. When I was nine, I climbed onto the subway tracks in Greenwich Village and was severely electrocuted. They said I took 7700 volts that day."

"Well, that explains a lot, but it doesn't make you an expert on reincarnation."

"The doctor said I was pronounced dead three times, but I kept coming back to life."

"You don't remember it?"

"No, and that's the problem. I don't remember anything. There was no shining light coming toward me. My life didn't flash in front of me. And I didn't even get a peek at the pearly gates. I think I just passed away."

"Are you sure?"

"Yes."

"There was nothing?"

"Nothing."

"No God?"

"I didn't see him."

"Angels?"

"I didn't see anyone."

"George Burns?" I asked.

"Nope."

"No 77 virgins?"

"Nope."

"The Devil?"

"Nobody. Not for me, anyway."

"And you didn't turn into anything?"

"Like what?"

"I don't know. Like a butterfly or a toaster or some kind of flower?"

"No."

"Are you sure? Maybe you don't get the works if it's a false alarm."

"Maybe. I just felt like I needed to tell you."

"Oh, sure. I can see that. Thanks."

"I'm sorry to be the one to say all this to you."

"I know you are."

"I'm just trying to be a friend."

"You are a friend."

"I wrote a new poem for you, man. Would you like to hear it?"

"Of course."

" '*Sweet David on the wire. Life can set your hair on fire. Knock you down and toss you back — like ass cancer or a heart attack. Keep your head, it's all you need. That, a bong and a bag of weed. You sir are a man in full. Don't succumb to the world's cruel pull.*'"

I said goodbye to Big Nasty and headed back to camp in a haze. For years I'd thought about greatness and waited for it to come my way. Then one day I began stalking it, never knowing that doing so is as much about the fear of success as it is about the fear of failure. Here I was on the precipice of something big; about to leap into a new world that held the promise of better days for me and my hometown, and yet I was afraid. I could lose my life or a loved one and my so-called bold act might make no difference at all.

twenty-four

Waking up at camp, I felt the ghost of Sam Patch starting to stir. On November 13, 1829, he made his fatal leap at 2:00 p.m. before an estimated crowd of 8000 people after reportedly shouting, 'Some things can be done as well as others.' It was not clear to me whether these words were the inane ramblings of a drunken madman or the profoundly significant thoughts of an important historical figure, but I chose to believe the latter because, frankly, it made me feel better. I took a deep breath. Today was the day the QWEAFS would go over the High Falls. And though my preference was to get the deed done by noon, the demands of prime-time television coverage and pre-game pundit analysis, not to mention the lack of affordable area daycare, meant the event would start at 8:00 p.m. and would be seen by millions.

As I climbed out of my tent, I saw that every inch of concrete at Brown's Race was covered with camera crews, protesters, tourists and cinemaphiles. Like a street fair on crack, the atmosphere was everything the Mayor had promised and then some. There were circus clowns, dancing girls, pony rides and hawkers selling everything from cotton candy and nacho hats to cell phone plans and fried dough. There was a country band, a bugle corps, a bagpipe team and six cheerleading squads from area high schools. The capper, however, now tethered to the Pont de Rennes Bridge, was the 50-foot high inflated dragon with the words 'I HATE AMERICA' emblazoned across its chest.

"Holy shit. It looks like the damn Macy's Day parade out here," Nubby said, observing the enormous balloon as he emerged from his sleeping quarters. "Where did that thing come from?"

"Where do you think?" I asked.

"Why does it say 'I Hate America' across its chest?"

With perfect timing, my cell phone rang.

"Hello."

"How do you like the dragon, . . . Dragon?" Mayor Candee asked, before heartily chuckling.

"Why the hell would you put that up, Candee?" I asked.

"Why the hell wouldn't I?"

"Because I don't hate America."

"Of course not, but I thought it had a certain ring to it."

"You're trying to turn everyone against me."

"Did you figure that out all by yourself? Not bad for a high school graduate. You did graduate high school, didn't you?"

"I want you to take the balloon down."

"And I want to meet a set of well-hung triplets with no scruples and a granny obsession, but it probably ain't gonna happen. Now, tell me: are you ready to die?"

"I told you a hundred times. Nobody is going to die."

"Oh, I beg to differ. Check the betting line in Vegas. The oddsmakers say somebody's gonna bite it."

"Why don't you bite it, you sick freak?"

I hung up on the Mayor, flustered by her harassment.

"God, she pisses me off."

"Just stay cool," Nubby said.

"What time is it?"

"Almost noon."

"Crap. I've got to go."

On this day of all days, I had promised Willa Nash that I would attend her skateboarding competition at an indoor skate park in Webster, a suburban town bordering the city. Making my way to the parking lot, I was surrounded by the press.

"Dragon, how about a few questions? Do you think you QWEAFS are going to make it out of this alive?"

"That's one of the goals," I said.

"Sam Patch died going over these falls. Why do you think you'll be any different?"

"Blind faith, I guess."

"Do you think you can you save the High Falls from development?"

"I hope so."

"Is it true you've been asked to be on The Tonight Show?"

"That's news to me."

"Why do you hate America so much?"

"I *don't* hate America."

I climbed into my Mustang and sped off. To date, I'd been able to convince Kit Nash that sending Willa away to prep school was a bad idea. After begging on her behalf, I had secured a one semester reprieve for her, after which Willa's grades, attitude and general state of juvenile delinquency would be assessed for improvement. If there was none, she would be sent packing for Rosemary Hall. Part of my plan was to show Kit that by allowing Willa to skateboard; something that she loved, she would flourish in the other areas of her life and perhaps eventually get into the kind of college Kit drooled over.

Arriving at Sharkey's Skaterama a few minutes late, I ran inside and looked for a familiar face.

"Are you Mr. Horvath?" The teenage girl working behind the front desk asked.

"Yes," I said, breathlessly.

"Willa's waiting for you. Go down this hall and make a left"

"Great."

Hustling down a concrete-floored corridor of exposed brick, wiring and plastic tubing designed to look hazardous; I turned the corner and ran into an unexpected crowd.

"SURPRISE!"

To my great wonderment, I stood face-to-face with my tennis students and their parents.

"Happy Birthday!" They said in unison, gathering around me.

"Are you surprised?" Willa asked.

"I'm stunned. You guys got me. You really got me. Nobody's every thrown a surprise party for me in my life."

"You are such a tool, David," Willa said, showing me affection the only way she knew how by poking me in the stomach with Plank.

"Happy birthday, David," Kit Nash said, sticking out his hand. "I didn't really want to throw this party, but Willa insisted. It's costing me an arm and a leg."

"Very gracious of you," I said, smiling to mask my contempt.

"You're not going to beat anyone up here, are you?" Kit asked, laughing nervously.

"No, you're all safe," I said, trying to play it off.

After making small talk with some of the parents, smashing a piñata shaped like an enlarged skateboard wheel and devouring a piece of red velvet cake, I was surrounded by my students.

"I've missed you guys. Have you been practicing?"

"Not really," Blaise said.

"Are you kidding?" Willa asked.

"We've mostly been playing X-Box," Boyle advised.

"And eating Easy-Mac," Blaise said.

"I've been practicing," Becky said.

"That's good, Becky. I'm glad to hear it," I said.

"Are you really going over the falls tonight?" Danny asked.

"Yes."

"If you get injured, make sure to call my dad. He'll help you file a lawsuit," Danny said.

"Got it. Thanks."

"I don't want you to do it, David," Becky said. "You could break something."

"I'm going to be fine."

"Can we come watch?" Boyle asked.

"If your parents say you can — then sure."

"They better. I think it'll be cool," Boyle said.

"Yeah — kind of like a real life video game," Blaise added.

"Maybe a little bit," I said. "There won't be a restart button though."

"I guess that's right," Blaise said. "That kind of stinks."

"So, Willa, I hear this party was your idea," I said, anxious to change the topic.

"Not really," Willa said.

"But your dad said . . ."

"You can't believe what he says," she said.

"But, Willa, the party *was* your idea," Blaise said.

"Was not," Willa protested, unwilling to show any vulnerability.

"Was too," Blaise said.

"Do you want to get pounded?" Willa asked, threatening Blaise with Plank.

"Hey, no violence, guys," I said. "It doesn't matter whose idea it was; I'm just glad you're all here."

"Why don't you open your present?" Becky asked.

"Sure. Where is it?"

From behind a curtain, Danny emerged carrying a large box wrapped in red and white striped paper with an enormous red ribbon tied around it.

"Whoa, that gift looks expensive," I said.

"We all chipped in with our own money," Becky said.

"I got mine from my dad," Boyle said.

"I appreciate the honesty, Boyle," I said. "Let me get a look at this package."

"Open it, David," Danny said.

"Yeah, open it now," Becky squealed.

I tore off the paper and ripped off the tape holding the box shut. Pushing aside an abundance of green tissue paper, I discovered two gifts: a life preserver and a bike helmet. I pulled them out and placed them on a nearby table, shaking my head in amazement at my students' thoughtfulness and concern.

"Thank you, guys. Thank you so much. I've never received better gifts on my birthday."

"We want you to be safe tonight," Becky said.

"Yeah," Willa said, poking me with Plank again. "Be safe."

"I will."

For the next hour, I watched my students take their skateboards off ramps and over jumps, fearlessly hurling their bodies in all directions. My turn to do something reckless in a very public setting was only hours away now; a fact that suddenly struck me as ironic driving away from the skate park, full of warm thoughts about my surprise party. The care these kids showed me made it clear I'd underestimated the impact I'd had on them. And though it should have been easy for me to see, like the sun in the sky, one beautiful truth had been hidden from me by clouds my whole life; that with simple acts done in ordinary settings, anyone can make a meaningful mark.

twenty-five

From the skate park, I went home to Mt. Hope Avenue. With her condition having stabilized, Beatie was out of the hospital and anxious to make me an early birthday dinner.

"Ya want honey chicken?"

"Sure. That would be great," I said. "Will you make it with rice?"

"Shoore," Beatie said.

Honey chicken represented the best of Beatie's culinary abilities; a chewy, gooey piece of baked chicken drenched in mustard and half a quart of Golden Blossom's finest.

"I'm tired of honey chicken," Biff said.

"Tough," Beatie replied. "It's David's birthday not yours."

"I think what you two are doing tonight is nuts," Biff said. "I want you to know that."

Although he had known for some time about Beatie's plan to join me in my imminent plunge, he had not accepted or endorsed the idea.

"You're going to kill your own grandmother. You realize that, right?" Biff asked me.

"It's my choice, Biff," Beatie said. "David tried to talk me out of it a dozen times."

"I don't care. I don't like it and I don't want you to do it," Biff said.

"Oh, hush," Beatie said. "I'm dying anyway. What difference does it make?"

"It makes a difference to me. That's what difference," Biff said. "The whole thing's asinine."

"Just eat yer cheese and crackers," Beatie said. "And open a Bud Light for Woofie while you're at it."

"He's not drinking my last beer," Biff said, trying to assert himself in the only way he could at the moment.

I hated to admit it, but I felt sorry for Biff. Even though he and I had never gotten along, I knew he loved Beatie and I couldn't blame him for being afraid of what might happen to her at the falls. She had been his companion — really the only person who could stand him and his bathrobe — for nearly 15 years, and that held meaning. Beatie wasn't the easiest person to live with either, yet Biff never wavered in his commitment to their life together and I felt sad about the possibility of him being alone in the house without her.

Dinner was mostly a silent affair save the clanking of silverware against plates and the occasional grunt from Biff. When time for dessert arrived, Beatie presented me with a cake that read, 'Happy Birthday Maude!'

"Got it half off at Wegmans," she announced proudly.

Few things in the world made Beatie happier than buying food on sale.

"I can't believe yer 40, David," Beatie said, before sighing and sipping her coffee. "Forty years old. My God. I wish yer mother was here."

"Me, too," I said.

"She'd be proud of ya," Beatie said.

"You think?" I asked.

"I doubt it," Biff said."

"Don't be a dumb bunny, Biff. Of course she'd be proud," Beatie said. "Go ahead and make a wish."

I stared into the flickering candle flames atop the cake hoping to find answers, just as I did every birthday. What did I want more than anything in the world? After 40 years of searching, all I knew for sure was that there had to be more to life than what I'd experienced. It would be nice to fulfill all of my mother's prophecies and become the world-beater she imagined, but what I truly wanted was more basic: extra time with Beatie, a loving wife and child of my own, an ongoing sense of purpose and the peace of mind I prayed would accompany those things.

After cake came presents, where Beatie gave me a calendar of cats in tuxedos that she'd found in a discount bin; an improvement, frankly, on last year's 'World's Greatest Lacrosse Mom' mug. Biff gave me an olive-colored bathrobe to match his own. "You're gonna wonder how you lived without this thing," he assured me.

As the sun began to set and the time came to leave, I took one last look at my bedroom; its walls still covered with the dragons my mother painted over 30 years before. The faded curtains, model airplanes and Farrah Fawcett poster revealed the life of someone who'd never really grown up; someone who, somehow, got stuck along the way and couldn't pry himself loose; until tonight.

Down Mt. Hope Avenue I drove my Mustang with Beatie and Woofie buckled up in back and Biff riding shot gun. Passing a convent, I said a silent prayer and a Hail Mary. Even though I wasn't Catholic, I had dated a few and I figured it couldn't hurt.

I didn't know what to expect upon arrival, but Brown's Race felt dangerous to me for the first time. Flood lights lit up the High Falls, the Pont de Rennes Bridge and large portions of the surrounding pedestrian areas, all of them teeming with people. Latin conga music played as bodies lined both sides of the Genesee River 50-deep and the city's frenzied atmosphere buzzed like Las Vegas on championship fight night. Neon marquees, temporarily erected on many of the historic district's buildings, illuminated the names of the actors and films that would debut in the coming week to great acclaim, tepid indifference or worse. All in all, Mayor Candee, who declared in her latest television ad that this would be the most exhilarating evening in Rochester since the 1968 race riots, appeared to be right.

After parking, we made our way through the crowd to meet Dixie and Nubby at a pre-arranged spot on the edge of the Genesee, about 50 feet up river from the rim of the High Falls, beneath a 10-foot high wooden tower built by protest volunteers. Located on a patch of grass between an abandoned warehouse and the edge of the water, the tower had a platform on top of it that jutted out above the flowing rapids and provided the perfect launching pad from which to enter the water and ride over the plummeting face of the falls. Situated a few feet away along the riverbank was an enormous soundstage where the Mayor would be acting as the master of ceremonies for the evening.

"Hey, Dixie," I called.

"You made it," she said, spying our approach.

"Of course I made it. You think I'd miss this?"

"I don't know. I thought about it once or twice," she said, smiling.

"Is Nubby here?"

"Not yet. Big surprise, eh?"

"Yeah, right. . . . Meet my family," I said.

"Hi family. I'm Dixie. This is pretty exciting, eh?"

"I'm just here to watch," Biff said. "These are the crazy

ones," he said, pointing to Beatie and me. "Are you joining them, too?" Biff asked.

"Yup. Over and away," Dixie said.

"Unbelievable," Biff muttered, tightening the belt on his robe.

"Sweetheart, can ya show me where the turlets are?" Beatie asked.

"Of course, come with me," Dixie said. "They're right over here."

"I don't think there's time to use the bathroom," I said. "This whole shebang is starting in 10 minutes."

"David, my shebang is starting right now and I need to find a turlet," Beatie said.

"Got it," I said. "Please just come back quickly."

With Dixie and Beatie off to the ladies room, I looked around and saw Mayor Candee, flanked by Denton Fink, walking toward me.

"Well, well, well, if it isn't Dragon Horvath."

"Go away, Candee," I said.

"Nice night for a tragedy, wouldn't you say?" Candee asked.

"Get the hell out of here," I said.

"Denton, don't you think this is perfect weather for a catastrophe?"

"Oh, yes, ma'am. Good breeze and plenty cold," Denton said.

"You're not losing your nerve are you, Horvath?" Mayor Candee asked.

"You wish."

"No, not really. What I wish is that society wouldn't automatically condemn every 87-year old, powerful woman whose boyfriend is still in high school. It's just not fair."

"You're deranged, Candee."

"And you're a dead man walking. Between the two, I'll take deranged."

Mayor Candee and Denton Fink walked away and climbed the stairs leading to the soundstage, where an assemblage of film festival organizers, mayoral assistants, media types and minor local celebrities sat chatting in two rows of folding chairs set up behind a podium and microphone. Also present were Pete Lee, who was assiduously avoiding eye contact with Dixie, Chuck Mangione, who held his flugelhorn on his lap, and the Chippendales bikini team. At 8:00 p.m. sharp, just as Dixie and Beatie returned from the bathroom, Candee finished saying her hellos, asked those on stage to be seated and approached the microphone.

"Hello Rochester! How's everybody doing?"

The crowd roared.

"I want to welcome all of you to this very special weekend of entertainment in Rochester, New York — the World's Image Center — or, as I like to call her, 'Rouletteville.' It's all being sponsored, as you may have guessed from the billboards, by the good people at Cockeye's. Come on down to Cockeye's for a 12-inch cock and mac snack, a delicious blend of rooster parts and macaroni salad on a foot-long kaiser roll, and tell them Mayor Candee sent you. Now, as you know, our city's annual High Falls Film Festival celebrating female accomplishment in cinema begins tonight and I want to say a special thank you to all the people gathered here who dedicate their lives to watching and making chick flicks. I don't know how they do it. I know I sure as hell couldn't. But, hey, better them than the rest of us, am I right, my loyal lieges?"

Candee's words drew no reaction from the masses this time.

"So, anyway, a hearty thank you to those folks and, of course, to Susan B. Anthony, one of the greatest actresses of her generation," Candee said, glancing back at the two rows of obviously perturbed festival board members behind her. "And, as if one big event isn't enough, we've got a second very special treat for you this evening. As you know, I'm talking about the daredevil theatrics of Dragon Horvath and his band of madmen, the QWEAFS, who plan to go over the falls just as local legend Sam Patch did nearly 200 years ago."

Applause and shouts echoed into the night sky. Over where we'd gathered on the grass, Nubby still hadn't arrived.

"Where the hell's, Nubby?" I asked, increasingly anxious about his absence.

"He'll be here," Dixie said. "Let's get everyone up to the platform."

"Right," I said.

After assisting Beatie to the top of the 10-foot tower, I climbed back down and scooped up Woofie in my arms. Slowly making my way up the structure's dodgy wooden ladder, I followed Dixie and a minute later, the four of us were gathered on the summit.

"You got room for one more?"

I looked down to see Bug Boone, dressed in an optic orange wet suit, standing at the foot of the tower.

"Bug, what in God's name are you doing here?"

Without invitation, he began climbing toward me.

"I quit my job. I'm headed to Los Angeles. I need a fresh start."

By the time Bug reached me, he was out of breath and placed a hand on my shoulder to steady himself.

"I need to be a part of this, David. It's going to be my baptism. Do you understand? Please don't say no."

"I'm not going to say no, Bug."

"Oh, good. I'm so relieved," he said, heaving up and down.

Something in Bug's eyes told me everything he was feeling.

How about some shtick?" Bug asked, suddenly revived.

"No shtick! I said. "Got it?"

"Got it."

Up on stage, the Mayor continued.

"In honor of these brave souls, the city has commissioned Grammy-nominated musician and native son, Chuck Mangione, to write and play a song. With his soon to be hit single, Hittin' the Rocks, please welcome Mr. Chuck Mangione. As Mangione walked forward, he pulled Candee aside.

"Uh, Madame Mayor, I still haven't gotten my check."

"Chuck, you'll have it in a week I swear," the Mayor said, pushing him toward the front of the stage. "Just an accounting glitch, I'm sure."

What followed next was haunting and beautiful as the melancholy sounds of Mangione's flugelhorn cut through the cold air and reverberated out across Brown's Race and the city. I might have gotten more emotional and contemplative, however, if I wasn't distracted by Nubby's continuing absence. Sure enough, as the song ended and the crowd cheered, Nubby showed up and began climbing up the tower's ladder to join us on the platform.

"Where were you?" I asked as he ascended. "I didn't think you were going to make it."

"Don't worry. I'm here," Nubby said. "Look, I've got to talk to you."

"You're backing out, aren't you?"

"I didn't say that."

"You didn't have to," I said.

"It's complicated."

"No, it's not. Either you're going over the falls with us or you're not. What's complicated about that?"

"I'm a match for Big Nasty."

"What?"

"I'm a matching kidney donor."

"But you told me you weren't."

"I know. I lied. I know it was wrong but I didn't want you pressuring me to have the surgery."

"Are you being straight with me? How do I know you're not saying all this now just to get out of going over the falls?"

"I'm being straight. I swear."

"But you said you didn't want to be a kidney donor even if you matched."

"Well, I've been thinking about that and maybe I do. Maybe doing this for Big Nasty is my way to show Anna that I'm worth her while. What do you think?"

As soon as Nubby asked me, I heard Mayor Candee's voice over the sound system. "If you'll kindly direct your attention to the group of maniacs standing on the platform to my left, we can get this show started." Suddenly, a spotlight was directed our way, momentarily blinding us.

"What do you think, David? Because I'll do whatever you want. If you want me to go over the falls with you, I'll do it. I'll be that Sancho guy. I owe you that much," Nubby said.

"You don't owe me anything."

"Yes, I do."

Having regained my sight, I looked around at the thousands of screaming people eagerly anticipating our stunt as the Mayor continued speaking. "What you're about to witness is a spectacle the likes of which we haven't seen here in Rochester since 1829. It didn't end well then and I don't expect it to end well tonight. But what the hell, I think we'll all have a good time anyway."

Beneath the bright spotlight, I shielded my face with an outstretched hand.

"Are you going to ask Anna to marry you?" I asked Nubby.

"Yes."

"Then you can't go over the falls," I said.

"I don't want to let you down," Nubby said.

"You're not. You're getting a life. Don't you see? You don't need the falls anymore."

Nubby paused to survey the scene before looking back at me.

"Do you?" Nubby asked.

A steady, unified chant rose up from both sides of the Genesee.

"JUMP! JUMP! JUMP! JUMP! JUMP! JUMP! JUMP! JUMP!"

"David, it's time," Dixie said, walking over to us. "What are you guys talking about? You're not ditching us, are you, Nubby?"

"He's a match for Big Nasty."

"Really?"

"Yes," Nubby said.

"Then don't jump," Dixie said.

"That's what I told him," I said.

I said goodbye to my friend and watched him descend the ladder to safety. Nubby had found another way to matter and, though I'd miss having him by my side, I was happy for him. He was going to lose his kidney, but Nubby was about to become whole or at least as close to it as he could ever get.

"JUMP! JUMP! JUMP! JUMP! JUMP! JUMP! JUMP! JUMP!"

The impatient crowd, having caught sight of Woofie, soon changed their chant.

"THROW — IN- THE PIG! THROW — IN — THE PIG! THROW — IN — THE PIG!"

"Shut-up, ya jackasses," Beatie yelled.

"THROW — IN — THE PIG! THROW — IN — THE PIG! THROW — IN — THE PIG!"

Perched on our platform, we moved a few feet forward together and peered into the moving shadows of the Genesee from above.

"Looks fast," Dixie said.

Although I'd never been so frightened, I was determined to take in the moment as the conga drums beat in synchronicity with my heart and the chanting mob.

"PUSH — GRANDMA! PUSH — GRANDMA! PUSH — GRANDMA!"

"Okay, I'm giving everyone one last chance to get out of this. Does anyone have anything they want to say?" I asked. "Beatie, are you sure this is what you want?"

Beatie, now attired in the life preserver and bike helmet given to me by my tennis students, nodded.

"Dixie? Are you ready?"

"I'm ready," she said.

"Okay, then. We go on the count of three."

When my quest started, I had one simple goal: become great. Yet until Beatie told me of her last remaining wish to attend the Academy Awards, I couldn't find the pathway. Once I did, it led me to people, places and things I'd never imagined before, as well as causes bigger than myself, and for that I was grateful. If I'd learned anything during this search it was the power of self-reliance, a force that had been missing from my life for 40 years. Standing on top of the world now, I was ready to risk everything for something I believed in. It was a feeling unlike any I'd ever known — colored one cool shade of madness — and for a brief moment, although flames weren't shooting from my nose, I was a dragon.

"One . . . Two . . . Threeeeeeeee!" I shouted.

With a united leap, we crashed into the river. Momentarily submerged, I scrambled to the surface and attempted to get my bearings. The current was moving quickly and I knew we'd reach the lip of the falls within seconds. The water was colder than I expected and my inability to see Beatie in the darkness engendered panic.

"Beatie!" I shouted. "Where *are* you?"

"She's over here with me," Dixie called out.

Dixie said something else, but I couldn't hear what. The falls grew louder the closer we came, and soon there was nothing between us and the hundred-foot drop but a translucent wall of sound and water lit from below by television crews. Catapulted over the crest, I fought desperately to keep my feet beneath me, determined not to land headfirst. Once in freefall, however, buried deep under the torrent, I surrendered myself to the moment. We were either pieces of pulp about to be shredded and left strewn along the side of the Genesee, or spiritual sheets of paper about to be fed into one of Chester Carlson's karmic copiers, coming out intact on the other side, somehow new and different than we'd been going in. Silence and streaming light surrounded me now, and I felt relieved to be on my way and at peace about my decision. Unfortunately, I still had to land.

Facing the river as I rocketed southward, like a rogue skydiver out of formation, I clipped a rock with the left side of my body upon entry and was immediately engulfed by the kind of white hot poker pain hell must offer. Coming up, I gasped for air as wild yelps erupted from both sides of the river. I tasted blood in my mouth and knew right away that my ribs were broken. My first instinct was to call for Beatie, but I couldn't breathe. I tried to speak, but my words were staggered and close to inaudible.

"Beatie — where — are — you?" I gasped.

A search and rescue team pulled me to shore and a group of paramedics took over. Blood I hadn't noticed before ran down my face, its origin unknown.

"Did — the — others — make it?" I asked, straining to raise my voice above a whisper.

"They're all being pulled from the water, sir."

"I — need — to — know."

"Save your strength, sir. You've been injured."

"Are — they — okay?"

"Sir, we've got to get you to the hospital."

The EMTs loaded me into the back of an ambulance and off it sped. My dragon dream was still alive.

twenty-six

Opening my one good eye, even the slightest bit, blinded me.

"Mr. Horvath? . . . Can you hear my voice? . . . Mr. Horvath?"

Through tiny slits, I saw a blurry figure standing over me.

"Who are you?" I asked.

My mouth was dry and cottony.

"I'm Dr. Marx and *you*, my friend, are lucky to be here."

"Where's here?"

"St. Mary's Hospital."

Every part of me ached as I surveyed the room, much of it filled with flowers.

"Are these flowers for me?" I asked.

"Yes, they're from well-wishers."

I felt dizzy and disoriented.

"What day is it?" I asked.

"January third. You've been in a coma for almost seven weeks. You woke up for the first time yesterday, but I doubt you remember. It was only for a few minutes."

"A coma?"

"Yes. You suffered multiple lacerations to the head, broken ribs, a collapsed lung and a broken right tibia. Given the height of your fall, however, it could've been a lot worse."

I weighed his words for a moment before the inevitable questions entered my mind.

"Is my grandmother here? Are my friends here?" I asked.

Dr. Marx took a seat next to my bed.

"Mr. Horvath, your friends survived the jump, but I'm afraid I've got some bad news about your grandmother. . . . She didn't make it. I'm very sorry."

"But, Doctor, I don't understand. What happened?"

"I didn't treat her personally, but the autopsy report said that she drowned."

"What? That can't be," I said.

"I'm sorry, Mr. Horvath."

Dr. Marx left the room and my emotions surged. For the next six hours, I cried on and off as disbelief turned to anger then sadness then shame. Beatie was gone and it was my fault. What had I done? Greatness. Immortality. Transformation. I had accomplished none of it for myself or my city. I'd only succeeded in making my life lonelier and, like an icy gust of air; I felt it chilling me immediately. I pressed the call button. I had to escape and another long sleep was my only chance.

"What can I do for you, Mr. Horvath?"

"Nurse, I need morphine."

"I can't give you any more yet."

"Please."

"You've got an hour to go. Is there something else I can get you? Let me change your bedpan while I'm here."

"I don't care about my bedpan. I need something to take away my pain. Please."

"I wish I could, but you'll just have to wait for . . ."

The nurse was interrupted by a knock on the door, which then swung open to reveal Nubby, wearing a hospital gown and sitting in a wheelchair.

"It's about time you woke up," Nubby said, rolling himself inside.

"Nubby, what are you doing here?" I asked.

"I'm collecting for Jerry's kids. What do you think I'm doing here? I'm recovering from kidney surgery."

"Oh, Christ, that's right. I'm so glad to see you."

"Right back at you. You gave me a scare, you dick. How are you feeling?"

"Not so good."

"I'm sorry about Beatie."

The nurse excused herself and left us alone.

"I don't think I can forgive myself, Nub."

"What are you talking about?"

"Beatie's death."

"Why?"

"Because I'm to blame. If it wasn't for me, she'd still be here."

"Don't say that. She wanted to go over the falls. She wanted that experience and you gave it to her. I don't think you realize how proud she was of what you were doing or how happy she was to be a part of it."

"If that's true, then tell me something. Just *what* was I doing? What was the point of it all? The whole thing feels like a sham. It didn't prove anything and it certainly didn't change anything."

"That's where you're wrong. Everybody's still talking about what you did."

"I'm not a dragon, Nubby."

"No, you're not. You're something better. You're a hero."

"A hero?"

"Well, not like Dale Earnhardt, Jr. or Blind Lemon Jefferson, but, yes, a hero."

"Hah. What a joke. I'm the farthest thing from a hero. I'm a complete failure."

"I'm telling you you're a hero."

"What for? What makes me a hero? Because I survived some stupid stunt?"

"No, not that. You're a hero because you helped people."

"I killed my own grandmother. I certainly didn't help *her*. Who did I help? Nobody, that's who."

"What about me? Two days ago they cut my kidney out and gave it to Big Nasty. Now he's going to live. That wouldn't have happened without you."

"You did that yourself. I had nothing to do with it."

"Yes, you did. I'm not exactly sure how, but with all your questing and Sancho Panza crap, you got me thinking about things I never thought of before . . . like other people. And you got me believing in things I never believed in before . . . like myself."

"That's very touching, but it's nonsense."

"Is it nonsense that Anna and I are engaged?"

"Really?"

"I told her everything about me."

"Everything?"

"Well, everything except my delinquent tax returns and nasal spray addiction. I didn't want to overwhelm her."

"See, I told you she'd still love you. Congratulations, that's amazing."

"If I hadn't had the courage to go under the knife, I'm not sure she would have. I give you credit for that."

"Me? What for? That was your idea."

"Yeah, but you gave me an example to follow."

"Look, all I know is that these things would be happening for you with or without me."

"All right, you stubborn mule, what about the Mayor's plan to develop the High Falls?"

"What about it?"

"It's dead."

"What?"

"They arrested her for attempted murder once word got out that they'd used the raceway to try and drain water off the river the night you went over the falls. She was trying to kill you."

"I can't believe it."

"There's more. Dixie's father came forward and admitted that Compost Country was just a front for Candee Land and that gambling and prostitution had always been part of the Mayor's plan. He's going to testify against the Mayor. So, one way or another, it looks like Candee's going to jail for a very long time. Isn't that the best?"

"Yes, but when am I going to jail?" I asked, suddenly remembering my own impending incarceration.

"You're not. After he saw the jump and heard about Beatie, Judge Kerfoot commuted your sentence to community service."

"So I'm free?"

"Yup."

"I'm stunned. I'm completely stunned. I really am."

"And did I tell you Big Nasty's poems are getting published?"

"No shit."

"Now that definitely wouldn't have happened without you."

"God, that's great. What about Dixie? Where is she?"

"Believe it or not, she's in Sri Lanka helping refugees. After she reconciled with her father and got out of hospital she decided that's what she wanted to do next. It was hard for her to leave with you still in here. She was really broken up, but she's coming back soon to visit."

"That's good. I'm glad."

"I haven't even told you the best news yet. Guess what."

TWO MONTHS LATER

For the first time, both Nubby and I are wearing tuxedos.
"Are you nervous?" I ask.
"A little," Nubby says. "You?"
"No. Just a walk in the park, right?"
"Right."
"I wish Beatie was here."
"She is. You just can't see her."
In the back of our limousine, I look around at the faces of my friends: Dixie, Big Nasty, Nubby, Bug, Biff (still in his bathrobe), Willa (still enrolled in the local public school) and Woofie.
"Everybody ready?" I ask.
The limo stops and the driver gets out to open the door for us. One by one, we step onto the red carpet as cameras click away and stars stride by without taking notice of our arrival at the Eastman Theatre. I grab Woofie's leash and we begin walking the gauntlet of reporters and paparazzi.
"Stay together," Dixie says. She is Dorothy and we're off to see the Wizard.
Inside the theatre we take our seats, unable to stop gawking at the recognizable faces everywhere. Tom Cruise, Jack Nicholson, Meryl Streep, Tom Hanks.
"Can you believe this?" Big Nasty asks. "Reminds me of a poem I once wrote."
"Not now, Nasty," Dixie says. "The show's starting."
"David, I have to say it. You did it. You really shocked the world."
"No, I didn't, Nub. You've got it all wrong. I didn't shock the world. The world shocked me."
The lights go down and the orchestra plays a stirring introduction. Seconds later, Billy Crystal appears to uproari-

ous applause as he starts one of his famous medley tributes to the best picture nominees. The crowd erupts again when he's finished and winded, he steps up to the microphone, covering it while he catches his breath. Pretending not to have noticed the audience's presence, he begins by acting startled.

"Oh, hello. I didn't see you there. Were you waiting for me?"

Crystal pulls a perfectly folded handkerchief from his breast pocket and dabs the perspiration on his forehead before returning it to its proper place.

"Ladies and gentlemen, it is my distinct honor and privilege to welcome you to this year's Academy Awards. You know, I never thought I'd say this in my entire life, but I have to admit: it's great to be in Rochester, New York."

Made in the USA
Charleston, SC
17 May 2014